Praise for **Terra Nova**,
the second Molly Stout Adventure

"Molly's back! *Terra Nova* packs the same page-turning action as *Dominion* did and with every bit as much of the imaginative, thought-provoking, enviro-political clout. Molly Stout is as brave as ever but she has matured, grappling with what is wrong and what is right—questioning her motives. I think Arbuthnott has come up with a whole new subgenre; let's call it Spirit Punk. I love it!"

—*Tim Wynne-Jones, award-winning author*

Praise for **Dominion**,
the first Molly Stout Adventure

"Molly is an independent and thoughtful character, and her skill as an engineer enhances her appeal...Arbuthnott creates an intriguing steampunk world with a smooth combination of technology and magic... A fast-paced read with a strong female lead, this will leave steampunk and adventure fans looking forward to a hinted-at sequel."

—*School Library Journal*

"Molly's heroic rebellion against everything she has been brought up to believe and value is at the heart of an action-packed narrative. Heroes and rogues can be male or female, the engineer is as likely to be a woman as a man...How refreshing."

—*Quill & Quire*

"This book will appeal to both historical fiction and science fiction fans. I found myself unable to put this book down and envisioning it as a movie much like the beloved Harry Potter series."

—*School Library Connection*

"What a fabulous read! A truly moving book. I hope there are many more to come."

—*Tim Wynne-Jones, award-winning author*

"Feisty young Molly will keep readers grounded in this page-turning mystical adventure."

—*Kirkus Reviews*

THE MOLLY STOUT ADVENTURES

Dominion
Terra Nova

TERRA NOVA

Shane Arbuthnott

ORCA BOOK PUBLISHERS

Library and Archives Canada Cataloguing in Publication

Arbuthnott, Shane, author
Terra nova / Shane Arbuthnott.

Issued in print and electronic formats.
ISBN 978-1-4598-1444-8 (softcover).—ISBN 978-1-4598-1445-5 (pdf).—
ISBN 978-1-4598-1446-2 (epub)

I. Title.
PS8601.R363T47 2018   JC813'.6   C2017-904566-0
C2017-904567-9

First published in the United States, 2018
Library of Congress Control Number: 2017949709

Summary: In this fantasy novel for middle-grade readers, Molly has been fighting to free the spirits, but she fears her rebellion is only putting people and spirits in danger.

Orca Book Publishers is dedicated to preserving the environment and has printed this book on Forest Stewardship Council® certified paper.

Orca Book Publishers gratefully acknowledges the support for its publishing programs provided by the following agencies: the Government of Canada through the Canada Book Fund and the Canada Council for the Arts, and the Province of British Columbia through the BC Arts Council and the Book Publishing Tax Credit.

Edited by Robin Stevenson
Design by Rachel Page
Cover images by Stocksy.com and Shutterstock.com
Author photo by Erin Elizabeth Hoos Photography

ORCA BOOK PUBLISHERS
www.orcabook.com

Printed and bound in Canada.

21 20 19 18 • 4 3 2 1

To my parents, who never stopped me from leaping before I looked but were always there with bandages afterward.

ACT ONE
REBELLION

ONE

Molly clenched her hands, trying to hold them still, but it was no use. Her whole body was vibrating, her heart beating so fast it felt like it might shake itself loose from her chest. She hated this part. The moment before action, before chaos. It felt like standing at the edge of a cliff, knowing you were about to fall.

Ariel, her companion aetheric spirit, floated up next to her. The blue whorls of her body coalesced into a slender human form, and she crouched down next to Molly. "You will have to be careful with this one," she whispered. "The spirit in the furnace is agitated beyond reason. Once released, I cannot predict what she will do."

Molly took a deep breath and gripped the cornice of the roof where she perched. "Any idea how strong she is?"

"She is old, and quite strong, but very, very tired."

The factory squatted in front of them like a fortress. Its soot-blackened walls were broken only by a few small windows up near the roof. The front doors were made of inch-thick iron, and Molly already knew they were barred and bolted. The only way in was through those tiny windows. They glared out of the dark wall like fiery eyes.

"Are Rory and Kiernan in place?" Molly asked.

"Yes."

Molly nodded. "I guess we're ready then. I mean, are you ready?"

The aetheric spirit glowed briefly, her eagerness apparent. "I have brought as many winds as I could gather," she said. Molly looked up and saw bright streams of color swirling in the sky above the factory—slow, warm oranges, frigid whites and stately blues. Molly lowered her eyes, blinking the bright streaks away. Over the past year she had grown used to her ability to see the winds, but sometimes they were still blinding.

She looked to Ariel. The spirit's edges flickered, as they often did when she was excited.

Molly gripped the brick cornice tighter. "Okay. Let's go."

Ariel's human shape dissolved into blue filaments of wind. She flowed around Molly, wrapping around her as tight as bandages until Molly's entire body was covered in glowing blue light. Ariel lifted them both into the air, and Molly felt a momentary joy as she left the rooftop behind. She loved nothing so much as flying with Ariel. But they weren't here to enjoy themselves.

They shot forward like a bullet. Ariel sent a stream of wind before them, shattering the nearest window, and Molly and the spirit flew through.

She only had a moment to survey the factory—she saw winding conveyor belts, countless faces looking up at her, and the huge furnace looming against the back wall—before Ariel dropped her to the ground just inside the doors. Molly met the eyes of the factory workers nearest to her. Their backs were bent, their eyes sunken. They were so small—even the oldest couldn't be more than fifteen years old, like her—but their tired faces gave the impression of incredible age. They, like the spirits that powered the machinery, were prisoners here, not allowed to leave until they were too broken to be useful. A burly man in an ill-fitting suit—one of the foremen, Molly guessed—hurried down a set of metal stairs toward her, and anger bloomed in her chest.

She reached up, and a bright white wind flowed in through the broken window, rushing down to twine itself around her fingers. She cast it forward, hitting the foreman in the chest. He flew back several feet and collapsed against the wall.

She turned back to the gaping workers. "Um, hi," she said, then cleared her throat. "I'm Molly Stout. We're here to free the spirits." Eyes widened in recognition at the name, but none left their stations. "So, you know, you should probably leave." No one moved. Molly noticed one young boy, no more than eleven, still piecing together the metal parts of an iron trap that, once complete, would have been used to cage even more spirits.

"Don't know why I bother," she muttered. She turned to the door. The bar across it was sturdy, but it was locked in place by only a thin chain. She pulled the bolt cutters from her belt and cut the chain, pushing the bar away. It fell to the ground with a loud *clang*.

The sound of the falling bar did what Molly's words had not and pierced the workers' exhaustion. Several of them screamed and dropped their tools, running pell-mell for the doors, and the rest followed. Molly pushed the doors open wide. Her brothers waited on the other side.

As the first of the workers ran through the door, Kiernan stepped forward. "All right, everyone follow me!" he shouted in his deep, commanding voice. Despite the general panic, most of the crowd heard him and followed as he ran down the street to the north. *Why can't I do that?* Molly wondered. Her other brother, Rory, chased after the stragglers and sent them in the right direction.

The factory was almost empty now. The foreman was pulling himself to his feet. Molly walked over to him, and he cowered away from her.

"You can leave too. But don't follow the kids." He stared up at her for a moment, then nodded and scrambled out the doors. She sighed, slightly disappointed. *Looked like he might try to fight me for a second there.*

"Molly!" Ariel called. She was hovering beside a tangle of machinery near the back of the factory, where the conveyor belts began. "Several aqueous devices here. A good place to start."

Molly nodded and jumped up to grab the walkway beside the conveyor belt. With the agility born of a childhood spent in the rigging of an airship, she clambered up over the railing and jumped across the conveyor belt to the far side, where Ariel and the spiritual machines sat waiting.

"The iron looks cheap," Molly said. "Shouldn't be hard to break."

"Cheap or not, it is burning the spirits inside. This place is so full of iron that the air itself feels caustic. Please be quick."

Molly pulled her pry bar from the back of her belt.

Working swiftly, she and Ariel made their way through the factory, opening the spiritual machines to free the spirits inside. Three aqueous spirits, four aetheric and ten small igneous spirits from the lamps, all told. Most were too disoriented or weak to move, but Ariel carried them gently out to the open air, away from the iron. Once the smaller machines were taken care of, Molly turned to the furnace.

It was huge and clearly sturdier than the rest of the machinery in the factory. Thick iron plates, heavily patched, covered it from top to bottom, and it belched fire and smoke from narrow vents. It was still smelting the iron for the traps, despite the empty factory around it.

To its right there was a heap of coal and wood to feed the machine. *Might be able to get in through the feeder*, Molly thought, *but an access hatch would be better.* She jumped down from the walkway and surveyed the base of the furnace. This close, the heat from the fire brought out beads of sweat on her forehead.

Finally, tucked against the wall, she found what she was looking for—a small maintenance hatch, its hinges rusted shut. A few hard pushes with her pry bar broke up the rust, and she pulled the hatch open. A tangle of wires spilled out. Molly shoved these aside, not caring that a few came loose in her hands. Beyond the wires she found the plain metal box that housed the spirit—a spirit trap, just like countless others made by this very factory. She climbed halfway into the hatch.

The trap was strong, clearly meant to hold a powerful spirit indefinitely, but it had not been maintained. At its bottom she found a small vent through which the spirit would get the oxygen it needed to keep its fires burning. Rust had begun to eat away at it, weakening the metal, giving Molly a way in.

She used the back of her hand to wipe the sweat out of her eyes and brought out a chisel and hammer.

"If you can hear me in there, and if you can understand me, I'm about to set you free," Molly said as she chipped away at the rusted metal. "I'd appreciate it if you didn't burn my face off." There was a rumble from inside the trap, which she hoped was a signal of understanding. She felt the heat on her face dim a little. "Okay. It should just be a moment more."

With a few more taps, the chisel broke through. Molly turned it and pried at the vent, pulling it halfway off. She saw flames flickering around the edges of the opening, and a bright red claw emerged.

"Wait, wait!" she shouted, but the claw punched through, knocking the vent to the floor. Flames blossomed from the hole, and Molly dropped her tools and slithered backward out of the hatch. She felt fire lick the side of her head as she rolled out onto the factory floor, slapping at her hair to put it out.

"Molly!" Ariel called, and a cool wind rushed in over her. Molly opened her eyes as Ariel landed beside her and saw a fiery form battering its way out of the maintenance hatch. A beak emerged, and flashing claws, and then the iron cracked and bent, and a vast bird made entirely of flame forced its way through, rising up into the air above the conveyor belts. Where it had touched the iron of the furnace, there were angry black streaks across its red skin, and one of its wings looked bent. Nevertheless it hovered in the air, angry and powerful.

"I thought you said she was tired," Molly said to Ariel.

"And desperate enough to overcome that, it seems."

The spirit flapped her wings, and a blast of flame slammed into the furnace. The machine's iron plates glowed white-hot and buckled under the heat. The spirit kept striking out until the furnace was nothing but a molten heap.

"You should leave!" Molly shouted to it. "We don't have long!"

The spirit did not seem to hear her. She shrieked, and the air around her ignited, melting conveyor belts and walkways.

Molly threw her arm over her head and turned away. "She's going to burn the whole building down! Ariel, can you talk to her?" she shouted.

"I will try!" The aetheric spirit rose into the air, struggling against the drafts created by the fire.

Molly looked around. The floor between her and the door was already on fire, but to the right she thought she saw a gap between walkways that she could pass through. Molly rose and started toward it, then stopped.

Something had moved beneath one of the conveyor belts. She crouched down to look again and saw a small boy huddled on the ground, his arms around his head. The conveyor belt above him was in flames.

"Hey!" Molly shouted. "Get out of there!" She ran toward the boy, who did not move. "Bloody hell." The rubber conveyor belt billowed smoke, and the flames flared higher as the spirit raged above them.

Molly reached up with both hands, calling all the winds that would listen, and sent them forward across the fire. Streams of bright blue light flowed in through the factory doors and buffeted the conveyor belt, damping the flames. The boy finally looked up at what was happening. He saw Molly running toward him, and his eyes widened.

"Go!" she shouted. "Go!"

He still didn't move. Molly sprinted to his side, pulling at the winds that now swirled around the factory. They gathered at her back as she wrapped her arms around the boy's chest and pulled him out from beneath the belt, and then the winds lifted them both off the ground, sending them arcing over the flaming machinery and down through the open door.

The ground rushed up toward them. They were falling too fast for her to land on her feet. "Try to stay relaxed," she muttered to the boy, and she curled herself around him, twisting to put her back to the ground.

She landed hard, and all the air left her lungs. For a moment, black and white streaks warred across her vision. She closed her eyes and rolled away from the boy. After a few painful moments, her lungs relaxed and her breath returned. Her vision cleared.

She rolled up onto her knees, one arm wrapped around her stomach.

"Sorry about that," she rasped. "That wasn't what I meant to do. But you should be saf—"

The look on the boy's face stopped her. He was lying on the ground, seemingly unhurt, but his eyes were fixed on her with naked terror.

"Hey. It's okay," she said. He only whimpered and dragged himself backward a few inches. "I'm not going to hurt you." The boy still didn't move. Molly rose to her feet and took a step toward him. The boy screamed and finally found his feet and bolted down the alleyway.

"Hey, that's the wrong way!" she shouted. "The foremen or the police will catch you that way!" The boy did not heed her. Molly thought about chasing him, but the image of his terrified eyes stuck her in place. She bent down and breathed deeply until the knot in her side undid itself, then turned back to the factory.

The igneous spirit from the furnace was still bellowing inside, and two of the upper windows burst from the heat. She hurried to the door and peered inside, but the way was now blocked by flames.

"Ariel!" she shouted.

A jet of fire shot out the door, and Molly threw herself backward. *Oh God*, she thought. *It's too hot. Ariel can't survive in there. What do I do?*

She looked up to the sky for any winds she could call on, but the force of the heat was pushing them back. "Ariel!" Molly called again, her voice barely audible over the roar of the flames.

A moment later the heat subsided, the flames withdrawing into the factory. Molly moved forward cautiously. The factory was a burned-out husk now, the walls and roof charred coal black. The machinery had all melted. In the center of the factory, the great, flaming bird still hung, beating her wings slowly, but her violent heat had cooled. Molly could make out sooty black feathers beneath the fire.

"Ariel?" she called tentatively.

The igneous spirit turned her red eyes on Molly.

"I am here," Ariel said, dropping down from one of the windows. "She refused to leave until she had burned it all."

"We don't have much time before Disposal arrives."

"I know." Ariel rose until she was level with the flaming spirit and made gestures toward the sky. The great bird bowed her head and then looked upward. With one powerful beat of her wings she shot up, bursting through the factory roof, and disappeared to the west.

"Good. Now we—"

An engine rumbled outside. Molly turned and saw a hulking vehicle with a silver sword emblazoned on its side pulling into the street. Men and women in dark coats began pouring out of its doors.

"They're here!"

She ran and slammed the door shut, pushing the bar into place just as the first agents reached it. Fists pounded on the other side.

Ariel dropped down beside her. "I will have to carry you out," the spirit said, and with a nod from Molly, she flowed around her and lifted them both off the ground. They flew toward one of the windows on the back wall.

Just before they reached it, a man came flying through. He had dark goggles over his eyes and a metal box strapped to his back, flashing with the energies of an aetheric spirit. A flitter, Molly realized. *They're getting smarter. We've always had the advantage of flight, but if they're using flitters now, that's gone.* The man carried a weapon—some kind of gun, thick with rivets and flickering with inner light.

"Hello, Ms. Stout," he said.

The voice made her recognize his mustached face, despite the goggles obscuring it. *Howarth*. Agent Howarth had been chasing Molly since before she brought down the *Gloria Mundi*, the flagship of Haviland Industries. Lately, she seemed to be seeing his face more and more.

"I don't suppose you would surrender," he said.

Ariel turned to take them out another window, but agents were flying in from all sides now, all kept aloft by the flitters on their backs.

"I thought not," Howarth said, raising his weapon. Molly pulled her pry bar from her belt and threw it. It hit Howarth's shoulder, and his shot went wide. A stream of flame, bright as the sun, passed only a few inches to her right.

"Get us out!" Molly shouted. Ariel started for the gaping hole in the roof, but the agents were training their weapons on them. Molly closed her eyes.

A bellow like thunder shook the building, and winds whipped in through the gap in the roof. The winds slammed into the agents, pressing them back against the walls and pinning them there. Molly looked up and saw the wooden hull of their airship hovering above the factory. Beyond the airship, Legerdemain's vast blue wings stretched across the sky. The huge aetheric spirit flexed and curled its wingtips, commanding both the winds that held the airship aloft and the ones that trapped the Disposal agents.

"Oh, thank you," Molly whispered.

Ariel took them both up, forcing their way through the hurricane winds. They reached the ship's deck, and Ariel released Molly onto the deck boards. She spread her fingers across the pale, time-worn wood. The ship began to ascend.

Her heart was still hammering in her chest, though, every muscle in her body tight, as if she was still under fire. *Safe. Home*, she told herself. She pressed her cheek into the deck and breathed it in. Slowly her knotted muscles began to unravel themselves.

Thick hands grabbed her shoulders, and she looked up into her father's bearded face.

"Moll, are you okay?" he asked.

"Yeah. Thought I wouldn't be for a second there." She probed her ribs, and her back, finding plenty of bruises but nothing permanent. Her father reached down and touched the side of her head where some of her hair had been burned away. "Just got my hair," she said. "Nothing serious."

She pulled herself up and walked to the ship's gunwale. Down on the street there were more Disposal trucks, and dozens of agents, but those with flitters were still pinned inside the factory. The others on the ground brandished their weapons ineffectually, firing bright-red shots that faded long before they reached the ship. "They got here quick. And they brought some new gear."

"Done this too many times," her father said.

Molly sighed. She knew he was right. But despite dozens of raids, they had hardly scratched the surface of the problem. As the ship lifted up, taking them swiftly away from the factory, Molly looked out over Terra Nova's industrial district. There were hundreds of factories like the one below, still laboring on, driven by the energies of countless spirits in countless iron prisons. *And for every one we crack open, another two seem to spring up.*

Molly's father gripped her shoulder again. "There's only so much we can do," he said, as if reading her thoughts.

Molly nodded. "I know that, but..."

The ground receded below them, the huge factories turning into tiny squares as they flew out, away from the city and over the Atlantic Ocean, where Disposal could not find them.

"Did Kiernan and Rory get everyone away?" she asked.

"We'll find out when we pick them up in an hour."

Molly took her eyes off the factories in the distance and tried to think of the spirits and the laborers they'd freed. Her brothers would get the children far from the factories, into the hands of the Unionists. They were going somewhere better. And the spirits were free to find their way home now, back through the fonts that joined the human world and the spirit world.

We're doing good. Even if it's not enough. The face of the small, terrified boy flashed into her mind. *What else am I supposed to do?*

She stood up straight. "Thanks for coming, Da," she said. He nodded and squeezed her arm.

"Yes, thank you," Ariel said. "I do not think we could have escaped if you had not arrived." Molly's father nodded again.

Molly went to the mainmast and pulled herself up. Despite her sore back, she climbed quickly to the crow's nest at the top. She had been climbing that mast for what seemed like her entire life, and its handholds were as familiar to her as her berth inside the ship. Once she was in the nest, she sat down on the small wooden platform and put her legs out between the posts of the railing, leaning against the mast. She looked up at Legerdemain, the spirit that carried the ship, and found comfort in the blue-white curve of his belly and the flash of his wings. She watched his long tail swish through the air behind the ship, its flukes curling to cup the wind.

"Thanks for saving me. As usual," she said. The spirit responded with a high trill, and through the strange connection they shared, she felt his pleasure at having her close again. "It was a risk, you know, coming like that. You're a pretty big target."

A deep rumble of displeasure.

"I know, I know—they could have caught me too. But here we both are."

She looked out across the ocean to where the lights of Terra Nova bled into the sky, masking the stars and illuminating the fug of its factories.

Looks the same, she thought. *Looks exactly like it did before any of this. Before the* Gloria Mundi, *before the factory raids ...* She closed her eyes and tried to let the wind wash her troubled thoughts away.

TWO

Molly stared at the face on the poster. She had seen the Wanted posters before, declaring her and her family enemies of Terra Nova and the British Empire, but she had never really looked at them. In the drawing they had made of her, she had sunken eyes and wild hair, and her mouth seemed to barely contain a snarl. She looked like a murderer. *Which I guess I am. Sort of.* Her stomach churned. *Do I really look like that?*

She pulled the brim of her cap down lower and kept walking. An elbow dug into her ribs, and she turned to find Rory at her side.

"Don't tug at it like that," he said. "Makes it look like you're trying to hide."

"I am trying to hide," she muttered back. "Did you see how many posters are out now?"

"I know. But the more you look like you don't want people to notice you, the more they'll notice you. Relax."

He grabbed her cap and pulled it down over her eyes. While she was pulling it up, he stomped on her toes.

"Ow! Hey!" she shouted, but he was already running up ahead, past Kiernan and their father. Molly gave chase. "That hurt!" Rory grinned back at her. She bent low and ran. Now that her legs had grown a little, she thought she might be able to catch him, despite his three-year advantage.

"Hey, stop!" called Kiernan. She turned. Kiernan gestured to the building beside them. "We're here."

A short set of stairs led down to a basement entrance. Beside her, over the front door, there was a battered wooden sign carved with the figure of a rooster and the words *The Bantam's Rest* in faded gold lettering.

They descended the stairs, Kiernan leading, then their father, then Molly. When Rory circled back and fell in behind them, Molly punched him in the shoulder. He only grinned wider.

They stepped inside. The roof was low, and the room ill-lit. Two shadowed figures perched between wooden kegs and stacks of chairs. No one spoke until the door was closed and locked behind them.

"Well, from what we've heard, the job is done," one of the figures said. He was a dark-skinned bald man, wearing a collared shirt and a well-worn vest. He was often present at these Unionist meetings, though the other faces changed regularly. She had heard one of the other Unionists call him Bascombe, though they weren't supposed to use names.

"Did you have to cause such damage?" asked the white-skinned, gray-haired woman next to him. "We could have sold some of that machinery, if you'd left it for us to collect."

"You know spirits are unpredictable," Molly's father said. "The furnace spirit—"

"Not unpredictable," Molly said. "They're all pissed off, every single one. Some of them are just too weak from the iron to do anything about it."

The Unionists, and her father, all furrowed their brows.

"No matter," Bascombe said. "The job is done, the factory shut. Thank you again."

"What of the children?" Kiernan asked. "Are they safely away?"

"They're fine. They're fed and safe. Tomorrow we'll be looking to find them better prospects."

"There was a boy," Molly said. "Didn't leave the factory with the others, ran off the wrong way. Did you…?"

Bascombe shook his head. "No one else came, apart from the group your brothers brought. Sometimes you can't save them all."

The woman stood up. "Spare the details. We haven't the time."

Bascombe nodded. "True. We should discuss your next target. There is a textiles factory on the west end that is forcing its workers to—"

"Next target?" Molly's father said. "Already? Disposal was waiting for us this time! We can't hit another factory so soon."

"Too dangerous?" the woman said, staring straight at Molly. "I thought you were the great and terrible Molly Stout, who brought down the *Gloria Mundi*, the greatest ship that ever sailed the skies."

Molly glowered. "I'm not—"

"Damned right it's too dangerous. We would be stupid to move again so soon," her father said.

"Da? Maybe we should—"

"This factory is going through laborers like they're chaff!" Bascombe pleaded. "Dozens have already—"

"We can't help anyone if we're captured because you're too stupid to—"

"Da!"

Molly's shout brought all eyes over to her. She hunched her shoulders. "Da, can we talk for a minute?" She gestured to the corner of the room. Her father, still glowering, turned and walked over. Molly and her brothers followed.

"Molly, you know we can't do this again," he said.

"We didn't talk about this beforehand. We should talk."

"Didn't think they would have the gall to set us on another raid right away," Rory said. "I'm with Da on this."

"We need to let things settle for a while," her father said.

"But the spirits still need our help. We can't just run and hide."

"I'm not saying we tuck our tails between our legs," Molly's father said. "Maybe something less dangerous for a while though. We could try distributing copies of Haviland Stout's true journal again, show people that the official histories are lies, that the spirits aren't evil, like they've been told. Maybe we could change some people's minds."

"Oh no," Rory said. "I'm not wasting my time with that again. Hours of bloody copying just to have the pages thrown back in our faces." He massaged his right hand with his left, as if reliving the cramps he'd suffered after all that writing.

"He's right, Da," Molly said. "We tried that. No one listens when we try to tell them the truth. At least if we go after another factory, we can free a few spirits ourselves."

"Factories aren't the only place we can help the spirits," Kiernan interjected. "I think Da's right. If we hit another factory, Disposal will be there waiting. But if we choose another target, we might catch them off guard."

Everyone thought for a moment.

"That makes sense," Molly said. "We could go after the air purifiers in one of the wealthier districts maybe. Or some harvesters."

Her father's grimace hadn't disappeared. "Couldn't we stop for a few days?"

"I don't want to stop," Molly said. "But maybe you could, Da. You and the boys."

Kiernan shook his head. "In for a penny," Rory said.

Her father growled. "Fine." He stalked back to where the Unionists were waiting, all on their feet now. "We won't be hitting another factory for you."

"I knew we couldn't count on them," the gray-haired woman spat. "They're spirit-touched."

"We don't work for you," Kiernan said.

"Come now, Mr. Stout," Bascombe replied. "We can't stop now. The children in those factories are still—"

"Then crack open the damned factories yourselves!" Molly's father roared. "My children have shut down a dozen, all while being chased by Disposal, while you sit in basements and plan where to send us next! We are not your dogs!" He spat on the floor, turned and stormed out of the basement. Rory followed quickly.

"He's not wrong," Kiernan said. "Yours might be a good cause, but we can't win it for you." He turned and left. Molly followed after him, but Bascombe caught up to her and grabbed her shoulder. She turned, ready to push him off, but the sadness in his eyes caught her.

"Please. You know how bad it is for the children in those factories."

Molly nodded. "I know." *Not just for them*, she wanted to say. But she knew even rebels like Bascombe weren't ready to sympathize with spirits, to think of them as more than monsters. She shrugged off his hand and followed her family out. As soon as the door closed, she could hear the woman shouting inside.

Kiernan waited at the top of the steps. She could see Rory and her father, already half a block away.

"Um, can you tell Da I'll catch up later?" Molly said. "I want to go see something."

Kiernan smiled wearily. "I thought you might. Don't spend too long there, okay?"

"Okay. I'll call Legerdemain when I'm done, and he can send Ariel to get me."

Kiernan squeezed her arm, then jogged off after their father and brother. Molly turned and scanned the crowds. No one seemed to be looking at her, but all the same she cast her eyes down and turned her collar up as she moved farther into the city.

※

Ingrid Bledsoe
    Francis Bourne
    Samira Bukhari

As Molly scanned down the list, the names began to blur together. She swiped at her eyes, trying to clear the tears, but they wouldn't clear.

Last time she had visited the *Gloria Mundi* memorial, they hadn't started carving the names of the dead. It had just been a ring of tall standing stones surrounding a statue of the huge iron-plated airship. It had been hard enough being here without the names. So many names.

None of these people care if you cry over them, she told herself. *Stop it.* She ran her sleeve over her eyes, and this time they stayed clear. She forced herself to look up at the names again. She moved along the stones to the last in the row.

Blair Sawyer

Cosmo Stathakis

Christine Sullivan

She scanned down to the end. *It's not there.* Her heart thudded in her chest, and she put her finger where Brighid Stout, her sister, would be. *How can it not be there? Maybe they left her off because of me?*

She went through all the names again, on all the stones, but Brighid wasn't on the list of dead. *Could she have survived?* Molly almost didn't want to think about it. Poking at the memories, at the guilt she felt over her sister, was like prodding a bear that could wake and consume her at any moment.

Her eyes moved back up the stone to another name. *Meredith Peterson.* She leaned closer. *Is that her?* She couldn't see any other Merediths on the list. When she had arrived on the *Gloria Mundi*, terrified and knowing no one, a girl named Meredith had taken an interest in her. She had teased her about her height and kept her from feeling lost. And then

Molly had freed the ship's spirit and sent them all crashing to the ground. *If that is you, Mer, I'm sorry. I'm so, so sorry.*

She didn't need to look to know that Charles Arkwright's name wasn't there, even if he had died in the crash. No one was supposed to know he was still alive, kept from death for over a hundred years by strange spiritual machines. Below the *Gloria Mundi*'s statue, she could see Tyler Arkwright's name instead. He had been the current head of Haviland Industries and was meant to be Charles's great-great-grandson, though he was only playing the part so Charles could stay hidden. There was a small statue of Tyler too, perched at the prow of the *Gloria*, resplendent in his dress uniform. Molly stared at it. *I wonder who you really were.*

"Molly," a voice whispered.

Molly spun around, legs tensing to run. But there was no one behind her. She scanned the area. There were a few people wandering among the memorial stones, but none of them were paying her the slightest attention.

"Molly, here."

The voice was a deep rumble that tickled her feet. In fact, it seemed to be coming from the ground itself. It took her a moment to understand.

"Toves?" she whispered. He was a terric spirit who had helped her, but she hadn't seen him since before the *Gloria Mundi*.

"Yeah. Now, can we get out of here? There are sniffers around."

"Sniffers?"

"Ferratics."

Molly's eyes snapped up, searching the alleys. Ferratics were spiritual machines designed to hunt rogue spirits, but she'd had plenty of them hunting her too. Even the word sent a jolt of fear through her chest.

"Go south a ways. We'll talk there," Toves said.

Molly started walking. She tucked her hands into her pockets, hunched her shoulders and tried her best to disappear as she made her way into the crowded streets.

The memorial was situated in the commercial district of Terra Nova. Molly took a risk every time she came here—more people meant more chances to be recognized, and this was the busiest part of the city. The floating island of the docks loomed far above, airships arriving and departing constantly. The docks were connected to the ground by the umbilical, a steel cable a dozen yards thick, with cable cars swarming over it like bugs on the bark of a rotting tree. Everywhere there were shopkeepers hawking their wares; sailors on leave from the airships, pockets full of fresh coin; and pickpockets hoping to relieve them of it. Molly kept her head down as she moved south in the direction Toves had sent her.

After a few blocks she started to relax. Shops gave way to houses and then warrens of broken-down buildings. The crowds of people were replaced with detritus, heaped in corners and lying in the streets. Weary faces peered out from windows. An old man sat on a stoop, hammering tacks into the sole of a cracked leather shoe. He looked up at her, staring openly, but said nothing.

"Alley on your left," said Toves from the ground. She turned, trying to look like she knew where she was going.

The alley was crowded with old boxes crumbling from age and weather. She made her way around the piles to the brick wall at the end of the alley. She checked behind her for watching eyes and then crouched down.

"Are you here?"

Beside her, the ground crumbled and reformed itself into a pile of stones. The pile formed legs and pulled itself up.

"Should be fine here," he said. "Sniffers never come this way."

"Why aren't you in Knight's Cove? It's not safe here for you."

The pile of stones rumbled. "Don't have to tell me. 'M not new at this." Toves's voice was like stones rubbing together, and it made her bones vibrate uncomfortably.

"But why?"

"Why do you think? Looking for you. Watched your house for a while, but you didn't come, and then Disposal set up camp there and that was that. The memorial was the only place I thought I might catch you."

The spirit fell silent. Molly waited, but the stones didn't even move. "Toves?"

"Gimme a minute. This ain't easy for me. Not used to asking for help."

"You…want help? My help?"

The stones pulled themselves up until they towered over Molly, standing on two legs as thick as pillars.

"I want to go home. Want to get out of this godforsaken place."

"You can't get away? But there are lots of terric fonts not far from—"

"Oh, well then, wish I had thought of that. I'll just nip down. Ta, Molly."

"You don't have to get pissy about it."

The stones hunched lower. "Don't know much about terric fonts, do you?"

Molly shook her head. "Spent all my time with the aetheric ones."

"Terric fonts don't move around. They sit in the ground, spittin' out nice juicy spirits like me from time to time. Which is why humans have set up camp at every terric font for a hundred miles, with their big iron drills and ferratics and enough traps to hold every spirit on the other side."

"So you can't go alone?"

"Not if I don't want my rocks chewed into dust by some big metal beastie."

"You don't think you could find an undiscovered font if we got you out of Terra Nova?"

"I'd bet my boulders Haviland Industries has got every font this side of the Atlantic staked and claimed."

"And you think they'd all be manned?"

"Yeah. Some more than others, of course. Maybe we could find a nice quiet one somewhere, but I wouldn't know where to look."

"Okay." Molly took a breath and closed her eyes. *Can we do that? Break into a harvesting operation just to get one spirit home?* It would be a big risk. Even without Disposal there, the harvesting crew and the ferratics would be a lot worse than the factory foremen they'd faced so far. *But we were looking for a new target. It would help a lot of spirits if we could actually shut down a harvest. Oh sod it, I wish Kier or Da were here.*

"I think we can do that. Try to help, I mean. But I have to talk to the others first."

Toves heaved himself up onto his pillar legs. "Fair enough. You do that, then come pick me up when you're ready."

"Okay. I'll see you soon. Are you okay getting back to Knight's Cove?"

"No, Moll, I'm scared. Please hold my hand so the big bad Disposal blokes don't—"

"Okay, okay, I get it! You're fine. I'll come see you."

The stones flowed down into the ground with a scraping noise, leaving behind no trace of them in the dirt. Molly made her way to the mouth of the alley to make sure no one had heard the conversation. She ducked back inside, closed her eyes and felt her way through the connection she shared with Legerdemain. She tugged at it like a rope and felt a returning tug. Then she sat to think things through until Ariel arrived.

THREE

They flew close to the water, the choppy waves below occasionally rising up to slap the ship's hull. The air here was damp and salty, but Molly was getting used to that. They had been spending more and more time over the ocean, where Disposal wasn't likely to catch them. There were places on the island around Terra Nova where they could be safe— the city itself only covered a small part of the land mass, despite its enormous size. But the island was dotted with harvesting operations, and you never knew when you might run across an aetheric harvester. They all felt more at ease out here, over the water.

"You really want to break into Haviland Industries?" Rory said, pulling Molly's thoughts back to the present. "I mean, we pull some crazy stunts, but this…"

"It makes sense," Kiernan said. "We need to know where a font is and where we're likely to find the least resistance. For that information, there's only one place to go."

"And once you get to their offices, how do you get in?" Molly's father asked. He hadn't stopped frowning since Molly proposed this new plan.

"Croyden," she said.

"The infusionist." Ariel's voice was cold. Molly realized that the last time Ariel had seen Croyden, he had stuffed her inside a spiritual machine—at the request of Molly and her father.

"He helped me with the *Gloria Mundi*," Molly said. "He might be willing to help again."

"He just might at that," her father said. "So when do we go?"

"Tonight, after dark. But I don't think we should all go." Her father's frown got even deeper.

"Of course we shouldn't all go," Rory said. "We can't descend *en masse* into the lion's den. We'll be spotted in a second."

Molly nodded. "I think it should—"

"No," her father said gruffly. "You can't go alone, Molly. And don't pretend that wasn't what you were going to suggest."

"Actually, I was going to say me and Ariel. I need her help."

Her father huffed. "Take Rory with you too. He's better at this sneaking-around stuff than you are."

"Always knew I'd make you proud, Da," Rory said.

Their father just scowled. "I'd tell you to be careful, but you wouldn't bloody listen anyway. At least have some supper before you go." He turned and went belowdecks, heading for the mess. Molly's brothers followed after.

Molly turned back to the waves for a few moments. She watched them churn, the light from Legerdemain reflected and refracted on their surface.

I really should eat something. She turned away from the ocean and followed her family below.

A few hours later they were sailing fast through the upper atmosphere, far above the clouds. Molly's breathing quickened—a response, she knew, to less oxygen getting into her body. Usually Legerdemain and Ariel—and Molly herself, changed as she was by her connection to Legerdemain—gave off enough oxygen to counter the higher altitudes. She knew the airship must be very high indeed for her to feel the effects.

Below them the lights of Terra Nova appeared through gaps in the clouds, tinged brown by the city's smog. *That looks like the industrial district. We must be close to the docks now.*

Legerdemain dipped his wings down, cupping them to catch the air, and the ship slowed to a stop. "Looks like this is where we get off," Rory said. "Ariel, are you sure you can carry us both down?"

"I am not," she said. "I have never tried to carry more than one person. But I believe I can get you to the docks safely."

Rory swallowed.

"Let's not wait," Molly said. "The longer we're here, the more chance there is that Legerdemain will be spotted." She looked up at the huge spirit, his pale-blue belly glowing against the dark sky. She could feel Legerdemain's fear for her through the connection they shared. He did not want her to go, though he would not try to stop her. Over the past year their connection had only grown, until at times the spirit felt like an extension of herself, or she an extension of him. She tried to send reassurance back to him, but he could feel the anxiety she was masking.

Molly and Rory walked to the gunwale and each put a foot on it. Far, far below, Molly could see glimmers of the docks through the clouds.

"That's a long way down," Rory said.

"Only a couple of miles, I'd say," Molly replied.

"If you are ready," Ariel said. She broke apart into a bright-blue cloud and wrapped herself around both of them. Rory took Molly's hand.

"Try not to move too much, please," Ariel said.

A small whimper escaped Rory's lips, and then he stepped off the ship with Molly. Ariel's winds tightened around them, pulling against gravity. Molly looked up and saw the ship shrinking away above them, disconcertingly fast. She looked back down. "Are we falling a little too fast, Ariel?"

Rory's hand tightened, making her fingers ache.

"It will have to do," Ariel replied breathlessly.

"What do you mean, *it will have to do*?" Rory hissed.

"You are much heavier than your sister," Ariel said. "The difference had not occurred to me."

"It's okay," Molly said, though she felt a lump growing in her throat. "If we find somewhere soft to land, we'll be fine."

They were nearing the clouds now. As they entered, the moist air chilled Molly's skin, setting her shivering.

Her brother's face was hazy through the thick cloud, but she could see that his eyes were screwed shut.

They emerged from the clouds, and Terra Nova appeared beneath them, huge and raucous. Just below their feet was the floating island of the docks. From above it almost looked like a huge flower, its inner districts dark and decrepit, its outer circle more lively and colorful, the airships and floating cranes like bees buzzing around the petals. The tangled metal cords that made up the umbilical curved away below the docks like the flower's stem. The endless lights of the city spread out around them as far as Molly could see.

"Take us to the center of the docks, Ariel," Molly said. "All the shops there are boarded up, so no one should see us." She squeezed her brother's hand. "Almost there now."

"That's what I'm afraid of," he wheezed.

The strands of Ariel's body wrapped tighter around them, winds as strong as ropes digging in to Molly's skin. The roofs of the buildings were coming up fast now. And they seemed to be accelerating.

"Ariel? Are you okay?"

"I...am...trying..." The spirit's voice was a whisper now.

"Oh crap, oh crap, oh crap," intoned her brother.

They were falling too fast—not quite in free fall, but they would break bones landing like this. Molly cast her eyes around.

There was a groan from Ariel. "Molly, I cannot—"

"I know! I'm looking!" Molly scanned the area and finally found what she was looking for. Behind one of the buildings, several large nets were strung between wooden poles. "There! Ariel, take us over that roof!" Molly summoned the nearest winds, which swept in around them and buoyed them up above the building.

"Don't fly into the nets, Ariel," Molly warned. "They're iron-laced. Just drop us."

"I don't believe I'll have a choice," Ariel said.

"Oh crap, oh crap, oh crap," Rory went on.

They skimmed across the roof of the shop and out into the yard. There was a small net directly below them, stretched out horizontally between four posts.

"Drop us now!" Molly said.

Ariel released them, and Rory yelped as they fell into the waiting net. They landed on the hard ropes, and then the entire net slid down off its poles, dumping them onto the ground.

"Ow," Rory said, his leg draped over Molly's stomach. "You're not allowed to make our travel plans anymore."

He stood and disentangled himself, working his left elbow up and down. Ariel descended, reassuming her human-like form, though looking a little ragged.

"Anyone see us?" Molly asked.

"Not that I could tell. Are either of you hurt?"

"No, that was perfect. Croyden's shop is just a few streets away."

They ran to their destination through the ill-lit streets. The infusionist's shop was closed and locked, but Molly could hear a rhythmic banging coming from inside.

"I should not be here for this meeting," Ariel said. "If you are wrong about the infusionist's sympathies, it would go badly for me. When you need me, call to Legerdemain and I will come."

Molly nodded and watched Ariel ascend to the clouds before knocking on the door. The banging inside did not stop. Rory pounded on a window. There was a moment of silence.

"The store is closed!" someone shouted from inside.

Molly recognized Croyden's dry voice, even through the door. "It's Molly, Mr. Croyden."

More silence. Molly cast her eyes down the narrow street but saw no one.

"Think he's called Disposal yet?" Rory whispered.

The door suddenly swung open. "In, in!" Croyden hissed. Rory hurried inside, and Molly followed.

The shop was just as she remembered it, cluttered from floor to ceiling with machinery. A row of chairs for customers sat empty to her right. Farther inside the shop the machinery was piled so high that she could not even see the workshop at the back.

Croyden closed the door and threw the bolt. He turned and stared down at them from his considerable height, leaning to the left because of the stiff metal apparatus that stood in place of his right leg. His frown was so deep that she could barely see his eyes.

"I never expected to see you here again. I thought you smarter than that," he said.

Molly nodded, unsure what to say.

"What are you doing here? On the docks, of all places?" Croyden asked. "No, wait, don't answer that. Come away from the windows."

He led them through the clutter to the small clear space of his workroom, hung with tools and half filled with the iron-plated table where he infused spirits into machines. With a grunt he sat down on a low bench, his mechanical leg sticking out straight in front of him.

"Now," he said. "What on earth are you doing in my shop?"

"We..." Molly took a deep breath. "We need your help again."

Croyden let out a huff of air that might have been a laugh. "The last time I helped you, the greatest airship in the history of the world ended up a twisted wreck."

"Yeah," Molly said. "Thanks."

This time he laughed in earnest. "You know, you don't look nearly as murderous as the posters suggest. No blood-shot eyes. No fangs."

"Just me," Molly said.

Croyden nodded. "Just you." He sighed, then reached down and rolled up the pant leg that covered his mechanical leg, revealing its long piston and a dizzying array of gears and springs. He reached up to the wall above him and pulled a wrench off a hook, using it to turn a nut on the side of his thigh. "And how does 'just you' know I won't turn you in?"

"Because you have a history with our father, and you helped me before."

"I don't think any amount of friendship with your father could warrant helping the most wanted criminals in Terra Nova," Croyden said. "I could be locked away, my shop closed, everything taken from me, just for talking to you. I owe your father much, but not that."

Molly didn't respond, watching him work on his leg. The metal piston gleamed in the light in a strange way. She'd taken it for iron the first time she'd seen it, but this didn't look like iron. He finished unwinding the nut and pulled a plate off the small box that sat near his hip. She had thought it was a spirit trap, but as she watched, he pulled a pitcher of water out from under his bench and refilled a reservoir inside the box. He removed a small metallic lump from a separate compartment and placed this inside the stove in the corner. He took out another lump from the stove, this one red-hot, and put it inside his leg. As it slid in, a hiss of steam escaped from the heel of his foot plate, and the piston flexed. Croyden began putting himself back together.

"How often do you have to replace the coal, or whatever that is?" Molly asked.

The infusionist stopped his work and looked up at her cautiously. "Every hour or so. More if I move around a great deal."

"It's steam-powered? Like the old trains?"

"One or two orders of magnitude more complex, but yes. Like the old trains."

Molly smiled, feeling more at ease. "We need to get into the Haviland Industries offices. You work for them sometimes, I know, so I hoped you could help."

"Is this more sabotage then?" He returned to screwing the nut back into place.

"We just need information."

"Why?"

"To help a spirit get home."

Croyden didn't look up. "And now we've come to it. Aiding spirits."

"It's what we do. What we're trying to do."

"And what makes you think I might help you with that? Spirits are, after all, the natural enemies of humanity."

"I don't think you'll help, for the record," Rory said. "Molly thought you might. I'm just hoping you'll give us a running start before you call the agents in."

"You helped me against Arkwright before," Molly said. "And I think you might want to help the spirits too, because there are spiritual machines all around you, yet you're walking around on a steam-powered leg."

The infusionist stopped and set his wrench down on the bench beside him. He didn't say anything for a long time. He seemed to deflate, his slender frame folding until his head hung down so she couldn't see his face.

"Will you help us? Or should we start running, like Rory said?"

"What you're really asking me is if I'm spirit-touched, like you. If I have sympathy for the spirits. But I work every day against them. I lock them in small metal boxes, where they will be forced into labor until they die or they escape. If I did that every day and also harbored sympathies for the spirits I imprison, what kind of man would that make me?"

Dozens of answers flashed through Molly's mind. She remembered the nausea she had felt when she found out for sure that the spirits weren't the simple, evil beings she had always been taught they were. And it hadn't been the injustice of it all that had made her sick. It was the realization that she had known the truth for a long time and had lied to herself because she didn't want to upend her life. She tried to remember what Ariel had said to her at that moment.

"I guess it would make you the kind of man who could help us now," she said carefully. "And if you feel sick, like I did, that's good. You *should* feel that way, because we've all been doing awful things for a long, long time. But feeling bad about it doesn't change it. A friend told me that a long time ago now. A friend who's made of air, and who I made you lock inside a flitter because I thought it would be fun to fly."

He looked up sharply. "The one who spoke? She's still alive?"

"Her name is Ariel."

He took a deep, shuddering breath, and his long fingers clenched and unclenched several times. His keen eyes wandered around the room, taking in his workspace, before returning to Molly. "What kind of information are you looking for?"

"We need to find a terric font that isn't being harvested right now or is lightly manned."

He nodded. "You'll be wanting the records offices then. What time is it?" He stood and strode across the room, knocking a pile of rolled onionskin parchments off a desk and revealing a clock behind them. The hour hand was verging on the nine. "The woman at the front desk is there late some days. We may just catch her if we hurry." He bent and pulled his pant leg down, then began limping toward the front of the shop.

"You'll help us?"

"Yes." He stopped at the door and turned, his eyes meeting hers. She saw a storm there—anger and fear and shame, all twisted together. She thought he might weep.

Instead he just turned and opened the door. "Come. We have to leave now, or we'll be too late."

FOUR

Molly thought the offices of Haviland Industries smelled of money. In the midst of the ramshackle docks, they were clean and austere, the white walls unstained by the pollution all around them. The windows of the second floor were dark, but an igneous lamp still burned above the entrance. The polished wood of the large front door glistened in the light.

Croyden stopped and spun to face them, leaning down to talk to Molly and Rory in a low voice. "There is an alley on the other side of the building. Two-thirds of the way down, you will find a locked door. Go there and wait for me."

Molly nodded. The infusionist strode quickly to the front door. He pulled it open and stepped inside. Molly heard him say, "Oh, good, Margaret—you haven't left yet," and then the heavy door closed behind him.

Molly and Rory sped along the street to the far end of the building. As promised, a narrow alley ran between the office building and another, dingier building beside it. She started down the alley, but Rory grabbed her sleeve and pulled her back onto the street.

"Rory, the—"

"No, you heard what the captain said. They'll cast off if we're not there in time." He was marching them farther down the street, away from the alley.

"What—" she began, and then a tall woman in a blue jacket strode past them, close enough to touch. The blue jacket was unmistakably the one worn by Haviland Industries sailors. The woman glanced briefly at them as she walked by.

"Honestly, this is the last time I let you disembark at the docks," Rory said sharply, slowing his pace but keeping his grip tight on her arm. He kept marching her forward until the woman turned a corner and disappeared. They both looked the other way, saw no one was coming and dashed back to the alley.

"Thanks," Molly said. Rory nodded.

They found the door and pressed against the wall nearby, trying to make themselves inconspicuous to people passing on the street.

"How long has it been?" Molly asked.

"Only a minute." Rory tapped his heel against the wall. "What do you reckon? Think Croyden can talk his way past the front desk? Or will he get cold feet and leave us here?"

"He seemed pretty determined."

Rory nodded again. "That he did. Nicely done with that, by the way. Surprised me. I'm still getting used to this new Molly, I suppose."

"What? Who?"

"You know, the Molly that actually speaks to people instead of muttering to herself and hiding up top of the engine. And not only speaks, but manages to convince people to help her, at great personal risk, with absolutely no chance of personal gain. It's a little scary, honestly. Maybe I should be glad you didn't speak to me all those years we were growing up."

Molly stared back at him, silent.

Rory waited a moment, then grinned. "There's the old Molly. Not everything's changed, I guess."

"I didn't convince him. He wanted to help already."

Rory nodded, but his grin didn't fade.

"And it was you who didn't talk to me when we were little," Molly said.

He continued tapping the wall with his foot, slow and rhythmic. Molly stared at the door, willing it to open. She could hear the sounds of ships a few blocks away—sailors shouting, the creak of wood, the chuff of the cranes. She closed her eyes and concentrated on the sounds. The *Legerdemain*—the ship, which still bore the same name as the spirit that carried it—didn't sound that way anymore now that it was only her family aboard and its days of harvesting spirits were over. Molly knew that the ships she heard now were bringing cargoes of captive spirits to market, imprisoned souls being sold like fuel. And yet these were the sounds of her childhood, and somehow they still calmed her. She gave herself a moment to relax into it, then opened her eyes again.

"How long?"

Rory pulled his watch from his pocket. "It's been eight minutes. Maybe we should scarper."

A few more silent moments passed, and then they heard footsteps on the other side of the door, and it opened. Croyden leaned out, checked the alley and beckoned them in.

"We won't have long," he whispered. "I'm meant to be fetching a few schematics."

Croyden held a lamp that lit their way. The rest of the building was already dark. He led them swiftly down narrow hallways toward the back of the building, closed doors passing on either side. Finally he ushered them into a room on their left.

Inside, they faced a single broad desk in front of ranks of tall cabinets stretching back a dozen yards. Molly gaped.

"I hope you know where to look," Rory whispered to Croyden, "or we'll be here for days."

"As a matter of fact, I do. Come." He led them past the desk, along the cabinets that lined the right wall. They passed a white door that almost looked like part of the wall. Croyden stopped on the other side of the door.

"Records of the terric operations are kept here. Surveying information should be kept..." He ran his finger across several of the drawers set into the cabinets, pulled one open and began riffling through the files. "Here." He pulled out a stack of files and handed several to each of them. "Quickly now." He strode away, and Molly heard him opening drawers elsewhere.

Molly could barely see in the wan light that Croyden's lamp cast across the ceiling. She squinted down at the papers. Each sheet was a record of a terric font, with codings for size and strength of spirits. She found a few that were marked with a red stamp declaring them *DEPLETED*. There were at least a dozen with the mark. *What does that mean? Fonts that don't have spirits coming through anymore?*

"This one says *PENDING*," Rory whispered, showing her one of the papers. "Think it—"

"Pardon?" a woman's voice said from the front of the room. "Did you say something, Mr. Croyden?" Molly and Rory froze, footsteps moving toward them.

"Ah, yes!" Croyden said from two aisles down. They heard the hiss of his pneumatic leg moving toward the doorway. "I was just saying that I've found the original here, but I couldn't find the copies I need. Could you assist me?" Molly gestured to the door just beside them, and she and Rory stepped through it. On the other side was a small carpeted room with a long table and a wispy plant in the corner. They pulled the door shut behind them.

Molly put her files on the table and took the sheet Rory had been trying to show her. As he had said, the word *PENDING* was scrawled across the top in red pen. The notations on the spirits indicated it was a medium-sized font, large enough for Toves to pass through but not much larger. Much of the rest of the form was incomplete—no list of workers, supply schedules or other details—but it gave a set of coordinates that she thought her father or Kiernan could work with.

"Think that's what we're looking for?" Rory asked.

"It seems like it's one they're not actively harvesting yet. We might be in luck," Molly whispered back. She folded the paper and slipped it into her pocket.

Outside the room she could hear Croyden and the woman still talking, and the clacking of drawers opening and closing. She wondered if they should try to sneak away while the woman was distracted, but she didn't relish the thought of finding their way back through the building in the dark.

"Moll," Rory whispered. She turned and saw him across the room. He was looking down at something that cast a golden, rippling light across his face. He beckoned her over.

As she got closer, she saw a strange device on the floor— a small curved disk rimmed in iron, with a cloudy glass center. The device was casting an image up into the air above it, just a foot off the ground. The image was cloudy, made of shifting amber light, but it was unmistakably their sister, Brighid. She was gesturing like she was explaining something, but there was no sound.

"What...what is this?" Molly whispered. Rory only shook his head.

The door opened and Molly turned, her heart in her throat. But it was only Croyden.

"She's gone," Croyden said, "but we have just a moment."

Neither of them moved. The infusionist took a step into the room.

"Did you hear me?" His eyes fell on the image of Brighid. "Oh. Have you not seen the projections before?"

"The projections?" Molly said. "I don't understand. Why is this thing showing Brighid?"

"They've been broadcasting her speeches over the projection network."

"Speeches?" Molly's brain was struggling to keep up.

Croyden knelt down beside them. "Did you not know that Haviland Industries has her making speeches decrying you and your family?"

Molly couldn't say anything. "We were pretty sure she died in the crash," Rory said.

"Oh. Oh." Croyden tapped his long fingers on the carpet. "Well, she didn't. But..." He looked over his shoulder. "You should really know what she's been saying. As long as this is one of the short loops." His fingers moved to the device, turning wheels along its outer edge. The sound of Brighid's voice faded up, whisper-quiet.

"...not try to reason with her, for she is beyond reason," she was saying. "Call for help, and seek Disposal agents as soon as possible. Thank you." There was a strange jump, Brighid suddenly leaning right when she had been leaning left, and she began talking again. "Hello. I am Brighid Stout, sister of Molly Stout. Haviland Industries has asked me to tell you about my sister—or the person who used to be my sister. When we were growing up, she often sought the company of our engine and the spirit inside. Even before she was made the ship's engineer, she was drawn to the engine. At the time I thought her eccentric, a moody child. It was only when she tried to kill me, and succeeded in killing dozens of souls aboard the *Gloria Mundi*, that I understood. She is spirit-touched now, lost to their vile influence. I believe it was inevitable. She sought this out like a moth drawn to a flame. I have no doubt that it was she who brought the spirit's influence to the rest of our family, and now they are lost as well. But my brothers and my father were good people once. Perhaps they can be saved, or treated. My sister..." She paused and bent her head, as if struggling. "My sister, I believe, was always insane. If you encounter her, do not try to reason with her, for she is beyond reason. Call for help, and seek Disposal agents as soon as possible. Thank you." Brighid's position jumped from left to right again. "Hello, I am—"

Croyden turned the wheels, and the image fell silent. "I am sorry, but now we really must go."

Molly was hardly aware of the building around her. Croyden took her by the elbow, and they were walking, but she couldn't feel her feet hitting the carpet.

"That projection thing. It's a network?" Rory was whispering. "So that speech is being shown in other places too?"

Her sister was alive. Her sister was calling her insane.

"Anywhere with enough money for a projector. The projections are beamed through the air and caught by receivers on the devices. They are common in the wealthier districts, and some have been distributed to public spaces recently. I had forgotten that being always aloft as you were, you might not know about them."

They were walking down a hallway. *She sought this out like a moth drawn to a flame.*

"And she's making a lot of these speeches?"

"Hush."

There was the door they had come through. *My sister, I believe, was always insane.*

Croyden pushed her gently through the door and into the alley. "Thanks," Rory said.

"Do not come and see me for a while," Croyden said. "But I wish you luck."

The door closed, and the alleyway was empty and quiet. A few blocks away, the work of the airships went on unimpeded, the sounds exactly the same as they had been before. The voices, the wood, the cranes.

She is beyond reason.

"Molly," Rory said.

She looked up into his face. His dark eyes, a lock of hair hanging down across the bridge of his nose. *It was only when she tried to kill me...*

Rory reached up and flicked her ear, hard.

"Ow."

"We've got to go now. Mission accomplished."

"Right. Yes." Molly brushed her hands across her face. "Yes. Let's get away from the building, and then we can signal Ariel."

They walked toward the front of the building and came back out onto the street. The sounds from the airships had grown louder now, and Molly could even hear the crack of ropes pulling taut as someone adjusted the sails.

"I don't understand why Brighid is saying those things."

"Because she's a sack of piss?" Rory said. "We're getting too close to the edge of the docks. Too many people." He turned left, and Molly followed after.

"No, I mean, why is Haviland Industries making her give the speeches? What's the point?"

"To make them afraid of you. You're spirit-touched, after all."

"But everyone already thinks I'm—"

"Look, maybe we can talk about this later. Or better yet, not at all. For now, let's shut our gobs and get out of here."

Molly stopped talking, but her sister's words ran through and through her mind.

FIVE

"It's only a short trip, right?"

Toves sat beside the device they had rigged to take him aboard the ship. It was a simple sheet of canvas, tied at all four corners and connected to a pulley they'd lashed onto the yardarm of the aft mast. Toves had put one tentative foot onto the canvas and stopped almost immediately.

"Well, it's all the way across the island, Da says," Molly told him. "West side, next to the Gulf of St. Lawrence. But Legerdemain is fast. Less than half an hour to get there."

Still Toves didn't move. They were down near the water, on an old wharf long since fallen into disrepair. It was just north of Knight's Cove, where Molly's family had once lived. Disposal did not spend much time in areas this poor, but Molly knew a spirit as big as Legerdemain could not go unnoticed for long.

"Toves, we should really go."

"Moll, hurry!" her father called from the deck of the ship. "Kier says there are airships!"

"Come on, Toves," Molly said. She gave him a hard push, which didn't move him an inch.

Toves rumbled. "Look, I don't do so well off the ground. Spirit of the earth and all that. Less than half an hour?"

"Yes! Now get on so we can get you home!"

"Home," Toves rumbled, and he finally rolled the rest of the way onto the canvas. Molly waved to her father, who backed out of sight. A moment later the ropes attached to the four corners of the canvas pulled taut, and Toves was lifted off the ground. Molly gripped one of the ropes to catch a ride up. She could hear Toves groaning inside the canvas.

"Are you okay?"

"Just get us there bloody fast." The groaning continued. It sounded as if his stones were grinding against each other. The sound made Molly's hackles rise.

Once they reached the deck, Rory stepped forward to pull them in. Molly's father let go of the rope he had been hauling, and Toves fell to the deck with a thud.

"Best go now," Kiernan called from the ship's prow. "One of the airships is turning our way."

Molly moved up next to her brother. Usually she could see airships from a long distance away—the winds they wove to stay aloft were incredible, and to Molly's spirit-touched eyes they made the ships blaze like beacons. But she could only see clear skies and undisturbed rivers of wind where Kiernan was looking.

"Where are they?" she asked. Kiernan pointed, and gave her the spyglass. She raised it and finally made out the dark outline of a ship, still miles away. It was a strange shape—shallow-hulled and wide, with no sails that she could see. "I don't understand. It doesn't have any winds around it. What's holding it up?"

"Whatever it is, it's got a silver sword painted on its side, so I doubt it's friendly."

Molly nodded. "Legerdemain, better get us out of here." The spirit lifted its wings and called a strong wind to them. They soared upward, banking out over the water before turning to the west. The dark airship they had seen was left far behind.

As they climbed above the clouds, Toves cried out. He was still struggling to heave himself out of the canvas, but he seemed to be having trouble moving. His stones kept scattering, and one escaped completely and rolled across the deck. Molly ran to catch it before it bounced overboard.

She brought the stone back to Toves where he lay flat across the deck, still half covered by the canvas. She placed the stone with his others, and it slowly sank into the spirit's body.

"Does it hurt?" she asked.

"Like blazes. Just get me back to the ground as fast as you can."

"Oh bloody hell. Molly, we've got a problem."

Molly's father was leaning out over the starboard side, spyglass to his eye. "What is it, Da? Another airship?"

He offered her the spyglass, and she looked through. Her breath stopped in her throat. "Oh."

"You see it?"

"I see it."

Up ahead, she could make out what looked like a mine shaft—the entrance to the terric font that was their destination. There was a huge ferratic perched at the edge of the shaft. It looked something like a badger, save that it was ten feet tall and bristling with metal plates. Its long claws flexed, digging furrows in the rock beneath it. Hunched and jagged, it loomed over several human workers who were unloading spirit traps from a lift that descended into the shaft.

"I don't understand. The record said it wasn't being harvested. There was no crew listed!"

"Well, I'd say it's got a full crew now, plus some security with muscle." He took the spyglass back from her. "We should make new plans, Moll. This isn't going to work."

Molly stared down at the activity below them, trying to will it away. The sun was brushing the horizon, the light changing from white to gold, and several large trucks began to rumble away over the hills, heading for Terra Nova. The day's work was ending. But dozens of workers remained, and the ferratic was going nowhere.

Beside her, she heard her father asking Legerdemain to skirt the mine, so they wouldn't draw attention. Molly kicked the gunwale and turned, striding back to the aft mast where Toves lay. She hadn't seen the terric spirit move for ten minutes.

"Toves, there's a problem. They're harvesting the font. Full crew, big ferratic. We might have to look elsewhere."

A few of Toves's rocks scraped across the deck, but he said nothing.

"Toves? Did you hear?"

"Yeah yeah." His voice was barely a whisper.

Molly stepped closer and crouched over the spirit. "Are you okay?"

"*Okay* is not the word for it," he muttered, and Molly bent closer to hear his faint voice. "Gotta get to the ground. Gotta get…home."

"But the font isn't safe, Toves. How bad is it? Can you hold up if we need to go somewhere else?"

The only answer was a long, rumbling groan.

There was a rush of bright wind, and Ariel swept in over the deck. "Molly!" she said. "There is a complication. The font is—"

"I know. We saw."

"You saw the tunnel rat?"

"Is that what that big ferratic is?" Molly's father said, and Ariel nodded.

"Tunnel rat. Bloody hell," Toves wheezed, and Molly pressed her hands to her temples. She and Toves had run into a tunnel rat once before, when he had helped her break into Arkwright's mansion. She hadn't seen the ferratic then, but she'd seen the way it could carve through solid stone like it was sand. Even Toves had been terrified of it.

"Maybe now that we're out of the city, Toves can find us a font," Rory said. "Terric spirits can find terric fonts, right?"

"I don't…I don't think…" Toves muttered, then fell silent.

"He's hurt or sick or something. From being up in the air," Molly said. "I think we have to get him home soon."

"But we can't, Moll," her father said. "We can't go up against a ferratic like that."

"We don't have a choice, Da! I said we would get Toves home."

"Not at the cost of our lives! We have to keep ourselves safe too!"

"If you can stop shouting at each other for a moment, I may have a way to do both," Ariel said. "As I said, this complicates things, but complications can be overcome. We must get ourselves down to the shore. There is someone we should speak to."

·•✢·

They found a spot on the shore where Legerdemain could drop them, hidden from the terric mine by jagged cliffs. Molly shoved the limp Toves back into the canvas, and they lowered him down. The stones of his body spilled loosely out onto the rocky shore, barely holding together. "Never doing that again," he muttered. "Bloody airships." He fell still and silent.

By the time they were all on the ground, the sun had vanished from the sky. Molly watched ribbons of wind wending their way eastward, stars glimmering between them. Legerdemain rose up and drifted out over the water, disappearing among the winds. Even after he flew out of sight, Molly could still feel his worry.

Ariel floated out over the water, her blue light frosting the low waves. Molly followed her to the edge of the rocky beach. "You said we were going to speak to someone? I don't see anyone here."

"Patience. She is coming," Ariel said, drifting back and forth. "There. Just below me."

Molly looked down, but saw only the dark water. Ariel made a strange burbling sound.

"Ariel?"

"She is nervous."

"She?"

The surface of the water broke, and Molly saw scales glimmering in the blue light. Two eyes emerged from the water and blinked up at her. It was some kind of fish, fat-bodied and iridescent.

"An aqueous spirit?"

Molly stepped forward, but the fish drew back, and the water hunched up around it as if to defend the small spirit. Ariel made the burbling sound again, and it stopped moving. Molly approached more slowly this time. The fish blinked up at her, silver lights in its eyes glowing and fading in rhythm with the waves.

"She has told me there is another way into the mine," Ariel said.

The fish raised her mouth above the waves. "There is a tunnel," she whispered, her wide lips bending awkwardly to fit the human words.

"Would it take us to the font?" Molly asked. The fish nodded. "Where is it?"

"Here. Below us."

"Underwater? But we can't travel underwater. I don't even know how to swim!" She looked down at the spirit, into her shining eyes. She seemed to shrink under Molly's attention. "Can you help us? Clear the water out?"

The small head shook. "She cannot move that much water," Ariel said. "She is young, and not as strong as that.

But I have looked, and I believe the tunnel is narrow enough that you could traverse it without much swimming."

"What about, you know, breathing?"

"I can provide air while we are underwater."

"But what if I can't get to you in time? I can't swim, what if—"

"Molly, the winds listen when you call them. You can bring your own air if you are worried."

Molly breathed deep and looked down into the water, but in the dark she could see nothing below the surface.

"What you need to be asking isn't if you *can*, but if you bloody well *should*," her father said. Molly turned, but in the shadows of the cliff she could hardly see him—just the curve of his shoulders and two glimmering eyes. "You want to dive down underwater, without knowing how to swim, to break into an active terric harvest with God knows what defenses. All we've seen is the surface. Who knows what we'll find belowground. And for what?"

"To help Toves," Molly said. "He's sick. We made him sick when we took him aloft, and he needs—"

"Why is his life more important than yours?"

Molly paused, caught off guard by the anger in his voice. He hadn't raised his voice to her in months now, not since the night he'd gotten drunk and thrown her out of their house, before he had read Haviland's true journal, before the *Gloria Mundi* and everything else.

"It's not more important. But it's not less important either."

"It is if—" he began, but stopped short. She could see his eyes staring out at her from his shadowed face. And then he turned, and she heard his footsteps retreating back toward the cliff.

"Da?" He didn't stop, and she was afraid to raise her voice further, lest the crew at the mine hear her.

"I can talk to him," Kiernan said beside her. Molly turned and saw him watching the aqueous spirit curiously. "It sounds like a good plan, Molly. It's just hard for Da. All of this." He shrugged and walked after their father.

Molly turned to the aqueous spirit. "Thank you for your help." The spirit nodded once and then disappeared into the water, leaving not even a ripple behind. Molly listened to the waves at her feet. "Ariel, can you show me how to bring wind underwater?" she asked.

"Call the winds, and hold them close."

Molly reached up. A small golden thread of wind broke away from the eastward procession and bent down to her outstretched hand. She wrapped it in her fingers, holding it tightly. It shimmered in her hand for a moment, then fractured and broke into filaments that dissolved into the air.

"Not so tightly, Molly."

"Then how do I make it stay?"

"You cannot make it stay. You can only ask."

Molly reached up again. When the wind came down she took it in her hands, but this time kept her fingers loose. *Come with me,* she thought. *Keep me safe down there.* As she thought the words, more wind flowed down through her hands and circled her arms, stirring the small hairs on her skin and making her shiver. The wind entwined itself about her entire body, shifting constantly. It felt almost the same as when Ariel held her.

"Better," Ariel said.

Molly knelt on the rocks and put her wind-wrapped hand into the water. The water parted as the wind touched it. When she withdrew her hand, it was dry.

"This will stay with me?"

"As you breathe it, it will lose strength. But it should be ample for your needs."

"Except we have to get back out again, and there's no wind at the bottom of a mine."

Ariel flew closer. Her human shape became more definite, more solid, and her hands reached out to Molly's shoulders. "You forget this from time to time, Molly, but you are not alone. I am here. Your family is here. I will be able to provide air for everyone on our return. Not every responsibility is yours."

Molly clenched her teeth. "I know that." *I might actually feel better if it was just me. Then I wouldn't have to worry about getting you all killed.* "With the factories, I knew what we were doing. This is new."

"As was the first factory. As was the *Gloria Mundi*, which was considerably more formidable than this small harvest."

"Okay."

Molly checked the wind still wrapped around her. She looked over to where her father had retreated, against the cliff. He met her eyes and scowled, but nodded his head. Molly moved closer to the heap of stones that was Toves.

"It's time, Toves. Can you move yourself, or do we need to rig something up?"

"No. I can do it." The stones heaped up and then fell again, but on the second attempt Toves formed his body and rolled down into the surf. "First the air and now the damned water," she heard him mutter.

"When you need a breath, come to me," Ariel said to everyone. "Stay close."

The waves parted around Ariel as she flew downward, water frothing around her. Rory followed, then Kiernan and their father. Molly put her foot into the water, and it immediately soaked through her shoe. She stepped in farther, and the water began to part around her legs and the wind that wrapped them. The water got through in small cold splashes against her skin.

She stopped. Ariel's glimmering form was sinking away into blackness below her. *It's always worse before you start. So start.* The beach fell away as she walked forward, and then she was in up to her chest, her shoulders, her mouth. She closed her eyes and let the water flow over her head.

Once she was submerged, she opened her eyes again, letting them adjust. She couldn't see well in the murky salt water, but Ariel glowed from below, easy to follow even when the rest of the world was a blur. Molly found handholds in the rocks and dragged herself downward. *Why didn't I ever learn to swim?* She vaguely remembered a day at the lakeside with her brothers and Brighid, Kiernan and Rory splashing her mercilessly, her sister ignoring them all.

Ariel's light illuminated the dark mouth of the tunnel, just a couple of yards below Molly. Molly couldn't see her brothers. *They must already be in the tunnel.* Ariel flew inside, her blue light going with her. By the dimmer light of her own winds, Molly watched her father follow Ariel. Toves went after him, flowing inside stone by stone, leaving Molly alone in the ocean. She put her lips to her arm and took a breath of the wind there before pulling herself through the opening. Ariel's bright light turned the others into silhouettes in the murky water ahead.

The tunnel was narrow enough for Molly to touch both walls when she stretched out her arms. She dug her fingers into the stones and pulled herself forward, legs out straight behind her. *Just keep moving.*

The walls narrowed, and the top of Molly's head brushed the jagged ceiling. Molly's breath escaped in a cloud of bubbles, and she raised her arm for another deep lungful. The golden glimmer of the wind flickered as she breathed, and Molly felt more water splashing through onto her skin. She closed her eyes for a moment. *Not far. Keep going.* Below her, Toves rolled across the tunnel floor like a slow landslide.

There was an opening in the ceiling ahead, and Kiernan pulled himself through. Molly watched impatiently as Rory moved into the opening. She took another breath and felt a strange fizzing against her skin. The wind around her chest was fading and fracturing, turning into a cloud of bubbles in the water. *No, no.* She snatched at the bubbles as if she could bring them back, but they flowed through her fingers. Her heart drummed in her ears. Her lungs began to burn. Her father was in the opening now, kicking hard to push through, and Toves was rolling forward. Molly kicked ahead of Toves. *Let me through, let me through!* She pushed up, tangling herself in her father's legs. His foot connected painfully with her nose, but she didn't stop—she needed to get up, to find air.

Toves pressed into her from below, and for a moment she thought he was going to crush her. But his stones lifted her and her father up, and her flailing arms splashed into open air—*Air! Thank God, air!*—and she rose onto her knees and breathed in deep. She rolled off Toves's back onto the craggy ground. She blinked the salt from her stinging eyes. There were hands on her shoulders now, and she looked up to see her father again.

"Moll, you okay? What happened?"

"I'm okay. Sorry, Da."

"Near gave me a heart attack, coming up at me like that."

"It was just…the tunnel, all that stone around us, and the water, and then my air ran out." She took another deep breath. "Sorry, Da. And thanks, Toves."

"Welcome," Toves said, his voice still sounding ragged. "Don't blame you for panicking. Not natural, all that water." His stones rattled together.

She pulled herself up to sitting and looked around. They were crammed together in a small cave, close enough that Ariel's winds made everyone's hair dance. Across from them was a low, dark tunnel, and Kiernan had crawled halfway inside.

"This looks like it leads out to the mine," he said. "It's a tight squeeze though."

"Toves, could you open the passage up wider?" Molly asked.

"No. If I move so much as a pebble, that tunnel rat will know we're down here."

"I think we can fit," Kiernan said, and with a grunt he pulled himself deeper into the tunnel. "Yes. I'm through. No one's here. But…what is that?"

Ariel flowed swiftly through the tunnel after him, and Molly heard her gasp. "Ariel?" Molly called. "Kier? What is it?"

There was no answer. Molly's father hurried forward. The tunnel was just barely wide enough for his shoulders, and Molly waited impatiently as he kicked and grunted his way through, finally emerging from it with Molly right on his heels.

She crawled out into a vast cavern with roughhewn walls. Not a single wind stirred. In the center of the cavern she could see the metal frame of the lift, though the lift platform itself wasn't there. Molly could see a small patch of sky at the top of the shaft, but she was shocked by how far away it was. "We're a long way down."

The cavern walls were lit by a flickering golden glow. Molly searched for its source, and her eyes finally fell on the terric font. It was unmistakable, though it was unlike any font Molly had seen before. It had a jagged black center, like the beginning of a tunnel that led…not down, not any direction Molly could discern. *Out*, her subconscious suggested. *It leads out.* Around the edge of the opening, gold and silver sparks pulsed, shining like fire and then fading to a dull glow in a rhythm she could not quite follow but that spoke to her deeper mind like music.

There was something strange about the font, Molly realized. It commanded her attention, like it was the only real thing in the room, but at the same time it was as if it wasn't there. It was solid and unmoving, but she could also see the bare stone beyond it. It wasn't transparent. It was more like she was seeing with two sets of eyes, and one of them did not see the font at all.

"What is this?" Toves said beside her.

"I think there's something wrong with the font," she said.

"He is not referring to the font, Molly," Ariel said from her other side.

Molly looked over at Toves. He was still having trouble holding himself upright, but his stones had hunched together, like an animal bristling. Molly finally looked past the font and saw a long rectangular machine with wires and pipes running its length. Closer to the font, a wide segmented tube protruded from the machine, its end ringed by small metal claws that reminded Molly of teeth.

Her stomach dropped. "No," she said. "This can't be here."

"What is it?" Rory asked.

"It is something terrible," Ariel said. "It is a harvester that pierces the fonts to extract spirits directly from the spirit world. I came to the human world to stop a machine like this more than a year ago."

"We did stop it," Molly said. "We brought the *Gloria Mundi* down to stop it. This can't be here!"

"Well, it looks like someone forgot to tell these blokes the news," Toves wheezed.

SIX

Molly rushed to the harvester, the font forgotten.

"You're saying this is like that thing aboard the *Gloria*?" her father asked as he ran after her.

"It appears to be," Ariel answered.

"That would explain the font looking so weird," Molly said. "Remember, Ariel? The way the other harvester broke the fonts it used?"

"You can't break a font," Toves said.

"They have found a way, I assure you," Ariel replied.

"But no one would do that. That would be insane."

"Why?" Molly's father asked. "What would that mean?"

"Our worlds rely on each other, feed each other," Ariel said. "Cutting the worlds apart would be like removing all the water from an ecosystem. Everything would simply wither away. In both worlds, in the case of the fonts."

"Bloody hell," Toves said, rolling himself slowly forward, the light from the font washing over his stones.

"Not to mention all the spirits it will capture before the font collapses," Kiernan said. Molly nodded.

"But you said that thing on the *Gloria Mundi* had a first-level spirit in it," Rory said. "They can't have captured another one so soon, can they? I mean, first-level spirits are huge."

"Not one of the great ones in there," Toves said. "Or a *first level*, or whatever you call it." He moved up close to the machine, stopping just short of the iron walls. "It's something big in here, a terric spirit like me. They must have found a way to do it with smaller spirits. But I can hardly feel this one. Think it's almost dead."

"But how?" Molly asked. Her heart was jumping, her skin crawling. "Ariel? How can they do this? We almost died to stop this thing!"

"We stopped one harvester. But an idea is much harder to kill." Ariel's voice was so low, Molly almost couldn't hear her.

"Maybe this is why the files didn't say anything about this font," Kiernan said. "It's an experiment, or they're keeping it under wraps."

Molly thought back to the files at Haviland Industries— the ones marked *DEPLETED*. *Is that what it meant? Are all of those fonts they broke?* There were so many…

"So what do we do?" Kiernan asked.

"We came to get Toves home," Molly's father said. "I say we send him home."

"Too right," Toves said, rolling his stone body toward the font.

"No, wait!" Molly said. "Toves, hold on!"

"Molly, keep your voice down," Rory hissed at her. For a moment they all fell silent, listening. The lift creaked slightly, but they heard no other sound.

"I'm sorry," Molly whispered. "But we have to shut this thing down. We might need your help."

Toves groaned, and so did Molly's father.

"She is right," Ariel said. "This is a bigger problem."

"There's always a bigger problem," Molly's father said softly.

Toves had stopped, but he was silent. "Look, why don't we just check it out?" Molly said. "If we can get the spirit free without your help, Toves, we'll send you home right away. But please just hold on."

"Fine, fine," Toves hissed.

"Okay. So, um, if it's like the *Gloria Mundi*'s machine, there has to be a feeding apparatus. Something they put traps in through."

"Traps? They feed it other spirits?" Toves asked.

"Yeah. At least, they did on the *Gloria Mundi*."

"Is there anything humans won't do to us?" Toves asked.

"Let's look for hatches, okay?" Molly said.

They all spread around the machine, examining it. Molly drew close to the machine's clawed mouth, and it bent toward her. She stepped back. "We're trying," she whispered to it.

"Could this be it?" Kiernan asked from the far end of the cavern. Molly and the others ran over to him. Against the back wall sat a small cluster of empty traps. And there, set into the wall of the harvester, was a small hatch with a lever and a keyhole directly beside it. Molly tried the hatch's handle, but it was locked.

"Damn it. Rory, can you pick the lock?"

"Really, Moll?" Rory said. "I know I can be irresponsible, but I'm not a bloody cat burglar. Of course I can't pick the lock!"

"So how do we get it open?"

"I can do it," Toves said softly. "I think I've got enough energy left to crack that door, if it's not too thick. But if I do, the tunnel rat is going to be on us pretty quick."

Molly stared up at the harvester. "You want to do it anyway, don't you?" her father said at her side.

"Yeah. I think we should."

"And you think we can still get away? Even with that ferratic after us?"

"If we can get the spirit out of here, it should cause a lot of chaos. We could get away while they're still trying to get things under control." She looked into his eyes. "We have to try, at least."

Her father hung his head and said nothing. Molly looked around the room, and everyone nodded. "Okay. Toves?"

Molly and her family stepped back, and Toves sank low to the ground. A huge stone broke free from the cavern floor, and Toves sent it flying into the hatch. The hatch bent. More stones came, and the hatch gave way. "Keep going," Molly said. "There will be a second hatch inside, like an air lock." Toves kept throwing stones through the hole in the side of the machine until the opening was clogged with rock. Molly started shoveling the stones out of the way, her brothers and father helping at her sides. Beyond the stones she found the second hatch. It hung off its hinges.

"You did it," she said. "We're in."

"Good," Toves said. "'Cause we've got company coming. I can feel the tunnel rat digging its way down here."

Molly was suddenly glad they were so far down. It might buy them a few moments.

She clambered in over the last of the stones and kicked at the broken hatch. It came loose and went clattering into the machine. Molly heard a soft breath from inside, but nothing else. She crawled through.

The interior was one large metal chamber, barely visible by the light leaking in from the hole. The bent hatch sat against the far wall.

"I don't see anything," she said. She peered around, and in the silence she heard a faint hissing coming from the hatch. She frowned and crept closer. Where the hatch rested against the wall, a thin trail of smoke was rising. Molly gasped, then scrambled forward and snatched the hatch away. What she had taken for the back wall of the chamber was made of stone, not metal, and where the hatch had been, there was a dark spot burned into it.

"Hello?" Molly whispered. She placed her hand against the stone. It was warm. This close, she could see that strange curlicues were carved into it, and dim golden lights ran through them.

She heard a scraping sound, and above her something shifted. She looked up and saw two dark eyes staring down at her.

"Oh. Um, hi."

The stone she was touching slid across the ground as the huge spirit pulled itself up onto four craggy legs, each larger than Molly. It loomed over her, and she stumbled back.

The patterns of light on its skin brightened as it stirred, save on its underbelly, where it had been resting against the iron floor. The stone was burned black there.

"My God," Molly said. "We'll get you out of here." She looked back toward the open hatch and up again at the huge spirit. *How the hell are we going to get that thing out?* "Can you, I don't know, make yourself smaller or something? The opening is small."

The spirit stepped forward, wobbling precariously over Molly. Each time it took a step on the iron floor, it let out a grunt that sounded like skittering rocks. It pressed itself against the open hatch, releasing a gout of smoke and a smell like burning tar. It grunted again and bellowed so loud that Molly covered her ears. The iron walls creaked but did not move, and the creature collapsed backward. Molly jumped away before it could crush her.

She looked again at the hatch and at the huge spirit. She could see it better now, closer to the light. A head like a boulder, broken only by two eyes and a crack for its mouth. Legs made of thick oval stones that somehow bent without breaking when it moved. It looked like a cliffside come to life. It looked big enough, and strong enough, to break the metal walls, if only the iron didn't burn it, if only it hadn't been trapped in here, growing weaker by the moment.

"Earth," she muttered, and scrambled to the opening. "Toves, we need something in here to feed it! It's too weak. It needs—"

Several stones flew through the opening, and Molly jumped back. More poured in, like water flowing through a hole in the hull of a ship, until stones covered the ground to the far wall and were piled against the spirit where it lay. The spirit turned its head and nuzzled into the stones, eyes closed.

"Okay, stop, stop!" Molly shouted. "I need some help in here. We have to pile the stones against the wall, give it a buffer so it can break its way out!" Kiernan and Rory scuttled inside, and a moment later Ariel flowed in, contracting herself carefully to avoid the iron. Molly pointed to the wall next to the broken hatch. "Here. Pile them up here."

Ariel used bursts of air to move the stones across the chamber while Molly and her brothers piled them up against the wall. As they worked, the spirit behind them pulled itself up onto its feet and opened its eyes, watching them. They piled the stones as high as they could and then moved out of the way. Molly gestured to the stones.

"There," she said to the spirit. "Do you think you can—"

The spirit raised one of its front legs and slammed it into the stones. The stones shattered into powder and fell away, revealing a long crack in the iron wall.

"Good. Again," Molly said. "Toves! More stone!"

"Better hurry," Toves said. "The tunnel rat's almost here!"

More stones poured in, and they bent to work again. Molly could feel sweat running down the nape of her neck and tickling her back. She shoved the stones up into the crack in armfuls, moving as fast as she could. As soon as she was done, she jumped out of the way, and the spirit hit the wall again. The crack widened, but the wall did not split. The spirit rumbled angrily and tried to hit it again, but its skin hissed and blackened on contact.

"It's okay," Molly said. "We'll do it agai—"

There was a crash from outside the machine, and a squeal like metal on metal. "It's here!" her father shouted. There was another crash, closer this time, and something slammed against the side of the harvester. Her father cried out.

"Da!" Kiernan shouted, scrambling through the open hatch. Rory started forward, but Molly grabbed his arm.

"Stay and help Ariel get the spirit free. I'll go and see if we can distract it."

Rory nodded, and Molly ducked through the hatch before she had time to second-guess herself.

There was a new hole in the roof of the cavern, next to the mine shaft, and the stone floor was torn and cracked where something had landed. Molly cast her eyes around and saw her father slumped against the harvester, hurt but still moving. Kiernan was at his side. Across from them, only a few yards from the font, was the tunnel rat. Its huge metal body was bent low, its head to the ground, tearing at the stone with its teeth.

"Where's Toves?" Molly called to her father. He gestured to the tunnel rat. Molly looked at it again and realized that the stones around the ferratic's jaws were moving, feebly trying to break free as the machine chewed into them. "No!"

She picked up a loose stone and hurled it at the tunnel rat. The stone clanged off its shoulder. Fire-bright eyes turned toward her, and a mouth the size of her head bared its teeth. Molly reached up and called for the wind, hoping against hope that she could find some this deep underground. A small silver glimmer answered from the mine shaft, swirling down and around her shoulders. *I hope it's enough.* She grabbed another stone and threw it at the machine. The stone hit its head, and the ferratic flinched and started loping toward her, mouth gaping open. *Oh hell.*

It crossed the cavern so fast Molly barely had time to react. As it bore down on her, she brought the wind close and thought, *Up.* The wind thrust her skyward, fading as it expended its energy. Molly rose into the air, then fell back down. The tunnel rat stood directly below her. She aimed her feet and landed hard on its back, wrapping her hands around the steel plates of its shoulders.

The tunnel rat reared up, but it couldn't reach her where she perched. It began thrashing around, and she held on tightly as the metal body beneath her bucked. Her toes found a gap they could fit inside as the machine bounded around the cavern, Molly clinging to its back.

Can I do some damage from here? she wondered. She looked to the iron plates below her hands, but they were fit so tightly against each other that they squealed when they moved. There was a long piston just below her right hand that contracted and hissed. She reached over and pulled at it, but it was too strong for her to break with her bare hands. She looked down at the gap where her toes rested. She could see a hint of wires and gears there, the inner workings of the machine. *There!* She let go of the rat's shoulder with one hand and crouched down to dig her fingers inside.

The ferratic leapt up suddenly and slammed itself sideways against the wall. Molly came loose, hitting the wall and rolling down. Beside her, the tunnel rat raised itself back onto its feet.

"Molly!" someone shouted. She turned her head and saw Ariel just outside the harvester. "Call the wind!"

The tunnel rat raised its claws, and Molly scrambled out of the way just as they came down. "I can't! There's no wind down here!"

"The font!"

Molly dove to the side as the tunnel rat pounced at her. Her shoulder banged painfully against the ground, and then she rolled back to her feet. She spun around, trying to get her bearings. There was the font, just beside her. "What do I—"

"Call the wind!" Ariel shouted again. Molly sprinted to the font. *Can I do that?* She called the wind, but nothing came. The tunnel rat was moving toward her again, rising onto its rear legs, its claws bearing down on her.

She thrust her hand into the font. It felt like rubber for a moment, resisting her, and then her fingers broke through and she felt cold air on her skin. She called the wind again, pointing her other arm toward the tunnel rat.

A fountain of wind burst through the font, bending around her. It was like no wind she had ever seen. It glowed a dark purple, and where it brushed against her arms it felt as solid as stone. It slammed into the tunnel rat's chest and threw the beast backward against the wall. There was a loud clang, and one of the pistons on its legs swung loose. It slid down the wall and slumped into a pile of jagged metal.

The purple spirit-world wind quickly unraveled, withering into nothing. Only a few small breezes were left to skid around the cavern. Molly pulled her hand from the font, eyes on the ferratic. *Please don't get up. Please don't get up.*

The tunnel rat's legs twitched. It raised itself back onto its haunches, crackling and growling as it moved. One of its arms hung limp, but the other came forward and gripped the ground, and it stood, eyes on Molly.

An earsplitting crack reverberated through the cavern, and the terric spirit spilled out of the harvester. Its entire body was covered in burns now, and its craggy face was fractured on one side, a portion of its mouth missing. But its eyes were bright and angry. The tunnel rat turned toward it just as the spirit raised one of its huge feet and brought it down.

The gravity in the cavern shifted, and suddenly Molly was sliding sideways, as if the entire space had been tipped. The lift groaned and finally buckled, the platform falling in a heap in the center of the cavern.

Whatever was happening to her and the lift, though, was nothing compared to the effect the shift had on the tunnel rat. It hurtled sideways, crashing into the rock wall. The terric spirit brought its foot down again, and the gravity pulled both Molly and ferratic flat against the ground. She struggled to stand, but it felt like trying to lift a ton of bricks. Even breathing was exhausting. But again, the tunnel rat got the worst of it. As it tried to stand, its legs broke under it, and with a groan the metal plates of its body bent inward. The ferratic crumpled, piece by piece, until all that was left was a small misshapen lump of metal. For a few moments all was still, and then the gravity eased, and Molly could rise again.

She looked to the spirit. It was lying still now, its stone cheek pressed into the ground, and it groaned softly. Outside of the harvester it looked even bigger, almost as large as the harvester itself. Its stony body was a rich red-brown where it was not burned black, and the glowing curlicues stood out in the shadowy cavern.

She glanced over to the wreckage of the tunnel rat. That too had housed a spirit—one driven beyond reason by the tortures it endured, but still a spirit. Now it was gone.

She couldn't help that spirit. But there was one who might still need her help. "Toves," she whispered as she rushed to the place she had last seen him.

Toves had not moved. He sat in a heap on the ground. The stones around his edges seemed whole, but at his core where the tunnel rat had torn into him was a pile of gravel. "Toves, can you hear me? Are you okay?" she asked.

The whole stones stirred and then contracted toward the center.

"Hell," Toves said.

Molly clenched her hands, her teeth, her entire body.

"It's going to be okay. We can get you through the font. You'll be better there, on the other side, right?"

"Maybe." The stones stirred again, piling briefly on top of each other before collapsing again. "Don't think I can move by myself."

Angry voices echoed in the mine shaft. Molly looked up to see more than a dozen figures standing at the edge, looking down at them and the broken lift. They were lowering ropes over the side.

"We've got to get out of here fast," Molly's father said.

"I know. But first Toves. Do we have anything we can use to carry him?"

Her father grimaced. "Moll, we don't have time."

Before she could answer, the ground shook beneath their feet. Molly looked over and saw the spirit from the harvester struggling upright. It stomped its front legs, and suddenly the light in the cavern dimmed. The mine shaft was closing itself, the rock walls flowing together like melted wax until it was blocked completely.

"Well," Molly's father said, "I guess that will buy us some time. But we'd best get moving." He looked down at her where she crouched beside Toves's broken body. She realized her cheeks were wet and turned away from her father to wipe her eyes. "Molly and I will get Toves home. Rory, Kier, you go with Ariel now."

"I will come back for you," Ariel said, "to give you air."

Molly nodded and watched as her brothers and Ariel made their way across the cavern to the small opening that would lead them out. The fight with the tunnel rat had dislodged a few stones at the opening, but they moved them aside.

Molly bent to Toves. "Is it safe to separate your stones? There's too much of you to carry in one go."

"Not too far," he said softly. "Try to keep me together."

Molly nodded, then pulled out the bottom of her shirt and started piling some of Toves's smaller stones into it. Her father did the same. "Thanks, Da," Molly said.

"Travel like a king, me," Toves muttered. "Nothing but the finest."

They had moved the first load of stones a few feet closer to the font and turned back to gather more when a horrible scraping sound echoed through the chamber. Molly clapped her hands over her ears and turned around. The spirit from the harvester was back on its feet now, bending down toward the small font. It was shoving its head against the dark opening, trying to force its way through. The font bent and shivered, and the light around its edges flickered. With a sound like stones cracking apart, the font widened and the spirit's head passed through.

"Hey!" Molly shouted, but she couldn't even hear her own voice over the scraping sound. "Wait! The font is too small, it's too damaged, it'll—"

The spirit forced its broad shoulders inside, then its front legs and its hind. The lights of the font flashed wildly, growing so bright that Molly had to look away. A cloud of dust washed across her, and the chamber fell dark. The ground shook like a ship in a storm, and she heard stones falling from the ceiling. She covered her head until the shaking stopped.

She looked to where the font had been, but there was nothing there. Small glimmers of light danced around the cavern, but they were only the small breezes she had brought through the font before. Molly called one of them close, so she could see by its wan light.

"Toves, the other spirit, it—"

"I know. I can feel it." Toves was breathing heavily, the sound like the patter of falling gravel. "Can't say I blame it. Spent enough years in a box like that myself. You can't think after enough time. You just want out. Home."

Molly fell to the ground. "But we can't get you home now."

"You should go," Toves said. "They'll be digging in here soon enough."

"I'm not going to leave you here like this," she said.

"She's right," her father's voice said, surprisingly far away. Molly turned and could just barely see him crouched against the far wall. "That quake caved in our escape route. We're not going anywhere."

"Oh," Toves whispered. "So we're all screwed then. Well, if you've nothing better to do, maybe you could bring those bits of me back here. Be more comfortable."

Molly watched her father feeling his way across the ground with his hands, back toward them. She realized he couldn't see by the light of the wind like she could. To him the cavern must be pitch black. She got up and went to her father, putting her hand on his shoulder and guiding him back to Toves's side. She began moving Toves's stones back together.

"What do we do now?" Molly asked.

"What do you mean?" her father said.

"I mean, what do we do?" Her voice echoed around the cavern. "How do we get out? How do we get Toves to another font?"

There was a scraping sound, and Molly turned to see Toves's stones shaking with laughter. "Don't stop, do you, girl?" he said.

"You have no idea," her father replied.

"You're not answering my question," she said.

"Because there is no bloody answer!" her father shouted, the sound amplified by the closed chamber. "There is nothing left to do! We're stuck here until Haviland Industries comes to dig us out, and then we either get locked up or shot!"

"There must be something we can do." Even to her own ears, her voice sounded small and lost.

"Does regret count as something?" her father said. "We shouldn't even bloody be here. I told you."

"But we had to try," Molly said. "None of us could have known that harvester would be here. If it hadn't been, Toves would have gone straight through and been home."

"Sure. Rub it in," Toves said. His voice was even smaller than Molly's—a sound that whispered along the ground and was swallowed by the shadows.

"But you don't always have to take the risk," her father said, sounding more tired than angry now. "You don't have to throw yourself into the middle of every damn fight."

"If I don't, someone else might—"

There was a thump above them, followed by a very faint whining sound. Molly and her father looked up, though neither of them could see the roof of the chamber.

"That'll be them," Molly's father said. "The harvesters. Or Disposal, most likely. Who knows how long it'll take them to tunnel in here."

"Maybe Toves can dig us out. If we can get him feeling better, he might be strong enough, and we could—"

"Stop, Molly. Just stop."

"No! We can't just give up, Da! Toves, what can we do to help? Do you need fresh earth? Your stones closer together? What?"

She stopped speaking, and a moment later the echo of her words petered out. The chamber filled with a silence so deep Molly could feel it pressing down on her.

"Toves?" she whispered. "Toves?"

Still no answer. She called the small winds closer so she could see, and knelt down to press her hands against Toves's stones.

"Is he…?" Her father put his hand on her back.

"Toves?" she whispered again. But the stones had no voice to answer her. They were gray and dry and growing colder by the moment. She leaned down until her forehead pressed against them, and she felt tears in her eyes. She let them run and bit her lip to keep from screaming.

No one moved. No one made a sound. Her father's hand on her back trembled. Or perhaps that was her trembling— she couldn't tell. She sat there, head pressed painfully into the dead stone that had once been Toves, not ever wanting to move again.

I wanted to get you home. But I asked you to stay. I made you stay.

"Moll?" her father said. She ignored him. "Molly, something's happening."

She hardly heard him. Her head was spinning with grief, with guilt. *Oh God, another one. He asked me for help and I killed him, just like Meredith, just like all those people and spirits aboard the* Gloria Mundi.

For some reason the image of the boy from the factory burst into her mind, his eyes wide with fear. Fear of Molly. *Maybe they're right about me. Maybe Brighid's right.*

"Molly, look!"

She noticed that the chamber was no longer silent. There was a strange rumbling above them, almost like thunderclouds. She looked up and saw blue arcs of electricity running across the ceiling, illuminating the rough walls. The electricity ran back and forth. Several arcs gathered into one point and then descended in a lightning bolt, striking the ground several yards away. Molly jumped to her feet.

"What is it?"

"Hell if I know. Maybe Disposal is doing this? Some kind of new weapon?"

The electricity was getting worse, moving faster, the crackling almost deafening. It sprang from the bare stone everywhere. Lightning struck the ground again.

"Da?" Molly shouted over the sound. She could feel panic rising like fire along her spine. "What do we do?"

"We need cover!" he said.

"There is no cover!" A bolt hit the ground only a few feet from her father. "Da! Look—"

Before she could finish, something impossibly bright descended from the ceiling and struck her, knifing through her. She felt as if her body was shaking itself to pieces, and everything went black.

⸙

"Molly. Molly."

Her skin felt like it was trying to crawl off her bones. Her fingers were shaking against the floor.

"Molly, wake up!"

Her eyes snapped open. Her father was leaning over her, his face covered with dirt and sweat.

"What...what happened? The lightning."

"It's gone now. Once it hit you, it stopped right away. How do you feel?"

She breathed deep. "Shaky. But I'm okay, I think."

"Thank God. The burns didn't look so bad, but I didn't know what damage it might have done under the skin," her father said.

Molly probed her chest with trembling fingers. There was a small hole burned through her shirt above her right shoulder, and a circle of raw and blistered skin under it. But that was all. She frowned. Growing up aboard an airship, she'd seen more than one lightning strike—it was a risk all aetheric sailors ran, and often it was fatal. *I shouldn't be okay. A strike like that, I should be dead.*

"How long was I out?" she asked.

"I don't know. Long enough that we won't be alone much longer." He pointed upward, and as she looked up, Molly realized for the first time that the cavern wasn't as dark as it had been. There were small holes where the mine shaft used to be, and as she watched, the head of a drill pierced through, showering down dust.

Molly flexed her arms. Other than the strange jitteriness and an ache in her chest, everything seemed to be working fine. *What the hell was that?* She stood.

She looked around for anything they could use to defend themselves and picked up a loose rock.

"Don't, Molly," her father said, taking the rock from her hand. "You can't win with that, and it'll only get you killed. Just let it be done."

She kept looking around. There were still a few of the purple spirit-world winds skittering around the cavern. She called them in closer, gathering them up. With all of them, she had a decent stream of wind. Her hair and clothes began to flutter.

"There's wind down here?" her father said.

"Some. Not much." She tried to recall how tall the mine shaft had been. *It might be enough to reach the top. But not for both of us.*

The drill was coming through again. Molly stepped back just as a slab of rock fell down from the ceiling. Sunlight poured in, making Molly blink. She brought the winds in tight around her. She could see the sky far above her, on the other side of a swarm of people.

"Molly, please. Don't fight anymore. I couldn't stand to see you get hurt."

"I know, Da. I won't fight."

Ropes were uncoiling now, slapping against the cavern floor. People were sliding down—clad in black with silver swords on their jackets, igneous rifles in their hands. As they came down into the cavern, Molly could make out more and more of the sky.

Thirty yards to the top, I think. I've never made a jump like that. But I think I could do it.

The Disposal agents were shouting, aiming their weapons at them, but Molly didn't hear their words. She was watching the patch of sky beyond the agents and whipping the winds faster and faster around herself.

The first agents hit the ground and ran for them. Molly looked at her father. Her heart was like a storm in her chest, and the winds she'd gathered roared in her ears. Her father's eyes met hers.

"I'm sorry," she said.

"No, wait—"

She brought all the winds under him, sending him up into the sky. His arms flailed, fighting the wind, and she saw him screaming, though she couldn't hear him. She focused all her will on the winds, pushing them higher, faster, through the dangling ropes, up the mine shaft, up until he reached the ground, far past the Disposal agents. The winds tipped him over the edge of the shaft, and then he was gone. Molly released her hold on the winds.

She felt a sharp pain in the side of her head, and suddenly she was spinning around. She saw the agent who had just hit her, his gun held like a cricket bat. She tried to bring her hands up, but they didn't respond, and she fell hard onto the stone. The agents were all around her, and her vision was swimming. There was a dark shape swinging down at her— *Is that a hand? A boot?*—that resolved slowly into a face with a dark mustache and darker eyes.

"Howarth."

"Hello, Ms. Stout," he said. "You'll understand if I don't want to take any chances with you, yes?" He didn't wait for an answer, but simply raised his fist and brought it down hard.

ACT TWO
INCARCERATION

SEVEN

The first thing she felt when she woke was relief.

She lay completely still, eyes shut. *It's over*, she thought. *I'm done. I can't do any more.* It felt like a huge stone rolling off her chest.

The pain came second. It occurred to her that her nose felt strange, like it no longer quite fit on the rest of her face. Her head ached too. And her shoulders. Something was pressing down on her shoulders.

She opened her eyes and saw a blank white ceiling above her. She was on a cot in a small, pristine white room. There was no other furniture in the room. The wall just beyond her feet held a door and a large window revealing an empty hallway. She sat up and watched, but no one walked by.

Now that she was upright, her head started to feel better, but her shoulders still ached. She looked down. Two hinged metal bars were wrapped over her shoulders, meeting above her solar plexus, where they were locked together by a circular clasp. *Iron. Some kind of harness.* She sat up and felt behind her. The bars of the harness crossed in the middle of her back, too, in a welded cross that dug into her spine. *Is this to block my connection with the wind?*

She tugged at the clasp on her chest, but it was locked tight. She was wearing a light cotton shirt that did nothing to cushion the pressure of the metal bars. She tried reaching for the wind, but of course there was no wind in the closed room. She couldn't feel Legerdemain anymore. Without that connection, it was like half of her emotions were missing, half of the world gone dark.

She felt her nose. There were bandages across it, and when she tried to pull them off, a lancing pain shot through her head to the base of her neck.

She stood and walked to the glass. Her room was near the bend in a hallway. To the left it continued straight, but to the right the hallway turned, and she could see several more doors and windows running its length.

There was a rap on the glass, and Molly turned quickly. Someone had stepped in front of the window while she was peering down the hallway. She took a step back.

The man on the other side of the window was slim, with a thick black beard. He wore a long white lab coat. For a moment they watched each other, and then he pointed at her bed.

"What?" Molly said.

"Move to the bed," he said, voice raised to carry through the glass.

"Oh, um…" Molly thought about refusing but found she didn't have the energy for resistance. She walked back to the bed and sat. The man watched her until she was still, then used a key that hung around his neck to open her door and slipped inside. He was holding a sheaf of papers in his hand.

"Before we begin," he said in a smooth, uninflected voice, "let me make something clear to you. This is a secure facility, with staff trained to subdue unruly patients. If you choose to attack me, you will be put down, most likely painfully, and you will face ongoing repercussions for your behavior. There are multiple reinforced, locked doors between here and the outside, so even should you escape this room, you will have nowhere to go. There is no use fighting. Do you understand what I am saying to you?"

"Uh, yeah. Yes." She frowned. "I'm not going to attack you." *Who do you think I am?* she thought, until the image of her own face on a Wanted poster appeared in her head. "I don't usually attack people."

"Hmm," the man said, flipping over a sheet of paper. He didn't move from his place near the door. "I am Dr. Van Orden, and this is the Twillingate Sanatorium. You are to be a resident here in perpetuity, and you will undergo treatment for your condition until such time as I deem you either cured or incurable." During all of this he did not look at Molly once.

"My *condition?*"

Van Orden shuffled some of the papers. "Pernicious influence of spiritual entities. You are spirit-touched, yes?" He looked at her. Molly said nothing. "Yes. Now." Here he finally stopped looking down at the papers and took a few steps into the room, looking Molly straight in the eye. "What I would like to know is, will you be a problem?"

"What do you mean?"

"I mean that I have no interest in fighting with you. If you pose a problem I will simply confine you to your room. Will that be necessary, or will you behave yourself?" The doctor stared down at her, his face devoid of emotion, waiting for her answer.

"What kind of problem can I be? I don't have any weapons, and you guys have me locked in an iron vest."

"I grant that you appear harmless, but the past year would suggest that you can be a very big problem indeed."

Molly sighed, weariness rolling through her. "I won't be a problem." *I did that. I'm done with that.*

"Good. On to medical questions then." He raised his papers and brought out a pen from a pocket. "Your nose was broken, but we were able to set it. How does it feel?"

"Fine. Sore."

"And your arrhythmia. Is that a previous condition?"

"My what?"

"Your heart beats irregularly. Not dangerously so, but it is something to watch."

"Oh. No, I didn't know about that. I never really saw doctors before." *Couldn't afford them,* she thought but didn't say.

"Can you think of a reason for it? A history of heart conditions in your family?" She shook her head. "Electrocution from your prior work with spiritual machines, perhaps?"

"I got hit by lightning."

His eyebrows rose, which was the first real expression Molly had seen on his face. "When was this?"

"Just before they caught me. I don't know how long ago that was."

He stopped writing and tapped his pen against the paper. "I see. Is that when you got the burn on your shoulder?"

"Yeah." Molly reached up to touch it. The skin still felt raw and tender, but she couldn't feel any more blisters.

"Hmm. That is all I need from you. One of the orderlies will be along to show you how things run here."

He rapped once on the door, it was opened, and he swept out. Molly thought momentarily about racing after him, trying to catch the door before it closed—some part of her felt like she should, even if it was pointless—but she stayed where she was.

She looked up at the single light set in the ceiling, a shaded glass globe with an igneous spirit skittering around inside it like a moth against a window. The spirit's frantic movements gave the light a flickering quality that Molly found slightly nauseating. Subconsciously she reached for Legerdemain, for the comfort of his connection. But it wasn't there.

It's over.

Molly waited for a long time before a young man with messy hair arrived to show her the way. He looked rougher than she thought a nurse or orderly should. But then, Van Orden had said the staff were trained to subdue patients, so this young man was probably more prison guard than orderly. He escorted her from her room and took her down the hall, past the other doors and windows. The rooms were mostly empty, but a few held pallid patients sitting on beds or slowly circling the small rooms.

"If you're not on confinement, we unlock your door in the morning, and you have access to the common area for a few hours. You can eat breakfast and lunch with the other patients. The doctors see people in the afternoons, and supper is in your room."

"Only a few hours outside our rooms?"

The orderly glanced back at her but didn't stop walking. "Sleep is good for healing."

They emerged into a large common room filled with small round tables and aluminum chairs. Everything was bolted to the floor. A few other patients, each in the same loose, white pants and shirt as Molly, were scattered around the room. Three were clustered near the far end, looking up at a small window.

"Code of conduct," the orderly went on. "You can talk to the other patients, but no touching. Any touching or shouting, we put you on confinement for the rest of the day. Do it to the staff and it'll be a week. Toilet's there," he said, pointing to a corner of the room where a low toilet and a sink sat. Molly had never lived anywhere that had working plumbing before. The head on the *Legerdemain* had just been a bucket, which could be dumped when they weren't over populated areas. But at least there had been a door.

"Isn't it a little open?"

"Yes."

"What if I need to go at night?"

"Knock on your door. We'll come if we can."

Molly's lip curled. The orderly walked her past the other patients to an opening in the left wall. Through it she could see a kitchen with two people buzzing around inside.

The opening was blocked by heavy wire mesh, save for a small slot at the bottom.

"You'll get breakfast and lunch here, at seven and twelve. No extra portions. Dishes and scraps back to the kitchen." He gestured at a closed door to the right. "Medical offices. The doctors will take you through there when they want you. It's always locked."

"I guessed."

The orderly pulled his watch from his pocket. "Lunch is in a few minutes. You can stay here or go back to your room."

"Umm..." Molly looked around. Several of the patients were watching her silently, though their eyes were strangely unfocused. "I'll stay."

The orderly turned without a word and went back down the hallway. Molly took a deep breath and sat in the nearest chair. She looked at the other patients. There were five women and three men in the large room. Most looked to be in their twenties or thirties, though there was one woman who looked considerably older. She had gray hair that contrasted with her dark skin. Her sharp eyes made Molly nervous.

She was also the only one not staring at Molly. No one was talking. Molly met some of the patients' eyes, but their vacant gazes were unsettling.

"Hi," she said to a black-haired man near her. He didn't reply.

"Won't get much from them," the gray-haired woman said without looking up. She had a small cup of water, and she took a sip.

"Oh. Why? Are they sick?" She turned back to the man. "Are you sick?"

"No more than they want us to be," the woman said. "It's the drugs."

"The what?"

The woman looked at her. "The white pills?" Molly shook her head. "Huh," said the woman. Her gaze was clear and curious. "That's interesting. And you've got a harness too."

Molly rose and moved to her table. "They put it on me while I was sleeping. The harness, I mean."

The gray-haired woman sat forward. "What's it for?"

"The iron harness? You don't know?"

"I've only seen one other patient with one like it, and he's not very forthcoming."

"Someone else here has a harness like this?" Molly looked around but saw only blank white tunics.

"He doesn't come out of his room," the woman said. "And even if he did, he wouldn't talk. Don't think he speaks English."

Molly tried to adjust her harness so it wasn't digging into her hips, but with little success.

"You haven't answered my question," the woman said. "But we can leave that for now. My name's Theresa."

"Molly. Stout." She waited for a reaction, but there was none. She held out her hand to shake.

"No touching," Theresa said, gesturing to the cooks in the kitchen, one of whom was watching them.

Molly dropped her hand. "You don't know my name?"

"Well, Stout is familiar. Any relation to Haviland?"

"Some."

She chuckled—a dry, crackling sound, like a wood fire. "A Stout, spirit-touched. I bet Arkwright and his crew are trying to keep a lid on that news."

"They don't tell you anything about what's going on outside? No newspapers or anything?"

The woman's sharp eyes fixed on her. "This is exile, sweetie. They send you here specifically to cut you off from the rest of the world. Why? Have I missed something interesting?"

"A few things." Molly wrapped her hands around her upper arms and tried to shrink lower in her chair. The others were still watching her. "Why are they all just staring at me like that? You said they give them drugs?"

"Give *us* drugs. Everyone here, usually before they even give the tour. Makes us placid."

She looked around at the others. *I guess that explains it.* "You don't seem placid."

The woman chuckled again. "Well, maybe once you get to know me."

A loud bell rang, and Molly jumped halfway out of her chair. The other patients, meanwhile, finally pulled their eyes away from Molly and turned to the kitchen. They shuffled toward the window. Theresa rose slowly, watching Molly with a slight smirk, and joined the line for food. "Don't want to miss out," she said.

The first patient returned to a table with a battered tin tray. On it were a pasty white bun, a small pile of beans drowning in sauce, a wilted carrot and a paper cup of water. Molly grimaced, but her stomach grumbled. She joined the line just behind Theresa.

Once Theresa had her food, she stepped aside but didn't return to her table. Molly was handed a tray like the others. Theresa leaned in close to look at Molly's food.

"Huh," she said. "That's interesting."

Molly looked down at their food trays. "What is?" And then she saw it. On Theresa's tray, a thick white pill rested next to the cup. Molly's didn't have a pill.

Theresa took her food back to her table. Molly sat at the table next to hers and began crunching on her carrot as she watched the older woman surreptitiously crush her pill with her spoon and mix the powder into some of the sauce, smearing it across the tray until it was unrecognizable. She looked up and saw Molly watching her.

"You really should eat," she said, taking a spoonful of beans. "Being hungry doesn't help anything."

Molly followed her example and ate every last horrible bean on her tray.

⁂

They didn't turn the lights off at night. After she'd eaten her supper in her room and passed the tray back to the orderly, she'd been locked in, with nothing to do but lie on her bed waiting for darkness. But it didn't come. Molly closed her eyes and stared at the dull red of the back of her eyelids. She missed the dark of the open sky, far from city lights. She missed the sway of the ship as Legerdemain swam them through the air. With no sun to mark the passing hours, and no clocks anywhere, she couldn't even tell what time it was.

Still, no one's trying to kill me, and I'm not dragging my family into another fight with Disposal. Not promising another spirit help I can't give. I can get used to it. She slept in fits and starts, and in between she paced her room, just to be moving.

When the orderlies came along the hallway unlocking doors in the morning, Molly rose from her bed to leave, but Van Orden bustled into her room before she could even get to the door, holding gauze and tape in his hands. "Sit back on your bed, please," he said without looking at her. "How are you feeling?"

"Fine, I guess. Didn't sleep well."

"Hrrm. I'm here to look at your nose." He came to her bedside. "Hold still, please." She did, and she closed her eyes as he pulled away the bandages over her nose, making her face ache anew. Van Orden spent a minute prodding and pulling at her nose. It hurt, but Molly didn't complain.

When he was done his examination, he took a piece of gauze—smaller this time—and applied it to her nose with tape.

"It's healing," he said. Without another word, he walked out of the room.

Molly stood and rubbed her cheeks vigorously. Her nose still hurt, but it was nice to have the large bandage off. Her skin was oily though. It had been several days since she'd bathed. The orderly hadn't mentioned showers, but since she hadn't noticed any odor on the other patients, she figured there must be a way to get herself clean. *But just seeing the sky would be even better.*

She hurried to the small window in the common room, hooked her fingertips on the sill and pulled herself up. She could see a bright blue sky and the branch of an evergreen sitting somewhere close to the building. Pale yellow winds rippled across the skies far above. Molly watched them reshaping the gossamer clouds, breaking them apart and pulling them back together like sculptors working clay.

"Hey, get down from there!" she heard behind her. She dropped down and turned to see one of the cooks glaring at her through the iron mesh.

"Sorry," she said. "Just trying to see the sun."

"No climbing."

"Okay." She looked up at the window. A few other patients were edging in around her, their wide eyes flicking between her and the glass. Their pupils looked odd, she realized. Too wide for the bright light. "Looks like a nice day out there," she said to the woman next to her.

"Blue," the woman said. Just the one word. Molly nodded and stepped back out of the way, letting the woman get closer to the window. The meal bell sounded, and Molly joined the line at the kitchen window. A few moments later she had a tray bearing a slice of cheese, half a sausage and a biscuit half soaked in the sausage's oil. Her supper the night before hadn't been any bigger.

"That's all?"

The cook on the other side of the mesh looked at her with scorn and said nothing. Molly took her tray and sat down. She picked up the sausage.

"It's mostly salt," Theresa said, taking a seat next to her. "Just to warn you."

Molly was too hungry to care. She took a bite, chewed a few times and swallowed before she could think better of it. Theresa watched her eat while picking slowly at her own biscuit. Molly's breakfast was gone in moments.

"Still no pills?" Theresa asked.

Molly shook her head. "Do they ever feed you more than this?" she asked.

"Less, sometimes. Once I got Julian talking to me—he's the cook with the birthmark over his eye—and he told me it was bad harvests. Food's too expensive to waste on the likes of us."

Molly nodded. "Because of the fonts."

Theresa frowned. "I don't follow."

"The fonts. Haviland Industries has been breaking them, and the more they break, the worse things get. Less wind, less fertile soil, longer winters. That's what my friend says."

"Breaking the fonts? That's news to me."

"They started using harvesters that pass through the fonts and pull spirits directly from the other side, and it destroys the fonts in the process. I thought the only one was on the *Gloria Mundi*, but they're—"

"Extractors," Theresa said. "They were just a theory last I knew."

"You know about them?"

The woman nodded. "I'm Theresa Walker. Former public relations director of Haviland Industries."

"You...you worked for them?"

"Thirteen years. Five of them at Tyler Arkwright's right hand. And now you're looking at me like I just grew horns."

"Sorry." Molly dropped her eyes. "How did you go from there to here?"

"My boss, Tyler Arkwright, was the supposed president of the company, but you can only spend so much time with him before you realize he couldn't tie his own shoes without help. And then you start asking questions, and eventually you ask the wrong questions, and open the wrong doors, and you end up in here." She gestured around her.

"You found out who was really in charge? That Tyler Arkwright was just an actor playing the part?"

Theresa's eyes fixed on her, and Molly felt again how sharp they were. "You know about that?"

Molly nodded. "Yeah, I know Charles Arkwright was still running things."

"Not many do."

"Even in here?"

"In here?" Theresa chuckled. "Try telling these people anything. They don't even hear you half the time. But step back a moment. What do you mean, *was* running things?"

"Well, I think Charles Arkwright is dead, so—"

Theresa sat forward. "Dead? How?"

Molly squirmed. "That's a long story."

"And you have somewhere else to be? It's your turn. What have I missed?"

Molly glanced around. Some of the other patients were watching her, but she was getting used to that. *And if I can't tell my story here, where can I tell it?* Her harness dug into her spine every time she hunched down in her chair, so she sat up straighter. "Umm, okay. How long have you been in here?"

"I'm not sure exactly. What's the month?"

"Oh. It's, uh, September, I think. Early September."

She narrowed her eyes in thought. "Almost five years then."

Molly was silent for a moment. "Five years?" Theresa nodded. "And the doctors haven't decided you're cured yet?"

"Molly, the doctors are for show. They don't try to fix people here. They just contain us."

Molly exhaled. *Five years.* She tried to imagine five years under the unflagging lights, in the empty white rooms. She would be twenty after five years. A quarter of her life.

"Talk, Molly," Theresa said. "Tell me what's happening out in the world."

"Right, okay. Well, things were kind of normal until a little over a year ago. That's when I met a spirit named Ariel…"

While they talked, the small patch of light from the one window traversed the room. Other patients came and went. Lunch was served, and Theresa gave Molly her bun. She interrupted only once, when Molly described the crash of the *Gloria Mundi*, to ask, "Is the bastard really dead then?"

"I think so. I mean, how could he not be? But still, nothing's changed. Haviland Industries is still running along exactly like before."

Theresa only nodded. Molly went on with her story, describing their early attempts to spread the word about the spirits and Arkwright's lies, and their efforts to free the spirits themselves. Molly hadn't known she had that many words inside her. When she stopped, her throat felt raw.

"My God, girl," Theresa said. "I've missed a lot, and it seems like most of it has to do with you."

"I never did it alone. There was Ariel, and my family, and Legerdemain, and…and Toves." She sighed. "That's the one good thing about me being here now. I'm not going to put them in danger anymore."

A puzzled expression crossed Theresa's face, and she sipped her water before speaking. "So the good things you've accomplished, those you had help with. But the danger. The blame. Those belong to you alone?"

"Well, I mean, I started it. I got them to help, got them to keep doing it even when Da told me to stop." She pulled at her harness, shifting it to a new spot on her shoulders that wasn't so raw yet. "They wouldn't have done any of it if I didn't ask them to."

Theresa nodded. "That's likely true."

"But it's over now."

"You mean for you."

"For me?"

"The rest of them are still out there, aren't they? And I very much doubt they would say this is over. What do you think they're doing right now?"

"I don't know. Finding somewhere safe?"

"That sounds uncharacteristic, from what you've told me. And besides, I doubt it's over even for you."

Molly frowned. "What do you mean?"

"Aren't you wondering about the way they're treating you?"

"You mean the harness?"

"I mean everything. They're not trying to drug you. The orderlies have been keeping at arm's length from you. And is that a new dressing on your nose?"

"Um, yeah. Van Orden did that this morning. It's still healing."

"And what *aren't* they doing? You're a criminal, after all, and the rest of your crew escaped. But have you been questioned by Disposal? By anyone at all, for that matter?"

"No. I mean, not yet. I've only been here a couple of days."

Theresa chuckled. "Molly, they don't take their time with things like this. I'm surprised you didn't wake up in an interrogation room that first day, frankly. But they brought you here, and they haven't touched you since. They've got the kid gloves on with you. You don't wonder why?"

"No. I mean, I do now. But didn't you say they didn't care? That as long as we are contained, they don't care what we do?"

"Patients they don't care about don't get their injuries seen to. And none of us were involved in active rebellion against Haviland Industries like you were."

"So why are they treating me this way?"

"That one I haven't puzzled out yet," Theresa said.

"Hey," an orderly called from the hallway. "Time's up. To your rooms."

"Already?" Molly said. "Did I really spend that whole time talking?"

Theresa nodded and got to her feet but stayed looking down at Molly for a moment.

"I hope your family is safe," she said, then turned and went down the hallway.

"Come on," said the orderly.

Molly stood and followed him to her room, but she was barely aware of the building around her. Instead, she was trying to answer Theresa's questions.

What is my family doing right now? And why hasn't Disposal come to see me?

Hours later, her stomach feeling empty even after supper, she forced herself to lie down and close her eyes. *I need sleep.* Her thoughts and worries about her family were reluctant to let her go though. She could think of a million ways her family might be hurt, and most of them started with an attempt to rescue her. *They wouldn't do that, would they?* She squeezed her eyes shut tight. *Who am I kidding? Of course they would. So even when I'm trapped, I'm still dragging them into danger.*

She gritted her teeth and forced her worries away for the hundredth time. *Sleep.*

She breathed in and out, focusing on her lungs, her chest expanding and falling back down, slower each time, easing her reluctant mind into sleep.

And then the world went white, and she couldn't breathe.

Her back arched, her shoulders pressing painfully into the harness bars. Her eyes snapped open. Electricity was running along her chest and arms, and for a moment she couldn't move, every muscle in her body petrified. Finally her arms relaxed, and she batted at the blue arcs of electricity running over her. They gathered around her hands, like cobwebs, then slowly dimmed and faded.

Molly took a deep breath. Her mind spun from the shock, and for a moment all she could do was lie there, gulping air. The skin on her hands was raw and red. *That felt like when the lightning hit me,* she thought. *But where did it come from? What shocked me?*

She sat up and looked around. *Is this something they do to people here? Am I being punished? Tortured?* She explored her harness, reaching as far up the back as she could. She felt only metal bars and hinges—no spirit traps or devices of any kind. She looked at her bed, the walls, the floor, the ceiling. She saw nothing that might have produced the lightning.

Did...did I do that? Did it come from me?

She looked down at her hands, recalling the way the electricity had gathered in her palms like strands of wind when she took hold of them. She'd felt some level of control over it.

I've never done that before. Only wind. I don't even remember seeing Legerdemain control lightning, though I know some aetheric spirits can. The big one aboard the Gloria Mundi *certainly could.*

She sat down on her bed. *I don't see how I could have created lightning like that, but there's nowhere else it could have come from—not in the cave and now here too. But then, if it came from me, why did it hurt so much?* She stared down at her hands. There was still a giddy feeling in her chest, like her heart was beating out of control. She lay back down and tried to breathe slowly and steadily again. But sleep was gone.

EIGHT

By the end of the night, Molly was dizzy with exhaustion. Her door clicked, and she stared at it, wondering what the sound was. It was only after several patients had passed her window that she realized her door had been unlocked, and it was time for breakfast.

Molly opened the door and followed the other patients out. Her mind still felt muddy, but moving around seemed to help.

Midway down the hallway she heard a tapping sound on her right. She looked up and saw a man at one of the windows, staring at her. He had angular features and skin that looked like it hadn't seen the sun in too long. His hair was long and black, with traces of gray. His dark eyes stared at her so intently that she almost withered.

"Umm, hi?" she said. *Another drugged patient?* She looked at his eyes, but they seemed more alert than the others'. More like Theresa's. Still, he just stood on the other side of the window, staring mutely at her. "What is it?" she asked.

The man tapped at the glass again, at the level of her chest, and then tapped at his own chest. Molly looked down and noticed for the first time that he wore an iron harness just like hers.

Molly pressed her hand to the glass. "Are you like me?" He pressed his hand against the glass right where hers was but said nothing. "Did a spirit change you?"

"Molly?"

Molly turned to see who was calling her. Theresa stood at the end of the hallway, holding her tray. "I want to talk to you."

Molly looked back to the window, but the man had retreated. He sat on his bed now, head down, long hair hiding his face. Molly waited a moment more, but he didn't move, didn't show any sign of being aware of her presence. She tried his door, but it was locked.

"I'm coming," Molly said. She let her hand fall from the doorknob and walked down the hall to the common room. When she looked back toward the man's room, she saw an orderly walking in with a tray of food. A moment later the orderly came out again and locked the door behind him.

Theresa was sitting at one of the tables nearest the window. She gestured for Molly to join her.

"I just saw the other person with the harness. He was at his window," Molly said.

"Oh?"

"What do you know about him?"

Theresa chuckled. "About as much as you, I imagine. He's been here a long while, almost as long as me, but I've seen him out of his room exactly twice. I've never heard him speak a word. And until your story yesterday, I had no idea why he might be wearing an iron harness. I didn't know spirits could change people as they've changed you."

"But we're all spirit-touched here, right? No one else—"

"Most of us are here because we became inconvenient to Arkwright or his allies, not because we have a particular affinity to spirits. But this isn't what I wanted to speak to you about, Molly. I want to talk strategy."

"Can I grab breakfast first?"

Theresa waved a hand toward the kitchen. Molly went and fetched her tray—which was still without any pills— and sat back down.

"Good. You eat, I'll talk," Theresa said. "I've been thinking through your story. Particularly the way Haviland Industries has reacted to you. The Wanted posters, your sister giving speeches, siccing Disposal on you at every turn—and from what you've told me, I wonder if they've even been supplying Disposal with more advanced equipment. They've never done any of that before. And if I was still working for them, they wouldn't be doing it now." She pursed her lips and looked at Molly. "You're what, sixteen?"

"Fifteen."

"Okay, I'm going to assume you don't know how this stuff works, but speak up if I'm wrong. While you've been fighting a guerilla war against their factories, Haviland Industries has been attacking your reputation and leaving it up to other people—Disposal, namely—to catch you. You know what that tells me?"

Molly shook her head.

"Haviland Industries isn't afraid you'll crash another ship or wreck another factory. They're afraid you'll start talking back."

Theresa looked strangely satisfied. She leaned forward over her forgotten breakfast. "They want everyone who hears your name to think of death and terror."

"Seems like it's working," Molly said. "I mean, the only people who would have anything to do with me were the Unionists, and they've all got warrants out on them too."

"I'd be surprised if the smear campaign hadn't succeeded. They own the projection networks, and the newspapers follow wherever the networks go. Not hard to dictate the conversation when you're the only one with a voice."

"So why are you smiling?"

"If I was there, you know what we would have said about you?"

Molly shook her head again.

"Nothing. Not a word. No one would have listened to you anyway, because they're already all too scared of the spirits. But now everyone knows your name. They made you the enemy, but along with that they made you interesting." She was smiling now. "You have everyone's attention. And that means you're at the table. You've got a voice, if you can find a way to use it."

"You mean if I *had found* a way to use it. But they caught me. It's over now."

Theresa shrugged.

⋯⋆⋯

Molly didn't know what time it was when the orderlies came for her. It was after supper, and she had finally fallen asleep after hours of trying to find a comfortable position in the iron harness. But it felt like her eyes had only been closed a moment when the door banged open and four orderlies burst into her room. They came straight to her bedside and grabbed her arms and legs.

"What...?" she muttered, fighting against both the orderlies and the sluggishness of sleep. They put leather straps around her wrists and ankles, binding her to the bed frame. Molly fought harder. She got her right leg free before the strap was fastened and kicked at the man there. He fell back, but the other orderlies came to help. They held her leg down while the strap was fastened.

"What are you doing?" she demanded. "Why are you doing this?"

None of the orderlies spoke. The one she'd kicked rubbed his jaw as all four filed back out of her room, leaving the door open.

"Hey!" Molly shouted at their backs. "Hey! Let me out!" She listened to their footsteps retreating down the hall. The straps dug into her arms and legs as she pulled at them. She couldn't move. "What do you want?"

There was a slow tapping, and then a figure came through the door into her room. For a moment, seeing him, Molly felt frozen. *This is a nightmare*, she thought. *I'm having a nightmare. I'm not awake.*

"What I want is a little hard to explain. It's very technical," the man said in a voice that was barely a whisper. But the words were undeniably there, in the room with her, in the waking world. He was really here.

Charles Arkwright. The man who murdered Haviland Stout.

But no. He can't be here. He died. I saw him falling from the sky.

When Molly had seen him aboard the *Gloria Mundi*, he had been attached to dozens of spiritual machines, all working to keep him alive despite his incredible age. But when she'd freed the first-level spirit, it had torn the ship apart and sent everyone—including Molly and Charles Arkwright—hurtling to the ground.

And yet there he stood. The same horrible face, wrinkled and hollowed like the face of a corpse save for his incongruous blue eyes. The muscles in his face only moved when he spoke, as if he were a simulacrum of a human rather than a real living being.

He came to the side of the bed and looked down at her. "You seem surprised to see me."

"How are you still alive?" She felt tears springing to her eyes, and she tried to wipe them away before remembering that her arms were bound.

"I think you overestimate your capabilities in that regard," he said. His movements were slow and delicate, and his breathing hard. He put a bag down on her shins and opened it, pulling something out and putting it across her feet where she couldn't see it. It felt heavy and angular. "You have inconvenienced me, to be sure, with the loss of my equipment aboard the *Gloria*. But I did not survive this long by being fragile, and I have found other ways to get what I need." As he spoke, he pulled dark leather gloves off his hands. Under his skin, his veins glowed a sickly green. "What you did succeed at, however, was setting the progress of the human species back years. It was no small thing to capture a first-level spirit, and I doubt the conditions to do so will arise again within this decade. Working with inferior spirits does more damage to the fonts, making the harvests far, far less efficient."

His face blurred as the tears gathered in her eyes. "Are you here to kill me?"

"No," he said. He bent over the device at her feet, and she heard a series of clicks and pings. "I have a use for you, and since you have cost me so much, it seems only fair that you give something back. You see…" Here he trailed off to work with the device, making a series of ratcheting sounds. "There. You see, it took a great deal of machinery to process spiritual energy for my needs. It was very difficult to achieve and never perfect. However, there are some for whom that process now comes naturally. Humans who have been corrupted by the spirits to make their energies more compatible." He stopped his work and laid a long-fingered hand on her stomach. Molly's skin crawled. "It makes you less than human, yes, but very valuable for my purposes."

His voice was calm, uninflected. Molly pulled desperately at the straps, already knowing that it was useless.

"I did have one question for you," he said, pausing. "The journal you stole from me, Haviland's journal. Is it safe? Do you still have it?"

"Why do you care?" she said through clenched teeth. "You don't need it, and we can't hurt you with it. No one even believes us."

"Is it safe?" he asked again. She didn't answer. With a long sigh, he reached into his bag again and pulled out a long-shafted key. He pushed this into the iron harness on her chest and twisted. The harness popped open, and Arkwright bent the shoulder bars back on their hinges.

As the iron lifted away, there was a pulling in her chest. *Legerdemain!* She could feel him, distant but clear. As he sensed her, she felt his joy and relief, and she echoed it. *You're okay! You're safe!* But the joy lasted only a moment. Molly's own panic crept into the connection, poisoning Legerdemain's happiness, and he began keening for her. As his call shook through her, the pale hairs on her arms rose, and the air around her seemed to thicken. Her muscles tensed, and electricity crackled across her skin.

Something heavy came down on her chest, and the feeling stopped. "None of that now," Arkwright said. She reached out for Legerdemain, but the connection was gone again.

Molly looked down at the device Arkwright had put on her chest. It was tall and angular, with multiple dials and gauges along its length. It wheezed through vents so narrow the air could barely escape. She shifted, trying to dislodge the machine, but Arkwright held it in place, pressing its four feet down into her ribs.

"You can relax," he said. "I have been told this does not hurt." He placed his hands inside two brackets on the side of the machine and turned a dial with his thumb. The machine's wheeze turned into a high whine.

He was right. It didn't hurt. There was a feeling in the center of Molly's chest like falling, but it wasn't her that was falling. Instead, every sensation and emotion seemed to tumble out of her, up toward the machine. First her panic ebbed away into it, and then the discomfort of the harness digging into her back. Her fear for her family. Her fear for herself. Her exhaustion. The physical sensations from her body flickered out piece by piece, like someone turning out the lamps in a house. It never hurt, not for a moment.

It was the single worst thing she had ever experienced.

When every sensation was gone, Arkwright thumbed the machine off. He lifted up the device, folded the legs and put it back into the bag that rested on her shins. His movements were quicker now, and the green of his veins was brighter. Molly began to shiver, though she did not feel cold. She did not feel anything.

He removed the bag and bent the harness back down over her chest, locking it in place. Molly felt a ghost of pressure as he turned the key.

"Perhaps I will ask again," he said, his voice stronger now. "Is Haviland's journal safe?"

Don't tell him, she thought, but it seemed only a reflex of resistance. She could not muster the will to care. "It was safe before I came here. My family had it."

Arkwright pulled his gloves back on. "Very well then." He picked up his bag and left, the door clicking closed behind him, leaving Molly hollowed out on the bed. She closed her eyes. She wasn't sure if it was sleep that waited for her there or simply the darkness on the inside of her eyelids. She retreated into that blank darkness and wondered how it could feel so horrible to feel nothing at all.

When she woke, everything hurt. Her muscles felt like someone had wrung them out, and even lifting her arms was painful. But she could lift them, she realized. Someone had removed her restraints.

She opened her eyes. There was no one in the room now, though she could see people moving outside her window. She thought she might hear the clink of plates and cutlery in the common room. She was hungry. She pulled her legs up and tried to sit, but her stomach muscles could not hold her. She closed her eyes.

A few moments later she heard her doorknob turn. She opened her eyes and shifted her head slightly to see Van Orden coming into the room.

"Ah," he said. "I expected you to still be asleep." He strode forward and put his hand to her neck. "You may want to rest a little longer this morning. The ache takes time to fade."

"You…you knew he—"

"Save your breath. Your body needs it, and there is nothing you need to say now."

"Arkwright—"

"I can give you something to make you sleep, if you insist on pushing."

Molly clamped her mouth shut. *This is why they're not hurting me,* she realized. *They want me in good shape for Arkwright.* She felt anger boiling up in her stomach, and it was so good to feel anything at all that she closed her eyes and held on to it.

"Good," said Van Orden. "You seem fine. I will check on you again in two hours."

He left, his feet shushing across the floor and out the door. Molly kept her eyes closed and then clenched them tighter as she felt tears building. She held herself as still as she could until the sadness passed, leaving only the anger behind.

Her mind pulled in two directions. One part was telling her to get up, move, find a way to escape so Arkwright could never, ever touch her again. The other, though, was lingering on the memories of her brief connection to Legerdemain. He had felt safe, calm, until her own fears had alarmed him. *He's okay out there. Okay without me.* The two thoughts warring in her mind were so distracting that she hardly saw the room around her. It took her several moments to realize she hadn't heard the door click shut when Van Orden left.

She tried to sit up, but she still couldn't. She twisted around until she could see that someone was holding the door open. The man with the harness slipped silently inside. He stood at the door, looking down the hall. Then he carefully pulled the door shut, making sure it did not fully close and lock him inside. He saw her watching him, put his hand to his lips and shook his head.

He walked to her bedside and opened his hand. In it was a small biscuit. She took it in shaking fingers. Even chewing the biscuit felt exhausting, but the food woke her body up. With each bite it was a little easier to move, to chew, to look at the man and not close her eyes. He split his time between watching her and watching the window.

"Thank you," she whispered when she had finally finished.

He nodded. "Food helps," he said in a soft, deep voice that crackled as if from long disuse.

"You talk," Molly whispered. "Theresa said you didn't talk."

"Better to listen, in a place like this," he said. "Quiet now."

He reached out and touched her harness, fingertips probing the lock. He placed his hand over the place Arkwright's device had sat, fingers hovering just above her shirt. His lips tightened until they almost disappeared, and he frowned.

"Does he do that to you too? Use that machine on you?" The man nodded.

I'm so sorry, she thought. *It's my fault. I knocked Arkwright out of those machines.*

The man said something, but Molly didn't catch the word. It sounded like another language. He repeated it more slowly: "Wisk-a-can."

"Wiskacan? Is that your name?"

"Wîskacân," he said again, the pronunciation slightly different in a way Molly wasn't sure she could replicate.

"Hi, I'm Molly." He tried out the word. At first he put the emphasis on the wrong syllable, but by the third attempt he had it.

"Hi," Molly said. "It's nice to meet someone like me."

"Not like you. You are of air. I am of fire."

"How did you know? That I was changed by an aetheric spirit—an air spirit?"

"I feel it. That is not important now." He leaned closer. "We must find a way to escape."

"You want me to help you get out?"

Wîskacân smiled slightly. "We will help each other."

"But how?"

He knelt on the floor and held out one finger. Molly managed to lift herself just enough to watch him. He took a series of deep breaths, then placed his finger on the floor. He began tracing a curve on the floor, and his finger left a thin line of embers behind. His breathing quickened. He drew a full circle with the embers and touched the center of the circle with the flat of his palm. When he lifted his hand away, there was something dark there, flickering with yellow light. Molly gasped.

"Is that a font?"

Wîskacân's breathing was rapid now, and he fell sideways onto his hands. The circle of embers flared and went out, and the dark point in the center of it vanished. There was no trace left on the floor of anything having been there.

"How did you do that?"

Wîskacân stood unsteadily and held the lock of his harness. "I cannot keep it open with the iron. We must break free of these."

"But Arkwright has the key. I can't—"

"Not yet, but soon. For now, think. Listen. We will find a way."

They heard footsteps coming down the hall. Wîskacân moved swiftly to the door, out of sight of the window. Two orderlies walked past carrying trays of food. Once they were gone, Wîskacân turned back to her.

"Find a way," he whispered to her, then slipped out the door and down the hall.

"But I can't. I can't help you," she whispered after him, knowing the words wouldn't reach him.

NINE

It took Molly another day to be able to get out of bed without falling. She hated feeling so helpless. But the electricity hadn't come back, and after a night of dreamless sleep, her muscles were working again.

Theresa was already in the common room when Molly arrived. She was sitting and picking at her food. The other patients milled around, moving in slow motion with their blank eyes wide. Theresa saw her and motioned for Molly to join her. *What does she want from me now? Can't she see I'm helpless—that all I ever do is make things worse?* Molly ducked away from her gaze and went to the kitchen window.

"Hey," she said to the cook who handed her a tray, "I could really use a bath."

"Talk to an orderly," he said, turning his back on her.

Molly took her tray to the table closest to the toilet, which always seemed to be empty. She could feel Theresa's eyes on her. *Please don't come over, please don't come over.*

Though Theresa watched her for a long time, she left Molly alone. Eventually she rose and walked away. Molly lingered until there were fewer people around and then used the toilet. She returned her tray and went in search of an orderly.

As she passed his room, she peeked in at Wîskacân. He was lying on his bed, looking as if he was asleep. There was a tray of untouched food beside him.

None of the orderlies were in the hall. She went past her own room. The hallway ended only a few yards down at a locked door, but on the right side of the hall there were windows that showed what looked like a staff room, full of men and women in white sitting around cluttered desks. Molly knocked on the window three times before one of them looked over at her. An ill-shaven man with white skin— one of the people who had restrained her—rose slowly to his feet and left the room. A moment later the locked door beside her opened and he stepped through.

"What?" he said.

"I need a shower."

He nodded, looking glum. "Go to the common room. I'll meet you there." He closed the door and disappeared. Molly hurried back to the common room, still empty, thankfully, and after a moment the door beside the kitchen opened. The ill-shaven man gestured her through, putting a towel and new clothes into her arms.

"End of the hall," he said. Molly walked down the hall and through the last door. Inside was a long row of showers. The shower stalls were divided by thin partitions but open on the side that faced the door. Molly looked at them in horror. *Please don't tell me I have to shower in front of someone.*

"I'll be just outside the door," he said, and Molly exhaled. "It'll be locked, so knock when you're done." He handed her a sliver of soap.

"Okay. Umm, thank you."

He closed the door, and Molly listened to the lock slide into place. She breathed deeply. It felt good to have that locked door between her and the world.

She put her clothes on the bench that sat against the wall and went to the far right shower—as far from the door as she could get. She stripped off her clothes, struggling for a few moments to get her shirt out from under the heavy harness. Finally she turned on the water.

She'd only used a shower a few times before—even when they were off the ship, her home had only ever had an old tin tub—and it took her a few moments under scalding water to work out how to adjust the temperature. But once she had it sorted out, the warm water splashing down across her back felt like sunlight on her skin, and she stood soaking in it. The soap in her hand dissolved to nothing. She raised her face to the water, letting it drum against her eyelids. Gently she pulled at the bandage on her nose, peeling it off. Her nose ached but seemed mostly fine, so she let the bandage fall to the floor. She ran her hands through her hair and scrubbed as best she could without soap, her fingers scraping off the grime and sweat of days.

When she was clean enough, she sat under the stream of water, feeling boneless. Waves of sadness rolled up and over her. She wrapped her hands around her upper arms and squeezed, pressing her lip between her teeth. She fought hard, but there was no denying her tears. She cried. And once she started, she couldn't hold back, and her anguish poured out of her in deep, racking sobs, her tears mingling with the water from the shower and trickling away down the rusted drain in the floor.

"Molly?"

The voice was so unexpected that Molly leapt to her feet. Her sobbing turned to short, ragged gasps, but she couldn't quite stop. She heard footsteps now, coming toward her from the door, and she backed up and covered herself with her hands as best she could.

Theresa stepped into view, a towel in her hands. She looked at Molly and nodded. "I thought it must be you. The medication stops things like that."

"I don't..." Molly struggled to speak through the tears. "I don't want to talk right now."

"I know. Did they do something to you? Hurt you?"

Molly pressed her arms tighter against herself. Theresa nodded, as if that was an answer. "Can I use the stall next to you?"

Molly nodded.

"Okay then."

Theresa walked out of sight, and a moment later Molly heard the shower next to her start up. Molly returned to her own shower. The flow was a little weaker now, shared as it was. She wanted to sit under it again, but felt too self-conscious. She stood, head down, watching the ribbons of water drop from her hair to the floor, and waited until the crying stopped and her breath came slow and even.

"He's not dead," she said faintly.

"What was that?" Theresa said.

Molly cleared her throat and spat into the drain. "He's not dead. Arkwright."

She heard the water turn off in Theresa's stall. "How do you know?"

"Because he came to my room two nights ago."

"Is that why you didn't come to the common room yesterday?"

"Yes."

There were splashing footsteps, and Theresa came around the partition, wrapping herself in a towel. She sat on the bench next to Molly's clothes.

"What did he do to you?"

"He had a machine. He needed my…He…" And just like that, the tears were back. *I hate this place.* The sobs grew harder and harder again, and she slumped down to the floor. A hand touched her shoulder. Theresa was wrapping her arms around Molly, and Molly wanted to pull away, to cover herself, but her self-consciousness was buried by a wave of anguish, and she found herself burying her face in Theresa's chest instead, feeling soft skin and rough towel against her cheek.

She didn't know how long they sat like that, but Theresa didn't move. She held Molly tightly against her, silent, cramped on the floor in the narrow shower. When her sobbing finally eased, Molly pulled herself away from the other woman and put her head under the flowing water. She scrubbed at her face, wiping away the salt and the snot from all her crying. Then she stood and reached down to help the older woman stand.

"I'm sorry," she said. "I didn't mean to do that in front of you."

"I have the feeling you try not to do that at all," Theresa said. She looked down at her sopping wet towel and grimaced. "Do you mind if I use yours?" Molly nodded. Theresa dropped her towel on the floor and walked over to the bench. She began drying her hair with Molly's towel. Molly noticed the way her skin wrinkled and sagged with age. So much life written on that skin. *What will I be like when I'm that old? Will I even survive that long?* And then she realized she was staring, and she looked down at the water splashing against the tile floor.

"So what comes next?" Theresa said.

"I don't know. Arkwright's using me, feeding on me to keep himself alive. He does the same to the man in the other harness. I don't know how often he does it."

Theresa's mouth tightened. "I wish he had the decency to die. But that wasn't what I was asking. What are *you* going to do next, Molly?"

Molly felt her shoulders knot up. "I don't know. I mean, I can't do anything. I'm stuck here."

"Really? You brought the greatest airship ever built down out of the sky, and a few walls are going to keep you in? With everything you've done, I'm surprised they've held you this long."

"I'm just a person. I can't break down walls or fight orderlies who are twice my size. I can't just escape."

"Can't? Or won't?"

The words echoed Molly's own conflicted thoughts so exactly that they hit her like a blow. She backed up against the wall, the shower streaming down between her and Theresa.

"I mean, I don't want to go through that again. It felt so bad. I don't want Arkwright to come back. But..."

"I can't hear you," Theresa said.

"I don't want to go!" Molly said, louder than she meant to. "I think—"

"You think you're better off here?"

"No. This place is awful. I don't want to be here. But everything I do just makes things worse. Maybe people will stop dying if I stay."

Theresa said nothing. She simply sat, watching Molly through the water. Her gaze was like a physical pressure on Molly's skin. Molly suddenly realized again that she was naked and brought her hands up to cover herself.

"There was a girl on the *Gloria Mundi*. Meredith. She called me Midget. She died in the crash. And there were so many others I didn't even know, but I tore the ship out from under them. And my sister. She was trying to keep the ship aloft. I...I left her there, ran to help Ariel instead of her. She didn't die, but she might have. I thought she would die. I left anyway."

Her voice was getting softer and softer. Theresa stood, set aside her towel and walked forward to hear. Molly didn't look at her.

"There was a spirit who helped me. Toves. He came to ask me for help, and when I tried to get him home..." She flexed her fingers. "He died. And my family almost got caught—I don't even know if my father got away or not. And before all this, before anything, my mother died when I was born, *because* I was born. Maybe I should be here. Maybe it would be—"

She was interrupted by a burning heat on her chest.

"Molly!" Theresa said.

The electricity was back, flowing along the iron harness. It burned where it touched, the bright arcs running down across her stomach, her thighs, toward the water on the floor. Theresa scrambled up onto the bench, getting her feet out of the water, just as Molly reached down and grabbed at the electricity, stopping it. She could feel its heat blistering her skin, but she didn't let go. She pressed it between her palms until it finally faded.

"Sorry," she said to Theresa as she turned off the water. "I'm sorry. I could have hurt you there. Even here I'm—"

"That was you?" Theresa said. "You made that?"

Molly nodded. "At least, I think so."

"Looks like it hurts." She gestured to the red marks on Molly's skin. "Is it always like that? So painful?"

Molly nodded. "Maybe it's good that I have the harness on. Keeps it in check."

Theresa pursed her lips. She backed up and sat down on the bench again.

"I'm sorry, I—"

"Stop that," Theresa said. "Stop apologizing to me. You didn't hurt me." She picked up the towel and carefully folded it. "I'm going to tell you something, and I want you to listen, because I don't want to repeat this. I told you they put me in here because I found out about Charles Arkwright. That's true, but the truth can lie if you tell it right. So here's the rest." She set down the towel and looked straight into Molly's eyes. Molly felt pinned to the wall.

"Eight months. I found out about Arkwright, and I kept working for him for eight months. It took me that long to grow the backbone to challenge him, and even then I was so clumsy about it that I never came close to hurting him. Part of me wanted to be stopped."

"Eight months isn't so bad," Molly said. "I think I knew for years that the spirits weren't the evil things people said, even before I read the journal."

Theresa shook her head. "No, you're still not listening." She sat forward. "It was my job at Haviland Industries to use stories to steer people, make them love the company. I was good at it. And I can tell you, that journal you found? It wouldn't have changed most people. Wouldn't have changed me."

"What do you mean?"

"You found proof that you were doing something wrong. That's hard to swallow—so hard that most people will just ignore it, explain it away, because it makes them feel bad."

Molly gritted her teeth. "It should feel bad! It *is* bad! We've been—"

Theresa cut Molly off with a raised hand. "I'm not saying you're wrong. I'm just saying it's not an easy sell, telling people they're guilty and they need to change. You saw it yourself when you tried to make the journal public and no one would listen. You want to know what usually works though? Give them an enemy. Show them the wool that's been pulled over their eyes, and the person who did the pulling. That's exactly what I had. And still it took me eight months.

"I've seen hundreds of people come through this place. And none of them, not one, did even close to what you did. If you really think the world out there is better with you locked away, then you're not bloody paying attention."

"So...what? What are you trying to tell me?"

Theresa sat forward. "I don't think you're trying to keep anyone safe by staying here. I think you're trying to punish yourself. People have died, and maybe you're responsible— I honestly don't know. But if this was really about them and not about you, you'd be doing everything you could to keep it from happening again instead of letting Arkwright bleed you dry. You want to stay because you think you deserve to stay."

Molly scowled. "No, I don't. You didn't feel what Arkwright did. No one deserves that. How could I think I deserve that?"

Theresa shrugged. "I don't know. But you're angry enough at yourself that you just burned yourself with lightning." She stood and stepped toward Molly.

"Don't," Molly said. "The floor's still wet. I might—"

"I'm not scared of you," Theresa said. "It's not me you want to hurt." She moved closer and gave Molly a hug, pressing the harness between them.

"I'm glad I met you, Molly," Theresa said, pulling away. "You're the most interesting thing that's happened to me in five years. And I wish to God you'd get out of this damn place." She walked away, out of sight. Molly heard her getting dressed, then knocking on the door.

The door opened. "Done?" said the orderly.

"Yes," Theresa said.

"What about you?" he called out to Molly.

"Umm, yeah. Yeah, I just need to get dressed again."

The door closed, and Molly was alone. She looked down at the red patches on her skin. *Is she right? Am I doing this on purpose?* She thought back to the night the lightning had hit her in the cavern, just after Toves died. *Am I trying to hurt myself?*

She dried herself as best she could with the damp towel, being careful with her burned skin. Getting her shirt back under the harness was much harder than getting it off. She didn't hurry. She felt empty, and her muscles trembled as they used to after a long day climbing in the rigging. When she was dressed, she sat down on the bench and closed her eyes as another wave of guilt hit her. She didn't cry again, though lightning crackled around her fingers, and she bit her lip to stop from shouting with the pain.

So what do I do now? I mean, what can I do? She thought of Wîskacân, and the hopeful look he'd given her. *Maybe Theresa's right. Maybe it's selfish to stay here. Maybe I should be trying to help someone, even if I don't want to help myself.*

After a few minutes the orderly came back in the door. "Long enough," he said. "You need to go back to the common area or your room now."

"Yeah. I'm done." Molly stood to follow him, her fists held tight at her sides.

TEN

A few minutes later, Molly sat on the floor of her room, cross-legged, and hitched the harness up. She closed her eyes and breathed deep, feeling the wind pass in and out of her lungs, the stirrings of her power whispering between her bones for a moment before the iron harness could kill them. She looked down at her hands, mottled red where she had burned herself.

Okay. Lightning.

She flexed her fingers, but nothing happened. She breathed deep again and tried to call the lightning in the same way she called the wind. Still nothing, except a feeling that the iron harness was growing heavier.

"Come on," she whispered, tugging at the iron harness. *This would be a lot easier without the iron. But Wîskacân could still make fire with the harness on, at least for a little while.* She calmed herself and tried again. And again.

Maybe I need help, she thought.

She opened her door and went out into the hall. Through the window in his door she could see Wîskacân under the covers on the bed, his dark hair splayed across the pillow. She made sure no one was watching her, then tried the door, but it was locked. She tapped lightly at the glass.

Wîskacân stirred but didn't look over. She tapped harder. His legs shifted under the covers, but his movements were so slow he might have been underwater. She was about to knock again when she noticed his eyes were wide open.

He's not asleep. He just can't do it. Can't even roll over. She had felt that way the previous morning. *Arkwright.*

She couldn't get in to see him. Couldn't even bring him a biscuit the way he had for her after Arkwright had drained her. She stared through the glass, knowing the pain he felt, knowing he'd been living with it for far longer than she had. *All because I had to mess with Arkwright and the machines that were keeping him alive.*

She felt a sharp pain in her neck. The iron suddenly was so heavy that it bore her down to her knees. She reached up to the burning spot on her neck, and her fingers came away flickering with lightning. She snuffed it out between her fingers.

Great. All I have to do to make lightning is think about how terrible I am. She paused. *Actually, I guess that's true.*

She sighed and went back to her room, then lay down on the floor and stared up at the light. She imagined she was lying on the deck of the ship, the grain of the wood against her skin, the sun bright and clear. The gentle dip and sway as Legerdemain beat his wings, carrying her across the sky. She closed her eyes, and she almost felt she was there.

But the illusion was marred by a sound like moth wings against a window—the sound of the igneous spirit beating against the glass of the lamp.

Molly's eyes snapped open, and she sat up.

She cursed herself silently as she got to her feet. *All this time trying to set spirits free, and I didn't even see the one trapped right above my head. I'm as bad as Arkwright!*

She stood up, gauging the distance to the ceiling. She got up onto her bed, aimed for the cage that held the small igneous lamp and jumped. Her fingers went through the bars of the cage, and she held tight. When she stopped swinging, she pulled herself up close to the lamp.

"Hello?" she grunted. "Can you hear me in there?"

The igneous spirit, which had been swirling around the edges of the glass, settled into the middle. All she could see of it through the frosted glass was an orange glow, which illuminated the fine iron mesh woven into the glass. *It's so small.*

"Can you, I don't know, flash or something? If you understand me?" Her arms trembled.

The light inside the lamp stirred and then flared red. Molly smiled.

"Good. I'm glad. I'm sorry I didn't talk to you sooner. I bet you've been trapped here a long, long time. But maybe we can help each other get out. Okay?"

The spirit glowed red again.

"Okay." She let go of the cage and fell back to the floor. She shook her arms out but stopped when an orderly appeared at her window. He glared in at her, and she waved uncomfortably. He moved on slowly toward the common room.

"It's nice not to be alone in here," Molly said and looked up to see the spirit sitting, still and calm, in the middle of the glass globe. Its light didn't flicker anymore. She wondered how long it had been burning, day and night, and how many other spirits this sanatorium might have killed just to keep the lights constant.

"I think I have an idea," she said. "But I'm going to need your help."

She sat on the bed and began working through a plan.

꙳

As she walked to breakfast the next morning, she counted the lights—six in the hall, four in the common room. All were the same design, as far as she could tell—a frosted-glass globe reinforced with iron mesh and covered by a cage.

She got her breakfast tray and sat down across from Theresa. She kept her voice low and calm. "I need your help with something."

The older woman smiled. "About time," she said. "You've been here a week already."

"If I needed to break some glass, is there something around here I might use?"

"Are we talking about a reinforced window, like the one to the office?"

"The lamps, actually. Thin glass, but I need something that can get through the bars of the safety cages."

Theresa pursed her lips in thought. "There are some utensils in the kitchen, but we can't get those. When patients are unruly, the orderlies have truncheons that just might fit in there."

"Good. That could work."

"If you're not too busy being beaten with them."

"One other thing. You said you got the cook talking to you once?" Theresa nodded. "Think you can do it again? I need a distraction while I talk to the lamps."

Theresa's eyebrows rose. "I see."

"And there's something you should know before you help me. My plan only goes so far, and I don't know if I'll be able to get anyone out, even myself."

"Ah."

"Will you help anyway?"

"Of course. Don't get me wrong—I'd tear down the walls with my bare hands if I thought it would get me out of this place. But barring that, I'll settle for shaking things up a bit." Theresa's voice was calm, but her eyes glimmered. "You think you might be able to get yourself out?"

"Maybe. If I do, I'll find a way to get you out later."

"You damn well better."

Molly took a bite of sausage, forcing herself to chew slowly though her heart was pounding in her chest. Theresa looked genuinely unaffected. Molly envied the older woman's composure and hoped she herself didn't look as nervous as she felt.

When Theresa had finished eating, she sauntered over to the kitchen with her tray. "Plumbing acting up again? Water tasted odd today."

"Yeah," Molly heard the cook say. "Think we might need to replace some pipes."

Molly hurried from her seat and jumped lightly up onto a table out of the cook's sight, positioning herself just under one of the lamps.

"Hi in there," she said softly. "In the lamp. Can you hear me?" The spirit inside flew faster, flickering around. "Well, I hope you can, and I hope you can understand. I want to get out of here, and I'm hoping I can get you out too. Sometime soon, in the middle of the night, the light in my room is going to go out. When that happens, I need you to stop shining too. Can you do that?"

The spirit batted twice against the glass, making pinging sounds.

"I hope that means yes."

She repeated her conversation with the other three lamps in the common room. While Theresa kept talking, Molly moved on to the hallway and went to each lamp there as well. Some seemed to clearly understand her, while others only looked more panicked when she spoke to them. It had been the same with small aetheric spirits she had talked to in the past—some understood human speech, but a few never seemed to grasp it. She just hoped her efforts would be enough.

Just as she was finishing, the door at the end of the hall opened and Van Orden stepped through. He stopped when he saw her.

"Is everything all right?" he said. "What are you doing here?"

"Just stretching my legs a little. Walking."

His brow furrowed. "Don't linger in the hall. You should be in your room or the common area."

"Okay. Right. Sorry."

She ducked into her room and sat on her bed. *I hope this works.* She looked up at the lamp on her own ceiling. The spirit inside seemed much more aware of her now, and she often saw it following her around the room.

"I've tried to arrange things with the other spirits in the lamps. Hopefully, most of them understood. But if the plan doesn't work—I mean, if I'm knocked out, if I stop fighting— you should stop fighting too." The spirit's light pulsed gently in understanding. "Good."

She bent down to examine her bed. It was good-quality metal, she could see: a solid steel frame welded atop four thick legs that were bolted firmly into the floor. In her years as the *Legerdemain*'s engineer, she had learned how to tell which welds would hold and which would not as the spirit in the engine incessantly struggled to escape. That knowledge had come in handy more than once when breaking spirits out.

The welder here clearly hadn't known his business. While the welds at the foot of the bed were sloppy but firm, at the head of the bed it looked like the metal had barely softened before the welder let off the heat. Cracks had formed in the weld, and when Molly pulled at the frame she could see those cracks widening. Molly checked the window to see if anyone was coming, then returned to the bed and lay down underneath it. With a hard kick upward she separated the frame from the legs, catching it with her feet before it could bang back down. Carefully, she stood.

The frame was made of four bars slotted together. It took some work to get the pieces at the head apart, and by the end she was sweating, but she got them loose and spent a few more moments cleaning off old rust deposits. Once she knew she could pull the bed frame apart easily, she put the pieces back together. She hopped up on the bed experimentally. The frame rattled but didn't buckle when she lay down. She allowed herself a small smile.

There was one more person she needed to talk to, so she got up and left her room. Molly stopped midway down the hall and looked into Wîskacân's room. She immediately pulled back.

Van Orden was there.

She leaned around the edge of the window to look in. Van Orden was bent over Wîskacân, his back to her. Wîskacân's legs were moving feebly, and his arms reached up to push Van Orden away. When the doctor forced his arms down, Wîskacân kicked his legs toward Van Orden, rolling off the bed as he grabbed at the doctor. They both fell in a heap. A moment later Van Orden pulled himself free, looking more frustrated than frightened. He walked toward the door. Molly hurried back, away from the window, as he put his head out the door and shouted, "Orderlies! I need a hand!"

A moment later five orderlies rushed down the hall and into the room. Molly waited a few breaths before returning to the window. The orderlies were holding Wîskacân down on the bed. Van Orden said something to him and pulled a long syringe half filled with a yellowish liquid from his pocket.

Wîskacân saw the syringe and redoubled his efforts to escape, but the orderlies had a firm grip on him. He shouted in a language Molly had never heard before, his desperation making the message clear even without the words. Van Orden ignored him.

"Hey!" Molly said. "Don't do that!" She pounded on the window, then thought better of that and tried the door. It was still unlocked. "Stop! Stop that!" she shouted, running into the room. The orderlies and Van Orden turned to her in surprise, but before they could get their hands on her she jumped between them to swat the syringe out of the doctor's hand. It flew against the wall and shattered, yellow liquid and glass sliding down the wall and onto the floor.

"What do you think you are doing?!" Van Orden shouted. "Get out of this room!"

"Leave him alone!" Molly shouted. Two orderlies grabbed her roughly, pinning her arms behind her back. She thought about struggling, but she knew it was pointless.

Van Orden stared at her with fire in his eyes. He looked for the syringe and saw its pieces on the floor. He turned back to her and took a deep breath through his nose.

"I warned you," he hissed. "Lock her in her room. Full restraints."

"Hey!" she shouted, and now she did fight. "Hey, no, wait!" But the orderlies were too strong for her. By the time they had dragged her into her room, she had stopped struggling, and she let them hoist her onto her bed. They strapped her down tightly, and Molly held as still as she could, praying they wouldn't notice how loose the bed frame was.

"How long am I going to be stuck like this?" she asked.

"Maybe we'll let you out tomorrow," one of them said, and they walked away.

"What?" Molly called after them. "Tomorrow? But it's still morning!" She heard the door click shut, and she dropped her head back down to the bed, groaning. The frame rattled underneath her.

It's okay, Molly. You can do this. She stared up at the spirit in the lamp and took a deep breath. "It's okay," she said. "I'm okay. Everything will be okay."

No one came for a long time. Eventually she drifted off to sleep, only to be woken again by pangs of thirst. Still no one came. She lay still for hours, feeling her stomach knotting up, until finally the unmistakable sound of footsteps just outside her door roused her from her reverie. The key turned in her lock, and her door opened.

"I understand there was an incident this morning," Arkwright said, coming to her bedside with his bag. She felt its weight settle onto her legs as she closed her eyes and swallowed. *Please let this work.*

"I can't say that I am surprised," Arkwright went on. "You are stubborn, as I have learned all too well."

Molly laughed despite herself. "I'm not the one who enslaved innocent spirits just to keep myself alive."

"Is that what you think I've done?" The machine was out now, and she heard the terrible ratcheting as he prepared it. She could see his arms trembling with effort, but his voice was as calm and uninflected as ever. "I suppose I should not expect better. After all, Haviland never saw the danger either. But at least he knew enough to seek some benefit for his fellow humans. You, it would seem, would rather allow the spirits to run rampant over humanity."

He reached back into his bag and pulled out the key for her harness. "But this is not why I am here. I do not expect to sway you, Molly. People like you are rarely concerned with reason or debate, and I certainly have nothing to gain by discussing such things with you. So let us dispense with that.

Now that you have been through the process once, it should take but a moment to complete."

He unlocked her harness and put the key away in his bag. His weak hands struggled to bend the shoulder bars back.

Now. Do it now, Molly thought as the iron slowly lifted off her chest. She closed her eyes and thought of people she'd left behind. Her sister, hammering at the *Gloria Mundi's* engine. Meredith, falling from the sky. The child from the factory, terror in his eyes.

She felt a crackling starting at her shoulders, but it died as Arkwright put the machine down on her chest. "I don't know why you insist on struggling," Arkwright said softly. He wrapped his fingers around the handles of the machine.

Toves. She thought of Toves, brash and powerful, coming to her for help in that alley. The tunnel rat tearing into him, his stones crumbling to dust. Toves, who'd only wanted to go home.

What was the last thing he said to me? She couldn't remember. They'd been in the dark, and she'd been talking about almost getting him home.

Sure. Rub it in. That was it. A thin joke over a deep well of pain. *He knew he was dying when he said that.*

Her back arched, and the lightning came.

It blinded her and made every muscle in her body spasm. The bed frame came apart as she shook, and her upper body tumbled down while her legs stayed strapped to the lower half of the bed. Arkwright's machine scraped across her cheek and fell past her head. She thought she heard Arkwright fall too, but the ringing in her ears made it hard to tell.

Enough, she told herself. *Enough. Have to stop now.* But the lightning continued, making her jaw seize so tight that she feared her teeth might crack. There was darkness swimming across her vision. *No! If you can't stop, more people will suffer.* Finally the electricity faded, and her muscles relaxed.

When she could open her eyes there were only a few traces of lightning running across her skin. When those too faded, she was in darkness. The lights were out, both in her room and in the hallway. She looked up at the lamp in the ceiling and thought she could make out a faint glow, but it might have just been the stars that still dotted her vision.

She raised her arms. Pieces of the bed frame were strapped to them, but they hung loose now, letting her arms move freely. She undid the restraints on her arms and struggled to sit up and reach the restraints on her legs. Her hands—her entire body—would not stop shaking, but she managed to dig out the buckles on the leather straps and then fell to the floor. She eased herself out of her unlocked harness.

She crawled over to the lump that lay beside her bed. It was Arkwright. Still breathing, but unmoving. She could see blisters on his skin where the lightning had burned him, just as it had burned her. For a moment she wanted to hit him, unconscious or not, but instead she rose and kicked his machine across the room, hearing it smash against the wall, parts scattering across the floor. She didn't waste any more time on it but went to Arkwright's bag on the far side of her bed and dug around in the darkness. Her hand closed on the heavy iron key.

She looked up at the lamp again. "Thank you," she said to it. "That was perfect. Now, we won't have long. Remember what—"

She didn't have time to remind the spirit of their plan. There were footsteps in the hall, and seconds later her door burst open. In the darkness she could just make out the orderlies rushing in. She closed her eyes tight and turned her face to the floor.

The lamp flashed, so bright that it was almost blinding even with her eyes closed. She heard shouts and someone fell to the floor. She blinked several times, until she could see their vague outlines, and jumped to the nearest orderly. As Theresa had promised, there was a truncheon clutched in his hand, and she snatched it away while he was still blinded. She ran back to the center of the room.

When she stretched, she could just slide the tip of the truncheon between the bars of the cage. She slotted it in, gripped it with both hands and jumped as hard as she could. She heard a crunch as the iron-laced glass gave way. She dropped the truncheon and heard it clatter on the ground.

A small flickering light flew out of the wreckage of the lamp to hover just above her head. Several wings fluttered along its back, and its orange glow illuminated the room.

"Thank you," Molly said. "Go now—get out."

In the spirit's light, Molly could see the orderlies gathering themselves. Two of them were still rubbing their eyes, but three were getting to their feet, standing between her and the door. Molly searched for her dropped truncheon and lifted it just as one of them rushed at her.

Before he reached her, the small igneous spirit streaked across his chest. His shirt caught fire. The spirit whirled between the orderlies, setting them all ablaze before zipping away down the hallway. While they batted at their flaming clothes, Molly forced herself between them and ran into the hallway.

She hurried down the hall, pausing at each lamp to crack it open. The freed spirits filled the space with flickering, shifting light that disoriented her, but she kept her eyes firmly on the ceiling above her, on the next spirit waiting to be freed. More orderlies ran into the hallway, but they shied away from the igneous spirits that zipped through the air. *They don't have iron weapons*, Molly thought. *They didn't consider the lamps a threat.*

After she'd finished in the hall she broke open the lamps in the common room. By the time she was done, the spirits had melted a hole in the window and were flying out through it. Molly doubled back.

Most of the spirits had cleared out, but there were still several in the hall, flashing with fire and darting at the order-lies like angry will-o'-the-wisps. Molly thanked them silently and ran to Wîskacân's door. It was locked.

Damn it! Should have grabbed a key from one of those orderlies. She looked through the window and saw Wîskacân staring at her from his bed. He sat up shakily. Molly tried kicking the door, but it barely moved.

She held the key up in her hand and he stood, almost falling in his haste. He looked unsteady, but he pushed himself along the bed toward the door as Molly kicked it again and again. The doorframe was iron-rimmed. The spirits wouldn't be able to help her here.

Wîskacân had reached the window. He pressed his palm against it and closed his eyes. A red light flared in his palm, and smoke began to rise from the glass. His jaw tightened as the red light grew, and the surface of the window blackened. He stumbled and cried out. Even on his knees he kept his hand on the glass, the light burning bright, until the harness overwhelmed him and bore him down to the floor.

But the center of the window was warped and charred now, burned halfway through. Molly wound up and swung the truncheon as hard as she could.

The sound of the glass shattering was deafening. It rained down on both sides of the window, covering Molly and Wîskacân in glittering shards. Molly shook herself to clear them, and looked down the hall. Theresa was standing at one of the windows, just a few feet away. She gestured impatiently and mouthed one word: *Go.*

Molly leapt through the broken window and landed next to Wîskacân. She crouched down and pressed the key into the lock on his chest. The lock resisted for a moment and then opened, the shoulder bars coming loose.

Wîskacân heaved them up and forced himself to his feet, stepping out of the harness. He stumbled against the bed and cried out, but the cry turned almost instantly to laughter. He stood and smiled at Molly. "Now we go."

Out in the hall there was a bang and a squeal. She turned to see the remaining igneous spirits rushing through the air toward the common room. One collided with the frame of the window and fluttered into the room with them.

Molly ran to the window. Down the hall there were two men wearing dark goggles, with silver swords on their shirts.

Disposal. How did they get here so fast? They held anti-spirit guns, and both men fired clouds of iron filings into the air. One of the igneous spirits was caught in the blast and flickered out like a snuffed flame. The others sped on.

Molly turned back to Wîskacân. He stood in the center of the room, arms wide. He was singing something under his breath, a song that pounded like a heartbeat, in a language she didn't understand. His hands traced a circle in the air, leaving a line of fire behind them. When the circle was complete he put both hands in the middle and pushed. The air inside the circle seemed to warp and shimmer, and then a dark hole opened. A wave of heat hit her.

She heard the guns go off again, just behind her. The Disposal agents were outside the window, the igneous spirits scattering ahead of them.

"Whatever help you're hoping to call through that font, I hope it—" She stopped when she saw what Wîskacân was doing. He stood with one leg in the font, beckoning to her.

"What? You want me to go through?"

"Come. Now!" he said.

She heard the crunch of broken glass behind her, and a Disposal agent grabbed her arm. She swung at him with the truncheon, and he let her go. Molly turned back to Wîskacân.

No choice, she thought, and she ran and dove through the font.

ELEVEN

She landed flat on her stomach on something soft and yielding. It felt almost like grass. She blinked hard, but her eyes wouldn't focus, and she closed them. She gripped the small grassy fronds with her fingers.

The fronds gripped her fingers back.

She leapt up, brushing at her face. Her eyes finally focused. She was standing on a hill covered in vivid orange blades of grass that probed at her bare feet like curious fingers. She lifted one foot uneasily, but the stuff didn't seem to be doing her any harm. She put her foot back down slowly.

With a snap the font closed behind her. She turned. There was a faint circle of flame in the air, but it guttered out quickly. And beyond it...

She was looking at a sky so full of stars that it was more white than black, and just above the horizon was the moon. She fell to her knees, head spinning.

The moon had wings.

At first she wasn't sure they were moving. But as she stared, unable to look away, the wings reached their zenith and began to flex downward, vast feathers spreading as they caught the air—or whatever was there for its wings to catch. The wings beat slowly—so slowly that after several minutes of her gaping up at them, they had barely begun their descent.

I'm in the spirit world. I went through a font, and I'm in the spirit world.

She realized she was gasping as if she had been running—or as if she was at high altitude without enough oxygen. The air in her lungs felt thick and heavy, yet even deep breaths left her feeling winded.

Wîskacân was standing a few yards away. He looked different here though. There was a reddish glow to him, as if a bed of embers sat just below his skin. His fingers crackled with a white flame. He stood there, breathing deep, eyes closed. His stooped shoulders slowly lifted, and his head came up. He seemed to have grown a foot taller.

He turned and looked at her with eyes that flickered with fire. He spoke, but the sounds warped and shifted, and she couldn't understand.

"I don't..." The heavy air in her lungs wouldn't cooperate, wouldn't let her form words. She hung her head and tried to breathe, but each breath left her feeling emptier. She felt Wîskacân's hand on her shoulder, and he was trying to help her stand. Her vision was beginning to spin. "Can't... breathe..." she huffed. "I need..."

Instinctively she reached out for air, for wind, and heard a whistling on the other side of the hill. Wîskacân gripped her shoulders hard and shouted something in her ear. "What? I can't hear."

Behind him, a glimmering river of wind rolled over the hill. It was huge, like one of the jet streams that crossed the upper atmosphere but flowing with dark purples and fire reds. The wind roared down on them like a tidal wave, and Molly tried to push it back, but it was past her control now, hurrying to meet her call for air.

It struck them both and sent them spinning. Wîskacân tumbled away, disappearing below as the wind bore Molly up, up, up, until she thought she might be lost in the sea of stars. It gathered around her, tangling her in its streams, spinning her head over feet across the orange hills.

She gripped at it, found solid purchase in the winds and finally stopped spinning. *Stop!* she tried to command it, but it would not stop. *Wait! Slow down. Please.*

At last it seemed to hear her, and the river of wind eased, dipping back down to the ground. When she was close enough, she released her grip on the winds and fell out of the river, tumbling down onto the orange fields. She lay there, holding herself as still as she could for fear that she might call the monstrous wind again, and watched the last streams of light flow away past the horizon.

She stood on shaking legs and looked around. Wîskacân was nowhere in sight. She tried to find the hill they had arrived on, but she couldn't pick it out among the rolling orange grasses.

I did that. I called that down on us. Where is Wîskacân?

She picked a direction and started running, scanning the ground ahead of her, but she saw no one. Her lungs burned. *What did I do? What if he's hurt?*

She tried to run harder, but she didn't have the breath. She climbed to the top of one of the hills and stared around. To her left there were tall trees clad in blue leaves that seemed to sway without wind. To the right there were only more orange fields. And between her and the horizon there was nothing, no one.

I did it again, she thought. *I tried to help him escape, and now—*

There was a *boom* in the sky above her, so loud it hurt. She looked up to see storm clouds blooming out of nothing, spreading across the sky. Lightning raced along the bottom of the clouds.

Oh no.

The first lightning strike hit her straight in the chest, and she fell, every muscle in her body rebelling. *I didn't mean to do this. I didn't want this.*

The lightning was striking all around her now, so fast that the *cracks* of lightning bolts sounded like rain. Fires started in the orange grass, and the fronds waved frantically. More lightning hit her, and her thoughts began to spin. She felt like she was on fire, the pain unendurable, and then she was beyond pain, dizzy with shock. The lightning kept coming, the world around her growing darker with each strike. *I think I'm dying.*

Legerdemain, she thought. *Da. I'm sorry.*

Her head lolled to the side, and she saw something in the distance. It looked like a person, but it held its hands up and caught the lightning when it fell. It came closer and closer, blue bolts crackling all around it.

Wîskacân? As the shape approached, it looked more and more familiar. The long limbs, the dark hair, the broad shoulders, the eyes glimmering with embers. *No, no, get away, I don't want to hurt you again.* She opened her mouth to call, but another lightning strike made the muscles of her jaw seize. Another bolt struck her, and another, but then Wîskacân was at her side, his hands held above her to catch the lightning before it struck. She watched the sparks exploding between his fingers until her vision began to swim, and she passed out.

⁘

Molly woke to the sound of water splashing. She opened her eyes—and immediately regretted it. Even her eyelids hurt. She tried to lift her arm, but the pain was too much.

She heard footsteps, and Wîskacân stepped into view, looking down at her with his dark eyes. He was holding some kind of leather bag in his hand, and he knelt down and put it to her lips. Water poured into her mouth. She swallowed it greedily and tried to follow the bag when he lifted it away.

"Be still," he said. "You are hurt."

"How long?" she asked.

"Two days. You are healing."

She groaned and tried again to sit up. Wîskacân put his hand on her chest and shook his head. She lay back.

Wîskacân drank some water himself and sat down on the ground next to her. "You must focus. This place listens closer than our world. It hears when you call. Dangerous, if you cannot control your heart."

Molly started to nod but stopped as she felt her burned skin pull taut. "Thank you for saving me." She took a few deep breaths. "I can breathe better now." When she paid attention to it, she could still feel the thickness of the air, but breathing felt much easier than in those first moments.

"Your body learns. This land can be hard at first, but it knows you as its own." He was watching her closely. "You have never been here?" She shook her head slightly, trying to avoid moving too much. "Your people do not come here, even when they are bound with spirits?"

"My people? Who?"

"The invaders. The ones who came across the ocean and built your city, Terra Nova." He didn't wait for her to answer. "Among my people, those who are bound with spirits all come to this place."

"I don't understand."

He shrugged. "It does not matter now. We are free. We have come home." He smiled, and she almost smiled back despite the pain. Seeing him here, free of the harness, he looked like a different person. Open, calm. *And I didn't kill him after all.*

He stood. "We must eat, but there is no food for us here. I will find us some. You should sleep while I go."

"Yeah. I think I could do that."

She watched him get up and listened to his footsteps as he walked away. She stared straight up at the sky, at the dizzying number of stars. The moon had gone where she couldn't see it.

She forced her arm up, despite the pain, and looked at it. The skin was badly burned—red and peeling, and so dry it cracked as she moved it. She laid her arm back down. The rest of her body felt about the same. She closed her eyes and let herself drift away.

＊

Something was sizzling, just to her right. She turned her head—only moderate pain this time—and saw Wîskacân sitting nearby, a fish in his hands. He was running his hands back and forth over the fish, and there was smoke rising between his fingers. The fish looked perfectly normal, and she wondered if he had caught it here or back in the human world. She didn't even know if there were fish here—maybe the only inhabitants of this world were spirits. She felt dizzy for a moment, contemplating all the things she didn't know.

The sun was high above them. It looked almost like the sun of her own world, save that the light pouring off it undulated across the sky like threads rippling in a slow breeze.

"You are awake. Good," Wîskacân said. "We have food, water." He had a knife and used it to cut open the fish, deftly removing bones and innards before handing her a small chunk of the meat. She moved her arm gingerly but ate quickly once she got it into her mouth.

"It's really good. Where did you get the knife?"

"I returned to my people while you slept."

"Your people?" she asked.

"I am Innu."

"I don't know them."

He laughed as if she had told a joke. "We live to the east. Not far to Nitassinan, our land."

"East? But…" She turned her head farther, as if she might see what he was talking about. But all she could see was an expanse of orange grass and a copse of the strange blue trees. "East is the mainland."

He nodded once. "Yes. Nitassinan is across the water."

"You're saying you live on the mainland? But no one can go to the mainland."

"We did not go there. We have always been there," he said, gesturing to his left. "My people and many others."

She opened her mouth to ask questions, or protest, but caught sight of his hand as it waved through the sunlight. "Can I see your hands?"

He watched her with narrowed eyes for a moment, then put the fish and knife down on the ground and held his hands out to her, palms open. The skin on them was a mottled red and black, peeling in places.

Burned. My lightning burned him.

"I did that. I'm so sorry, I—"

"No," he said sharply, closing his hands. "The choice was mine. The pain is mine. It is not yours to take." He returned to work on the fish. Molly struggled to suppress the surge of guilt in her stomach.

Not again. Don't call it again.

"Breathe," Wîskacân said.

Molly met his eyes, confused.

"You are afraid the storm might come back?"

She nodded.

"It could return, if you let it. Breathe. Think of your breath moving in and out, only of your breath." He began breathing deeply himself, hand moving back and forth in front of his chest.

Molly copied him, focusing her attention on the feeling in her lungs, her chest, the glimmers of bright wind passing out of her mouth. The guilt subsided, and no storm came.

"Good," Wîskacân said. "It is important to be able to still yourself while you are here. For you, very important, with two strong spirit links. This world listens very closely to you."

"Yeah, I—wait. Two?"

He looked at her sharply. "You do not know even this?" He put his hand over his face and muttered to himself in his own language. "Your people know so little but take so much."

"Legerdemain. I have a link with a spirit named Legerdemain."

He came closer and put his hand on her chest, closing his eyes. "Two spirits have claimed you as kin. One is in the human world, where you cannot feel it."

"Yes. Legerdemain."

"There is another, here in this world. A greater spirit. A piece of the sky, a storm."

"I don't know what that is. Unless…could it be the spirit I freed from the *Gloria Mundi*? It was huge—we call it a first-level spirit—and I almost got swallowed up in it. But I didn't think it changed me. Not like Legerdemain." She swallowed. "Is that what's happening? The storm I feel sometimes, the lightning? Did that come from the great spirit?"

"I do not know. But you have been twice honored. It is rare, even among my people."

"Rare? But it happens sometimes?"

"Sometimes."

People on the mainland. People who know about spirits, about the way I've been changed. "I don't understand all this."

"For now, healing is more important than understanding." He touched her arm lightly, running his fingers down to the back of her hand. "Good," he said. "It is good we are here. This is a healing place. Tomorrow you will move without pain, I think."

Molly looked down at her arms. They really were beginning to heal—though the crusts of peeled skin on the grass around her were slightly nauseating. "I do feel better."

"Good. Stay calm, breathe, and you will heal." He stood and stretched his legs. "I will go now, but I will return in two days' time."

"Go? Do you, um, do you think that's safe? I can't move really."

He smiled down at her. "You are safe here. I will leave the food and water. But I must go back to Nitassinan. That is my first home, my truest home. I must heal too, and I will do it better there, among my people."

"Oh. Yes. Yes, of course. Is there anything I need to know about the spirit world? Are there dangerous animals or things?"

"Only if you call them to you. Sleep as much as you can, and remember to breathe deep." He knelt and held her hand for a second, his cracked skin scraping against hers. She squeezed his fingers despite the pain. "I will return and see you back to your first home as well."

"Home. Right." She let go of his hand. "Thank you for helping me."

"We have helped each other." With a final smile he walked away. She pushed herself awkwardly up onto her elbow to watch him cross the grass, running lightly and easily, and disappear into the trees. Beyond the trees she could make out the faintest glimmer of water—the gulf that divided the island of Terra Nova from the mainland. She stayed that way until it became too uncomfortable and then lay back down on the grass.

Her movement seemed to stir the grass to life. She could feel its fronds through her shirt, gripping her, exploring her. It felt odd but not uncomfortable. She nestled in and closed her eyes.

When she woke again the sun was gone, replaced by the strange winged moon. Dark silhouettes crossed its face. They moved in a V shape, like geese, but they had no wings that she could see. Long, willowy tails trailed behind them.

She pressed her arms into the ground and succeeded in sitting up. Her skin felt tight across her body, but it no longer cracked when she moved. She checked herself over, then removed her shirt to shake all the dead skin out of it. Her skin was raw and red but much better than it had been.

How long have I been lying here? I don't even know.

As she pulled her shirt back over her head, she heard rustling in the trees on her left. She looked over and saw something emerge. It was small and white. It seemed to flow across the grass more than walk. Its shape was long and pointed—almost like a fox, Molly thought, but more like a painting of one, done in the simplest brushstrokes. It was moving straight toward her.

As it approached she stood, nervous, but it pulled up short a few feet away. It glowed slightly, and it floated just above the ground. It seemed to be made of wind.

"Hello?" she said to it. It made no sound but came a little closer, slowly, as if worried about scaring her away.

Its white tail curled around it, and it shivered slightly. Then the brushstrokes of its body seemed to merge, and new limbs appeared—ones that were straighter and more solid. Its body reformed into something like a small person, and two dark eyes appeared in the white, featureless face. It looked up at her and waited.

There was something familiar in the new shape. The dark circular eyes, too wide for the face, the straight limbs with a small bulge around the joints, the blocky body...

"Cog?" she said. "Is that you?"

The small spirit jumped forward, shifting quickly back into his previous brushstroke form. He skipped and flowed around her legs, and she laughed and crouched down. She put a hand to his back, and he pressed up against her palm. He felt soft and yielding, like cotton.

"It's really you, isn't it?" She gathered the spirit into her lap and held him for a moment. The spirit made a humming sound and curled into her arms. He looked so different now. When she had known him in the human world, he had inhabited a small cogitant—a foot-tall automaton, like a tiny metal man, used to do menial tasks aboard the *Legerdemain*. Despite the change, he felt familiar and comforting. "It's so good to see you. I didn't know what happened to you

...

after I let you go on the *Gloria Mundi*. You made it home!" She grinned down at him and felt tears pooling in the corners of her eyes. "That's good. It's so, so good to know you're safe. That I at least managed to help one spirit get home."

She felt a lump in her throat, and the tears began to fall from her cheeks, passing through Cog's insubstantial body. "Oh, Cog," she whispered.

She heard a rumble on the horizon, like a distant storm. The hairs on her arms stood up.

Breathe, she thought, and pulled in a breath and blew it out through pursed lips. *In and out.* She breathed deeper, slower, trying to concentrate on her lungs. The rumbling subsided. "Sorry. I'm a bit rough right now." She grimaced as she said the words.

Cog's head rose, and he leapt out of her lap.

"Wait! I didn't mean you have to go!"

Molly rose to chase him, but he stopped only a few yards away, bending to the grass. There was something there, rising up from the ground. It glimmered like gold and curled in the air. It looked like a tendril of pure light sprouting from the earth.

"What is it?" she asked.

There was a soft rumble, and Molly put her hand to her chest. But her heart was slow and steady. *Not a storm. Not me.* The rumble seemed to travel toward them, and now she could feel it under her feet.

The light that Cog had gone to investigate was joined by others. Cog leapt and danced between them as they continued sprouting, moving steadily closer to Molly. She backed away.

The lights reached her feet. They sprang up all around her, twining around her legs, glimmering between her fingers. The earth beneath her feet warmed.

The ground in front of her parted, and two huge black eyes set in a stony face peered out at her from the earth. A huge creature pulled itself up and onto the ground, tendrils of light all around it. The creature was covered in these tendrils too, like golden ivy clinging to a cliffside. But unlike ivy, these lights were in constant motion, growing and receding in dizzying curlicues.

It took her a moment to recognize the creature through all the light. It was the terric spirit they had freed from the extractor. Its pale golden glimmers had turned into something bright and alive and bigger than the stones of its body. Its blackened skin had healed—though she could still see the places where its stone had broken away, leaving its body uneven.

"You're here," she said, then shook her head. "Of course you're here. But why? I mean, why did you come here, to me?"

Its eyes were fixed on her, and she could see herself reflected in them. In the reflection she saw strands of light beginning to wind themselves around her legs, and she shook them off. The lights didn't climb her again. "Why did you come?" She felt Cog brush against her calves, but she didn't look down.

Strange colors swam around the edges of its eyes, and her reflection fractured. The lights swirled and formed an image—the terric font. And around it a cavern dominated by the huge harvester. The image broke up and reformed to show Molly herself, her family, and Ariel and Toves. Molly bit back tears.

"You want to know what happened?"

The spirit's huge head nodded.

"Well, I got my Da away—I got him out of the cave, at least, but who knows what happened after that. But Toves… You broke the font. He couldn't get home. He died."

The eyes fell dark, and the spirit made a deep, mournful sound that Molly could feel vibrating the ground beneath her. The sound grated on her nerves.

"Why are you here?" she shouted. The spirit didn't move or even pause in its sound. Molly felt like she was shouting at a cliff face. As her anger flared up, she felt a brief hum of electricity, and then it collapsed.

"I don't know why I'm mad at you. Toves wasn't even mad. Said you just wanted to get home. You're not the one who took him there. You didn't ask him to stay."

The spirit didn't seem to be paying attention to her now. It raised its head skyward and opened its mouth, its sound growing and changing slowly. *It's singing*, Molly realized. The sound fluctuated slowly but never ceased, humming through the ground around them. It was so low that sometimes Molly couldn't hear it anymore, but she could still feel it.

She waited for the song to stop, but it didn't. Molly's legs were beginning to tremble, and her skin was sore. Finally she sat, and Cog came to curl in with her.

"Do you remember Toves, Cog?" she asked him, letting her fingers play through the winds of his back. "The terric spirit in Knight's Cove? When Da kicked me out of the house, Toves let me stay with him." She paused, fearing she might be overwhelmed again, might call a storm in on them, but the big spirit's song was so slow, so steady, that it seemed impossible to feel panic or anger inside it—only a soft and somehow peaceful sadness. "He asked me to get him home, back here to the spirit world. But we found a harvester like the one on the *Gloria Mundi*, and this spirit was inside. I asked Toves to stay and help free it."

There was a pain in Molly's side. She lifted her shirt to discover a crack in her skin, a bright-red streak that glistened wetly. She sighed. *Moving too much. Take it slow.* Molly lay down, and Cog slid into the gap between her arm and her side.

"What if I didn't go home?" she said. "No more fighting. No more dragging people into danger. It's so peaceful here." She closed her eyes. "I mean, as long as I stay peaceful." She listened to the spirit's song. It vibrated through her, in her head, her skin, her bones.

She opened her eyes suddenly. She hadn't meant to drift off, but she could see the moon had moved halfway across the sky, and the spirit had stopped singing. But it was still there, lying just beside her. She could feel the warmth radiating off it, juxtaposed with the coolness of Cog, who was still tucked in on her other side. The glowing tendrils were all around them, but none touched her.

She sat up, and the spirit's head shifted just slightly, taking her in with the corner of its eye. She left Cog sleeping and moved closer to the other spirit, the lights on the ground making way for her.

"I'm sorry. About before. I shouldn't have yelled. It's just...it hurts. But I'm glad you got home." She sat again, a few feet from the spirit's head. "It was all so fast, we didn't have time to talk. But I know it must have been horrible for you in that box. I'm not sure I can even imagine what that was like."

The spirit shifted itself, turning its face farther toward her and resting its head on one of its craggy legs.

"Do you have a name I can use? I mean, one that a human could say?"

Its only response was a long, low rumble that hummed through her bones. She watched it, and it watched her. The spirit itself was absolutely still—not breathing, not shifting—but its lights were constantly in motion, growing and then fading to make way for new tendrils.

"I'm still thinking of you as an 'it.' With the other spirits, I started thinking of them as 'he' or 'she,' even though I know spirits aren't actually like that. What do you think you would be?"

Another rumble. Molly heard the far-off *whoosh* of the moon winging its way toward the horizon. She spread her fingers in the grass, feeling it move under her palm.

"I guess that's more about me than about you," she said. She paused. Something in the words echoed in her memory, but she wasn't sure why. She shook her head. "I mean, me wanting you to have a name I can use. Wanting you to be he or she. You aren't those things, and you don't have to be."

She took her hand off the ground and pressed it flat against the terric spirit's skin. It was warm to the touch, and the lights flocked toward her fingers. The spirit shifted closer, pressing into her hand.

She looked at her hands. In the spirit's light, she could see her red and blistered skin. It was a lot better than it had been, but she wasn't sure it would ever be smooth again.

She turned her hands over to look at the palms, and suddenly the memory that had tried to surface a moment before clicked into place. *When I tried to apologize for Wîskacân's hands, he said the pain was his, not mine. Not mine to take.* She brought her hands closer to examine them. *He was mad. Because I was trying to make it about me. I said it was my fault he was hurt, but actually it was his choice.*

"Oh God," she whispered to herself. "Is that what I've been doing all along? Even with Toves?" She looked up at the spirit—the spirit Toves had given his life to free. She wasn't remembering that Toves had died a hero. Instead, she'd turned him into a reflection of her own failure, a mass of guilt sitting in her stomach. *I asked him to stay, but he was the one who decided to do it, and now I've made it about me. All those people from the* Gloria Mundi *too. I've been carrying them around like...like I'm the only one that matters. But they were all people. They made the choices that brought them there. That guilt, that blame. It's not mine to take. Just like Wîskacân said.*

The spirit rumbled, and its head pressed forward until it touched her shoulder. Molly leaned into it, pressing her forehead against the warm stone. Vines of light sprouted from the ground and reached up to enwrap her.

"When did I get so self-centered?" she whispered into the spirit's cheek. She pressed her head harder against its stone. "What am I thinking, wanting to stay here? Everyone else is still out there, everything is still happening. It's just happening without me."

She stood up, her weariness swept away, but sat down immediately when the skin across her stomach pulled painfully. "I've got to get home."

The spirit rumbled behind her, and suddenly the ground shifted under her, sliding forward. She fell back but landed on a soft bed of the glimmering vines, which eased her into the grass and curled around her.

"Is that your way of telling me I should rest?" She laughed—and suddenly realized she couldn't remember the last time she had laughed. She felt lighter than she had in ages. "Okay. I guess I won't be much good like this, burned to a crisp. Besides, I have no way to get home without Wîskacân."

She curled onto her side but didn't close her eyes. She stared down at the glimmering vines that danced in front of her, watching them twine with the orange grass. The movement was hypnotic.

Unbidden, a song rose in her memory, and she hummed it lightly. It was the Irish lullaby her sister had sung to her in their long-ago childhood. The melody had stayed in her head her entire life. When she sang it now, it was tinged by everything that had come later between her and her sister.

But the tune and the vines reminded her of something else. A story Brighid had told her about the time she had visited their mother's family in Ireland. She'd said it was a place where green sprang from every corner. Growth everywhere. She'd promised they would visit someday, so Molly could see it. There had been a word her sister used to describe the ground in that impossibly green place.

"Loam," she said aloud, and rolled to look at the spirit. "Would it be okay for me to call you Loam? It's not your name, I know, but it would be nice to have something I could call you." The spirit rumbled low and long. Lights danced in its eyes. She wasn't sure what it meant, but it didn't seem like a rejection. "Okay. Loam."

She curled down into the grass and closed her eyes.

TWELVE

Someone touched her arm. She opened her eyes and saw Wîskacân leaning over her.

"You have found friends," he said with a smile and offered her his hand. She took it and stood. "You are well?"

"Yes, good." She ran her hand along her arm. "It doesn't hurt anymore. Though I still look like I've been boiled."

Wîskacân nodded.

"How are you?" Molly asked. "How is your family?"

"My family is gone. Since long ago now. But my people are healthy, and Nitassinan has been kind this season. It was good to be home." As he spoke, he set two leather bags down on the ground and pulled waterskins and some kind of bread from them, offering both to Molly.

"Thank you," she said after a long drink. "I still don't understand how you live there. Isn't it dangerous?" She sat down beside him, and Cog moved over next to her.

"Everywhere is dangerous," he said. "You mean dangerous for your people."

"People from Terra Nova who try to explore the Inner Continent disappear. Airships vanish."

"You bring your enemies in cages with you," he said.

"You're talking about spirits?"

He nodded. "There are many spirits on the mainland. They do not care to see their brothers and sisters caged, and when the caged ones are freed, they do not forgive easily."

"That's true," Molly said.

He shook his head. "How is it that you came to be as you are? You come from a people who capture the spirits, yet you set them free. You set me free. You have set yourself against your own people."

"It's a long story. I met someone, a spirit, and she taught me better."

"It is good that you could listen."

"She's a good teacher." She watched him for a moment in silence. His eyes were turned eastward, toward the mainland, as he slowly chewed a piece of bread. His eyes were still and peaceful. He was looking at the land the way she herself looked at the sky. "If you're from the mainland, how did you end up in that sanatorium?"

He stopped chewing his bread. "One of your ships caught my spirit kin. I tried to set him free, but I could not. They took me there."

"Then your spirit, is it still trapped?"

"No. He is gone now."

Molly shivered. She tried to imagine losing Legerdemain—that horrible sense of loss she had felt when they put on the iron harness, but stretching on forever.

"I'm sorry."

"Do not be sorry. You did not kill him."

"No. But I used to do that. Catch spirits. Before I understood."

He examined her and then bent to twine some of Loam's vines around his fingers. "Your friend must be a good teacher indeed. I wish her words could find the ears of more of your people."

"I want that too. My family understands now—or most of them do. But...I haven't found the right way to make other people hear the truth."

"If that is what you want, you should go where your people are. From this place they cannot hear you at all. Are you well enough to return?"

"Yes. I think so."

"And will you bring your storm with you? Hurt yourself again?"

"The lightning? No. No, I think that won't happen again. I figured some things out. I feel calmer now."

"Good. But remember, sometimes a storm is what is needed." He put down his bread and stood. "Come. I will make you a gate home."

Molly looked around—at the rippling sunlight above her, at Cog nestled against her leg, at the huge spirit she called Loam lying a few feet away. "Actually, do you think you could teach me how to make a font for myself? So I can come back here?"

He smiled at her, and she smiled back. "That would be a good thing. This is your home now as well," he said. "And when you are kept from your home, no matter where you are, you are in a cage."

⚜

Hours later, in the day's last light, Molly stepped through her font into the human world and sank ankle deep into water. *The shore's closer here than in the spirit world.* She splashed ashore and took a moment to look back at her font. There it sat, just as it had in the spirit world—an orb of woven wind, spinning with gold and blue, its heart a dark gateway. She grinned and dug her fingers between the strands of wind, plucking them apart. As the winds scattered, the dark center winked out—gone elsewhere, Molly knew, to another place where the winds of the two worlds danced together.

And then a roaring exaltation spread through her and knocked her to her knees. She laughed. She could feel Legerdemain again, and his joy at her return was so huge it swamped her own. *I'm here!* she thought. *I'm back! Oh, I've missed you so much.*

He wasn't far off, and she could feel him drawing closer as she climbed back to her feet. She waited, watching the far hills until she saw a blue glow rising against the darkening sky, growing bigger and brighter as it came.

He called to her, and she called back wordlessly, giddily, as his wings dipped to bring him to the ground. There were figures crowded at the prow of the ship below him: her father,

her brothers and, between them, Ariel, her own brightness almost invisible against Legerdemain's belly.

As they flew in close, a rope was lowered, and her family descended to the ground. Molly ran forward, arms uplifted. Before she could reach her family, bright streams of wind swept down around her, picking her up and drawing her in against Legerdemain, pressing her into his bright skin. Molly spread her arms across him, feeling the rushing of his winds. Legerdemain crooned softly, vibrating, and Molly laughed.

"That tickles," she said. "But I'm so, so glad to be back."

The spirit held her another moment and then let her go, the winds dropping her lightly to the ground beside her family.

"Hi," she said just before her father rushed forward and lifted her off her feet. Her brothers crowded in beside her.

"We didn't know where you were. We didn't know what happened," her father said softly into her hair.

"I know, Da."

"You were captured, and something was blocking Legerdemain from tracking you, and then he couldn't feel you at all, and—" He squeezed her until it hurt.

"Da, easy. I'm still healing."

He finally put her feet back on the ground but didn't let her go. "Healing? Are you hurt? Your skin. What did they do to you?"

"The burns were my fault. I'll tell you about that, I promise. But first, I'm sorry. I've been trying to do the right thing, and I've been doing it all wrong. I've been making it about me when really it's about all of us. I want to do better, do this properly, change things for good. And I think I have an idea what to do next—or, at least, I know someone who can help. But you might not like what I'm going to suggest."

"Bloody hell, Moll," Rory said, gripping her arm. "You got home a second ago, and you want to talk strategy? Give it a rest for a night!"

Molly laughed. "Yeah. Okay."

Rory was about to say more, but the words caught in his throat. "Really? Okay?"

"Yeah. You're right."

He stared at her for a moment. "Are you dying or something? What's wrong with you?"

"Nothing. Well, nothing new anyway. But it's good to see you all."

She hugged Rory, who stood stock-still, and Kiernan, who hugged her back. Then she walked up to Ariel and wrapped her arms around the spirit, feeling her cool winds against her skin.

"I missed you, Ariel."

"You have changed, Molly. You have been through something and come out the other side."

"I think, maybe, yeah. Thanks for staying with me, believing in me, even when I didn't appreciate it."

"I have nowhere else to be. This is my fight even more than it is yours."

"You're right. But I'm still in it too."

Ariel nodded. "Good. But your brother was right. We can talk about all of that tomorrow. Tonight we are back together, and that is where our focus should be."

"Okay." She and her family walked to the rope that trailed in the grass nearby, swaying as Legerdemain beat his wings. They climbed one by one back onto the ship that had been the only home Molly had ever known.

ACT THREE
REVOLUTION

THIRTEEN

"We have to put the ship down."

Molly could hear her father's gasp even from several yards away. Everyone stared at her. Molly looked down at the deck below her feet, at the shadow of the masts and rigging. It had taken her a long time to muster the courage to make this suggestion. *Don't back down now.*

"I know it sounds bad. But I've been thinking about this. Legerdemain has been carrying this huge, heavy ship for us for years now, and it's not right. It's not fair, and what's more, it's in the way. If we're going to win this, we need Legerdemain and everything he can do. The ship is holding him back."

"Molly, you know she's not made to be put down," Kiernan said. "The frame can't hold the ship's weight if she's not in the air. She'll—"

"Crack like an egg. I know. I got the same warnings from Da as you did, remember?"

"It took us half a year to put her back together last time she was set down," her father said. He wasn't meeting her eyes. "And we had the Unionists then to help get the planks and tools. If we break her now—"

"I know all of that. And I don't want to hurt her either. But..." She coughed, trying to clear the lump in her throat. "But the ship's not alive. And we can do more good without it."

She watched her father's face as he wrestled with his thoughts. "For now?" he finally said. "Just for now, and once we're done, we can pick her back up."

"For now," Molly agreed.

There was a moment of silence, and then Rory shouted, "Ha!" and slapped his leg. "New Molly strikes again. I'm in. Let's crack her open."

"Respect, please," their father said softly. "Show her respect. She's..." He looked around at the *Legerdemain*, his ship, and Molly could see tears in his eyes. "Oh, hell. Okay. Be gentle about it, Moll."

Once it was decided, no one seemed in a great hurry to see the task through, not even Molly. They stowed and battened down everything they could. They packed up any gear they thought they would need and even scrubbed the decks. At last, with every possible preparation made, they found a grassy expanse without too many protruding rocks and directed Legerdemain to begin. He lowered the ship until the keel just touched the ground and eased the rest sideways, down onto the port side of the hull. The masts creaked as the ship tilted, and there was a painful cracking from the frame that made them all wince. Molly's father turned away.

Once the ship was down, Legerdemain let go of the complex weave of winds that cradled it. The tangled skeins of wind had become so familiar, Molly hardly saw them. Without the winds, the *Legerdemain* settled fully onto its own weight. The masts bent, and with a *crack*, part of the hull gave in.

"Well, that didn't sound healthy," Kiernan said.

"If you broke my room, I get yours," Rory added.

Molly felt like something inside her chest had collapsed—her ribs, her lungs, her heart—and she couldn't speak for a moment. She'd been here before, seen her home laid low all those months ago in the derelict shipyard when she had finally set Legerdemain free from the engine. She suddenly felt like she was back there, young and lost, and her home was gone, and there was no one she could talk to.

Her eyes found her father. He still wasn't looking at the ship, but he had fallen to his knees, and his fingers were wound in the grass. *He feels it too*, she realized. *He loves her like I do, maybe even more. He first bought this ship for my mother.* Molly saw tears glimmering in the hairs of his beard. *And yet, when I asked, he still decided to let her go.*

"Da," she said. Her father looked up and met her eyes. He swiped away tears but held her gaze.

"So what comes next?" Rory asked.

Molly looked past the ship to the sky. Legerdemain swam through the air above them, stretching his wings without the great weight of the ship to carry. It had always seemed easy for him to carry them all, but watching him now, Molly realized Legerdemain moved very differently without the ship. He banked in the air, one long wing rising until it crossed the sun. Molly smiled as the light shone through the wing, illuminating it. It was good to see Legerdemain flying free. She felt his satisfaction suffuse her through their connection.

"Now we see how much damage Legerdemain can do when we're not tying him down."

They struck at five o'clock in the morning, half an hour before shift change, when the guards and orderlies of the Twillingate Sanatorium would be most tired. Legerdemain plunged down from the clouds, trailing an army of winds behind him, and sent them all straight into the back wall. The wall collapsed. And then, just as suddenly, the winds were all doubling back, gathering under Legerdemain's wings and carrying him skyward. The spirit was there and gone in less than two minutes.

As soon as Legerdemain was safely hidden in the clouds, Molly and the others burst from their hiding place at the foot of the hill where the sanatorium stood. They charged in through the broken wall. Two orderlies with truncheons stood in the middle of the common room, but they were staring in shock at the cracked wall and not moving. Molly had feared they might be prepared for such an attack after her escape, but clearly they weren't. She sent her own winds into the orderlies, knocking their weapons away. When Molly's father came at them, fists raised, they turned and ran.

Molly went straight down the hallway, beckoning her brothers after her. They carried a large log between them.

Theresa was standing at her window, watching them come, looking utterly unsurprised. She nodded to Molly, and Molly gestured for her to back up.

Her brothers swung their log into the doorknob. It took two strikes to crack the lock. Theresa opened the door and walked through.

"Took you long enough," she said.

Her brothers went to the other doors, breaking them each in turn. Her father roared commands to the patients in his best captain's voice, and even in their drug-addled states, they responded. Molly and Ariel hurried farther down the hall. The door at the end was open, and on the other side a mass of people were gathering, many in Disposal uniforms. *So they weren't completely unprepared then. Just mostly.* She called every wind she could reach and sent them down the hall, slamming the door shut before anyone could come through. She closed her eyes in concentration and kept up the pressure on the door as the guards tried to push it open. Ariel, at her side, added her own winds.

"You okay, Moll?" her father shouted behind her.

"Yeah! We can hold this for a while. Are the patients out?"

"Almost all!"

"Remember to check for spiritual devices," Ariel said.

Something was hammering on the other side of the door, trying to break it down. But the iron plating added to ward off spirits also made it impervious to battering rams. If Molly and Ariel could keep the winds up, no one could reach them. Her family was clearing the rooms just behind her now.

"Patients are clear" she heard Kiernan say as the last one followed her father out.

"Remember the igneous lamps in the rooms," Molly said.

Molly and Ariel backed down the hall, getting ready to make their exit. The pounding on the door had stopped.

"Ariel, can you check outside?" Molly asked. "They could come around the building to attack from behind."

Ariel flew away. Molly could hear her family banging through the rest of the sanatorium. "Almost done?" she shouted. No one answered.

The winds she was directing at the door suddenly shifted, bending sideways into the corners. Molly refocused them, bringing them back against the door. But a moment later they slipped off again. No matter how she tried, she couldn't keep them pressing on the door.

The doorknob began to turn.

"Hey!" Molly said. "Hey, I can't hold the door! It's—"

The door opened a crack, and a single arm came through. A thin, pale arm with a dark-gloved hand. Molly tried to still her trembling as Arkwright stepped through.

She pressed her winds forward, but they skipped away from him, barely ruffling his clothes. They couldn't— or wouldn't—touch him.

"I thought you might return," he said. "I hoped you might." He took a slow step toward her. The skittering winds found the door and slammed it closed behind him.

"Da!" Molly shouted.

Arkwright was halfway down the hall now. Molly dropped her winds and backed away around the corner. Arkwright sped up, his legs awkward and stiff yet carrying him forward with surprising speed. "Time to return to us now, Molly. Enough of this futile struggle."

Suddenly Ariel was at her side again, bringing a torrent of wind to bear on Arkwright. For a moment it pressed against him, and he paused, but it slid away just as Molly's winds had done. Arkwright moved forward.

"Why won't the winds touch him?" Molly shouted.

"I do not know, Molly. Something about what he is, what he has done to himself, perhaps. But we have no time to puzzle it out now! Molly, it's time!"

Molly swallowed, still walking backward. "I don't know if I can. I mean, I know it worked when I practiced before, but this is—"

"You must, Molly! The others have almost cleared the spirits. They need but a moment more, and we need to give it to them."

Molly flexed her fingers. "But I—"

"Molly, now!"

She balled her hands into fists and focused, feeling something bubbling up inside. Fear, frustration, anger, rage—not directed at herself this time, but at the man in front of her. The man who had changed so many lives, ruined so many, all to keep himself walking on those feeble legs a little longer. The man who had captured her and stolen from her without even a hint of remorse.

Her skin hummed and crackled, and electric blue arcs sprang up along her arms. They were hot, but they didn't burn her. Not anymore. She extended her arms, and the lightning jumped from her fingers to Arkwright, striking him in the chest. But it didn't seem to affect him. He strode forward, wreathed in electricity, face as expressionless as ever. And then, like the wind, the lightning veered away, unable to hold him.

"All clear!" Molly heard her father roar from the common room.

She turned the lightning away from Arkwright and instead poured it into the ceiling above his head. The broken lamps crackled with electricity, and the tiles burst into flames, falling down on Arkwright's head. He stumbled and fell to his knees.

"Go!" Ariel shouted, and Molly released the lightning as they both turned to run down the hallway, through the common room and out the hole in the back wall. Small spirits flitted through the air and along the ground with them, out onto the grassy hills, toward freedom. As Molly emerged she saw Legerdemain descending again, already scooping up the bewildered patients in complex knots of wind. Molly caught a glimpse of Theresa, shrouded in winds, and the wide-eyed look of surprise on her face almost made Molly laugh.

Ariel wrapped herself around Molly, and they rose to follow, all sailing up into the air and toward the safety of the clouds. Gunfire rang out behind her, and Molly turned to see Disposal agents on the grass below, but nothing struck them. She didn't see Arkwright emerge, and she turned her eyes away, back up to the sky.

Rory was just ahead of her, wrapped in warm orange winds, arms wide, laughing like he had just heard the best joke of his life.

We did it. He couldn't stop us.

Molly felt a thrill rise up in her chest, like the lightning but so much warmer, so much brighter, and she spread her own arms too. Her laughter joined Rory's, echoing across the brightening sky.

"I can't believe we did it! That was aces, Moll!" Rory was pacing back and forth, clapping his hands and gesturing wildly. "When Legerdemain came down I thought he was going to flatten the bloody building. Almost did! But we did it! Went off without a hitch! That never happens to us, you know. Something always goes wrong!"

Maybe that's why I feel so nervous, Molly thought. Her own excitement had faded quickly as they fled the sanatorium and set down on a remote corner of the eastern shore. Now she kept her eyes on the sky, watching for ships.

The patients were ranged across a nearby hill, most of them lying down, some clutching the earth like they might never let it go. The adrenaline from their flight seemed to have worn the edges off the medication, and they were watching her and the spirits with wary eyes. The smell of dew-soaked stone and moss was undercut by the scent of urine—one or two of the patients, confused and terrified, had peed themselves during the flight. Molly didn't blame them.

Theresa, meanwhile, looked even more nervous than Molly did. She sat at the crest of the hill, sharp eyes roaming the landscape. Molly walked up and sat next to her.

"We shouldn't stay here," Theresa said.

Molly nodded. "But we need to talk about what comes next."

"Yes. I suppose we do. What are your plans exactly?"

"We don't really have any yet. That's why I wanted to talk to you."

Theresa laughed under her breath. "You really are just fifteen, aren't you? No plans at all?"

"I want to change things. Not keep freeing spirits here and there, but change the way people do things. Change their minds. And we don't know how to do that, but I thought you might. You said Haviland Industries was afraid I would talk back. Well, I want to talk back."

Theresa sat forward, and some of the nervousness left her eyes. "So you were listening after all."

"Yeah. So where do we go from here?"

Theresa was silent for a moment, her gaze far away. "The first thing we'll need is the journal. Haviland's journal. You've still got it?"

"I have it," Molly's father said from behind them. He pulled it out of the bag slung over his shoulder, handed it to Theresa and sat down beside her.

Theresa leafed slowly through the journal, handling the pages delicately with her fingertips. "Good. Do you have a printing press?"

"Umm, no," Molly said. "But we tried that anyway. We made copies by hand and distributed them, but—"

"You'll need more copies, well done this time—not hand-made copies but proper replicas that look like the real thing. And the journal alone isn't going to change anyone's mind. Everyone's too invested in Arkwright's version of history for that. But we need to get it into people's hands anyway. It's like seeding the ground. We'll still need the rain, but first things first. Who do you know who might have a press?"

FOURTEEN

The Unionists were easy to find, if you knew where to look. Molly remembered they had mentioned a textiles factory on the west end of the industrial district at their last meeting, so she, her father and her brothers set up watches on the three textiles factories in that region. Soon they noticed people surreptitiously handing out pamphlets at one of the factories, and sometimes passing baskets of apples through the windows when the foremen were out having a smoke. After they had watched for a while, Kiernan and Molly followed one of the pamphleteers to a nearby market, where he bought himself a sandwich and sat to eat. They sat down at the table with him, their caps pulled low over their eyes.

"Oh, crud, is this your table? Sorry, I—" He stood to leave, but Kiernan grabbed his sleeve to stop him. The boy was around Molly's age and clearly nervous. Molly understood. The Unionists were almost as unwelcome as spirit sympathizers in Terra Nova. Molly raised her cap.

"Recognize us?" she said softly.

The boy's eyes widened, and he sat back down. "It's you," he said. "'Course I recognize you. You busted me out of a factory not three months ago."

He looked vaguely familiar—he had bronze, pitted skin, a delicate mouth and the permanent bags under his eyes that characterized the factory workers—but she'd seen so many faces during her time working with the Unionists.

"Glad you're still out," Molly said, pulling her cap back down. "We need your help. We need to meet with Bascombe."

"You do?" He wiped sandwich crumbs off his chin. "I'm...I'm sorry. I'm not supposed to tell anyone where we stay. They told me—"

"It's okay," Kiernan said. "Can you tell us your name?"

"It's Abdel."

"Abdel, could you take a message to the leadership for us? Would that be okay?"

"I...I think so. They haven't said anything about that."

"Okay. Tell them we'll be at the Bantam's Rest tomorrow morning at ten. We hope they'll be there."

"Sure. Okay, yeah. Bantam's Rest, tomorrow at ten."

Molly nodded. "Thanks." She and Kiernan stood up.

"Hold up!" Abdel said. "I, um, well, I never had a chance to say thanks before. That factory was an awful place, and they don't let you leave once you're in. You...well, thanks."

"You're welcome," Kiernan said, and Molly nodded.

They turned to leave. Molly scanned the crowd, but no one in the busy market seemed to be paying them any attention. She stuck to her brother's side as they made their way back out of the city.

They arrived at the Bantam's Rest a little before ten the next morning and made their way inside. This early, only the staff was around, and Carver, the surly owner, hadn't dragged himself out of bed yet. The cook knew them, though, and she opened the back door to invite them through. In the storage room there was a trapdoor. The cook pulled it up.

"Don't leave this way. Use the outer stairwell," she told Molly as her father and brothers descended.

"We will. Sorry to bother you so early."

The cook shrugged, and they waited in awkward silence as Theresa climbed slowly down. Once she was in, Molly jumped down, not bothering with the ladder. The cook kicked the door closed above them. Molly couldn't see anything in the dark, but she heard someone crossing the room and unlocking the outside door.

Molly's father found the lantern and lit it, then cursed. "Almost out of oil," he said. "We'll need to save it for the meeting. Means waiting in the dark." They all nodded, and he extinguished the light.

The pub's cellar was quiet. All they could hear were the banging pots in the kitchen and the shushing of a broom across the floor. Someone was speaking, and Molly could just barely make out the words.

"...what she's like now, but even when she was young she sympathized with the spirits. She spent hours with the engine, only leaving when the engineer chased her away. It was dangerous, but our father never stopped her. I think he was a little afraid of her."

It's Brighid. Her voice sounded strange, crackling and hollow. *She can't really be here. It sounds like one of her speeches about me.*

"Sounds like they're broadcasting her on the wireless now," Theresa said. "Smart. They'd never reach most people just through the projections."

A radio, Molly thought. They'd never had one aboard the *Legerdemain*.

The broadcast went on. "When I raised the issue with my father, about Molly's behavior, he told me to leave her be. I did. I shouldn't have. But I was scared, and I was young. I left the ship as soon as I was able."

You left the ship, sure enough, but not because you were scared. You left because you thought money and position were more important than family.

She felt a hand on her own. Her father's rough, thick fingers, wrapping around hers and squeezing. Molly held his hand lightly, afraid that clinging too hard might make him withdraw.

"Try not to listen," he whispered. "It's all nonsense."

"She sounds pretty certain," Molly said.

"Your sister's always been good at convincing herself she's the victim. And I don't think I…" Her father fell into silence, and the speech went on, outlining Molly's failings and flaws. "She's wrong. About all of it. But it's not entirely her fault, I don't think," he said finally. She held her father's hand tighter, and he didn't let go.

"You're okay with this?" Molly asked. "I mean, with us going on helping the spirits? You kept telling me I should stop."

She heard the fingers of his other hand scratching at his chin. "Well, I had some time to think. Truth is, I still wish you would stop. But I don't think you will. And it will only make things worse if I'm always arguing with you."

"So you gave up on convincing me?"

"I suppose I did."

"Oh." She tapped her heel against the stone floor. "You don't have to do it though. If you don't want to. I mean, I like having your help, but it's up to you."

His hand tightened around hers. "You think that's what I want? To send you off on your own? I just—"

"Footsteps," Rory said. "On the stairs outside."

The doorknob rattled just as Kiernan lit the lantern again, and they all blinked against the sudden light as the outside door opened. Bascombe stepped through and closed the door behind him. He wore the same ragged vest as before, but his coat was gone. His face looked more shadowed than Molly remembered.

"Only you?" Molly's father said, dropping her hand.

"Too dangerous to travel in groups now," Bascombe said. He nodded to them all, his eyes settling on Theresa. "Who is this?"

"Theresa Walker," she said.

"I know your face," Bascombe said, one hand still on the door. "I've heard your name."

"You have. I spent years dismantling your cause, back when I worked for Arkwright."

Bascombe's face darkened. "Yes, I remember. Your campaign against us did more damage to the union cause than even the police crackdowns."

"That's exactly what it was meant to do," Theresa said.

"Do you have any idea how many people, how many children—" he started, then bit off his words. "No. This is not the time for that." He looked to Molly. "You trust this woman?"

"We met in the Twillingate Sanatorium. She's no friend to Haviland Industries now."

Bascombe glowered at her again but nodded once. "Okay. Did you call me to begin our work together again? In your absence, things have only gotten worse for the workers."

"We've actually come to ask you for something," Molly's father said. "The pamphlets you distribute. Do you have your own printing press for those?"

"Yes. Why?"

Molly's father held up the journal. "We need to make copies of this."

Bascombe came forward and took the book. He examined the cover but didn't open it. "This is the journal you say is Haviland's?" Molly's father nodded. "Didn't you already distribute this?"

"We need to do it properly. Printed, bound," Theresa said.

"All official like," Rory added.

Bascombe sighed and handed the journal back. "Look, we have common enemies, but don't mistake that for a common cause." He looked around at them. "I know you. Despite my better judgment, I even like you. But I am no friend of the spirits. I simply consider a few rogue spirits an acceptable price to pay to see people freed from an unjust system."

There was silence in the room. Molly waited for her father to speak, but he simply stared down at the journal. She turned to Theresa, but Theresa was watching her, and she gestured for Molly to say something. Molly swallowed.

What was it Rory said? The new Molly, who speaks and convinces?

"I know you don't believe us," Molly said. "And I doubt I'll change your mind today. But what makes more sense to you? That every single spirit is wicked and intends us harm? Or that the same unjust system that can lock children in a factory until they're too sick to work might do the same thing to spirits? You already know you can't trust Haviland Industries and the other manufacturers. Why would you take their word on the spirits?"

"Because they've hurt people I know," Bascombe said softly. "I don't need anyone else's word on it."

Molly took a breath. "I'm sorry about your friends, whatever happened. The situation is more complicated than you know. But knowing that doesn't bring your friends back." Bascombe nodded, but his expression did not change. "Maybe, then, if you don't want to help us, we can offer a trade. Use of your press for another task. Another factory."

Bascombe's lips pursed. "That seems reasonable. But I should warn you, things have shifted in Terra Nova. They're accusing you of new crimes every other day, blaming the work of every rogue spirit on you, playing your sister's speeches on every wavelength, every network. You'll find no friends in Terra Nova now. And Disposal seems to have every cobblestone in the city under watch. I have something I'd like you to do, and I am willing to trade, but I don't want to send you into danger unknowing."

Molly and her family looked at each other. *I knew it was bad, but...*

"What could you possibly be smiling about?" Molly's father asked. Molly turned and saw he was watching Theresa, who indeed had a smile on her face.

Theresa grunted. "Well, it poses problems, sure enough. But they're acting out of fear. It's like I told you, Molly."

"They're putting attention on me, you mean?"

"So much that they might as well have built you a stage."

A lot of good that will do if we're all shot before we can say a word. "What is it you want us to do?" she asked Bascombe.

"There's a new factory we've been watching. Very new, very secretive—we haven't even been able to determine what they make there. But there is clearly a great deal of money involved. And workers are disappearing into it at a rate we've never seen before, and coming back out in black bags. Whatever they're doing must be extraordinarily dangerous. We'd like you to shut it down before more workers are killed. If you do, you will have use of our press and any materials you need."

Molly looked to her father, who nodded slowly, and then to her brothers.

"Okay," Molly said. "We'll do it."

***

It didn't look like any factory Molly had seen before. Sure, there was the name on the door—Haviland Industries, like half of the factories in the city—and sure, it was inside the soot-stained industrial district—surrounded, she noticed, by factories that had been closed and boarded up for quite some time. But other than that, it had no markings of a factory. The brickwork was clean. There was no smoke coming from its chimneys—no signs that its furnaces were even lit, from what Molly could see. And when she pressed her ear to the wall, she felt only cold stone, no thrum of machines.

And yet, just as Bascombe had told them, a new batch of laborers made its way in every eight hours and didn't come back out.

"This is weird," Molly said. "Something's not right with this place. I mean, more not right than usual."

"I agree," Ariel said softly above her. "I can sense spirits inside. Quite a few." She drifted along the wall, holding her arms out in front of her, but suddenly stopped and drew back. "There is iron in some of the brickwork."

"Iron in the walls? Why would—"

There was a hum above them. Molly and Ariel scrambled for cover in the stairwell of a nearby factory, where her father and brothers were still waiting. Once they were in the shadows, Molly looked up to see a black ship float by, the winds shying away from it. A spotlight pierced the darkness at its prow, roving over the rooftops of the nearby factories.

That's the ship we saw before, when we picked up Toves, Molly thought. The hull was black and shallow, the only color coming from the silver swords painted on either side.

"That ship has shown up every thirty minutes," her father said. "I think it's guarding this place."

Molly watched the black-hulled airship. *How does it fly without the wind?* And it wasn't just that it didn't use the wind, she realized. The wind seemed unable to pass near the ship, skirting wide around it. *A ship that disrupts the wind? It would be a good way to hunt spirits like Legerdemain. Maybe it's doing something to the gravity. Like a huge gravitic engine. But I've never known one that powerful.*

"Disposal, keeping watch on a factory?" Kiernan said. "But why?"

"Well, if Theresa was right that Haviland Industries is supplying Disposal with new equipment, maybe they owe Arkwright some favors," Rory suggested.

"Maybe we'll find out once we're inside," Molly said. "How do we get in? There are no windows, and the only things that go in are people and unmarked trucks."

"Are the trucks on a schedule?" her father asked.

"They come in at the same time as the shift change and leave again a little while later."

He nodded. "Seems like the best way in then. But we're going to have to do this one without Legerdemain. I don't think we can bring him in with that airship about."

"I was thinking that too," Molly said. Legerdemain was in the high atmosphere now, far above them. Molly tugged at their connection and thought, *Stay away*, trying to send an image of the black airship. She felt a gentle hum back from the spirit far above. "Ariel, with that iron in the walls it may be best for you to stay back too. What do you think?"

"I would rather come."

"Okay. Your choice."

"Anyone else worried that we're going into a place that's heavily guarded, without any idea what's inside and we can't even bring our heaviest hitter to?" Rory whispered. "No? Just me?"

"Of course we're worried, Rory," Molly's father said. "I'd rather sail a skiff into a hurricane than go in there. But this looks like the only way on from here, so this is what we do." Kiernan and Molly nodded their agreement.

"Okay then. Plan?" Rory asked.

"We could pretend to be laborers, get in with the next shift," Molly said.

"No. They'd recognize us," Kiernan said. "I think Da was right. The trucks are our best way in. Ariel, could you fly Molly in on top of one as it's coming in?"

"I believe so."

"Good. From there, we try to run it like the other factories. Molly, you get the doors open. We'll be waiting here. We need to be out before the patrol comes back."

"But Rory was right too," their father said. "We don't know how dangerous this is, what kind of resistance might be inside. Molly, take this one slow and quiet until you know more. We'll take our cue from you."

Molly pursed her lips and looked at the factory. *Why would they be guarding this place?* Suddenly she realized everyone was watching her. "Oh. Right, yes. Good plans. We'll do it the way you said. I sneak in, see what's what, then let you in. Out in thirty minutes, before the patrol returns."

"Thirty minutes," Rory said softly. "Well, we usually manage to do some damage in that amount of time."

◆

A few hours later Molly was skimming along the ground, held aloft by Ariel as they flew toward the supply truck's route. The sun had set long ago, and the abandoned factories around them were dark and still, giving them plenty of shadows to hide in. Molly closed her eyes and felt the goose bumps on her arms, and the giddy joy of flight.

I wish we could just go flying together instead of always skulking around, Molly thought. *But if that's what I want, I guess we have to make a world where that can happen.*

As they wove between the factories, Molly heard the thrumming of igneous engines and opened her eyes. A boxy truck passed the mouth of the alley ahead of them. It was a somber gray except for the engine, which glimmered sun-bright through cracks in its casing. There were two men sitting in the cabin. Ariel lifted Molly higher into the air, and they swooped in over the truck. Ariel set Molly down on the truck's roof and unwound herself. Molly listened for sounds of alarm, but all she could hear was the engine's grumble.

"I'll try to get inside," Molly whispered. She peered down over the back of the truck at the doors. A long latch held them shut, and Molly couldn't reach it from the roof. The road flew by beneath them. *A fall at this speed probably wouldn't kill me. I think.* She lowered herself over the edge

"Careful, Molly," Ariel said. Molly didn't respond. With her fingers gripping the roof of the truck, she felt down below with her feet until she found the latch. She kicked down, and it turned.

The door under her swung outward, carrying Molly with it. She fell, catching the latch with her hands, and looked down to see the road speeding by just inches below her feet. She pulled herself farther up.

Both rear doors had swung partway open, then stopped. As Molly got her bearings, she realized Ariel had stopped them with her winds, keeping them from banging open and alerting the drivers. "Thanks," she said to Ariel.

Molly reached carefully around to the other side of the door and found the interior latch. She used it to swing around to the inside of the door. With some effort—and an uncomfortable amount of noise—she got herself into the truck's cargo area. She gestured for Ariel to follow. Ariel flowed between the doors, still holding them with her winds. But as soon as she entered, she recoiled.

"Molly! Iron!" she hissed. Her grip on the doors vanished, and Molly lunged to grab them before they swung too far open. With the doors in her hands, and the road rushing by in the gap beneath them, Molly peered over her shoulder to see what Ariel was shying from.

The truck was filled top to bottom with spirit traps. Over the rumble of the wheels she could hear them wheezing, groaning, growling. They were full.

Ariel hung back from them, halfway into the truck. But they would be at the factory soon, and if the doors were still open, they would catch her.

Molly pulled one door closed and then used her free hand to pull out the neck of her shirt. "Ariel, get in! Stay close to me!"

Ariel did as Molly said, flowing down inside her shirt and wrapping herself around Molly's chest. They had kept together like this aboard the *Gloria Mundi*, that great iron ship, and Molly's spirit-touched air gave Ariel some protection from the iron.

Molly pulled the second door shut, and the cargo area grew dark. Molly could see the nearest traps by the faint glow of Ariel through her shirt. There were dozens of the traps in the truck, some quite large.

"What do they need them all for?"

Ariel's only response was a groan.

A moment later Molly felt the truck slow, and she heard the murmur of voices outside.

"Ariel, I have to get closer to the traps. They'll be opening the doors in a second, and we need to hide."

"Do what you must," Ariel hissed.

Molly stepped up onto the nearest traps, trying to keep Ariel as far from the iron as she could. The traps swayed underneath her as she climbed to the top and crawled farther back into the interior, where the shadows could hide her.

The truck had stopped now, and Molly heard the cabin doors opening, followed by more muffled voices. They moved around the truck, and then light poured into the back.

"Smaller load this time?" someone said.

"It's what was on the requisition," another replied. "We're running low on subjects, I think, now that we're not using the kids anymore."

"Not a good idea to slow down when we haven't had any success yet. I don't know if you were here last time Arkwright made a visit. It wasn't pleasant." There was a thump as someone stepped up into the truck. "Come on, let's get this unloaded. Most of the subjects are already in the rooms."

What are they talking about? What is going on here?

Molly listened as the first of the traps were unloaded, and waited until she heard the workers moving away from the doors. She crawled along the traps and jumped down to the truck floor. No one was in sight, and when she leaned out of the truck, she saw the backs of several people to her right, carrying traps away. While their eyes were averted, she jumped out.

"I'm going under the truck," Molly whispered to Ariel. "If you think you can slip out without being noticed, now might be a good time."

Ariel flew out of Molly's shirt and up toward the ceiling of the factory. Molly wished she could go with her to get a better view. But a flying girl would probably draw attention.

Carefully Molly made her way to the front of the truck and peered out around one of its huge wheels.

The room in front of her looked nothing like a factory floor. Along the walls were rows of cells with narrow metal doors, an iron-mesh window in the center of each door. Through the windows Molly could make out people, peering back into the larger room.

Is this some kind of prison?

In the far corner she spotted a huge stack of empty traps—more even than her family had carried with them aboard the *Legerdemain* back when it had been an aetheric harvester. She scanned the room but saw no spiritual machines anywhere, nor any of the equipment required for infusing spirits into machines. *What did they do with them all?*

The people carrying the full traps came into view, moving slowly under their burdens. "Bring them straight here!" a tall woman shouted, beckoning them toward the cells. "These subjects are ready." The woman wore an odd suit that glimmered in the lights above. Molly stared at it for a full minute before she puzzled out why. There was iron sewn into it, from an iron-banded collar down to iron-studded boots. Several other workers near the cells wore the same kind of suit, but another group standing nearby wore only loose white pants and tunics. Molly stared at the familiar-looking white clothes—they were the same as what she had worn in the sanatorium. *Are those sanatorium patients?*

Footsteps sounded above Molly, inside the truck, and she pushed herself farther back under the truck. More of the iron-suited workers emerged with traps, carrying them straight toward the doors. Once they were clear of the truck Molly eased forward again to see what they would do.

The tall woman took one of the traps. Next to each cell door there was a small hatch, and she fitted the trap carefully into one of them, fastening it in place. She then twisted a knob on the trap's side. A pale face watched her from inside the cell.

There was a hiss, and then a roar, and something iridescent green flashed in the window. Molly squinted to see through the thick mesh. Something bright and amorphous flowed past. *Are those scales?* She thought she heard a voice in the cell, followed by a thump. The woman and other workers moved forward, blocking her view. They recoiled a moment later as something crashed against the door.

The workers around the door chattered among themselves as Molly's stomach churned. *Did they just set an angry spirit loose on someone?* To the side of the row of cells, the people in sanatorium garb looked on with a vague, unfocused anxiety, but they didn't seem fully aware. Molly looked harder at their eyes. *They're drugged. They really are from a sanatorium. What is going on?*

"Not a strong candidate, really," the tall woman said, her clear voice carrying across the room. She was looking down at a ledger as she spoke. "No history of pro-spirit behavior, only mild sympathies. It was a poor chance to create a link. None of these look promising. Do we have anyone better in the new batch?" She looked up at the group of drugged people. "Come, dispose of the spirit, and we'll move on."

A link? Pro-spirit behavior? Molly's mind spun for a moment, and suddenly the pieces fit together. *This place is for Arkwright. They're trying to create more spirit-touched people like me and Wîscakân so he can feed.* She watched in horror as the trap was removed from its hatch and replaced with a small canister. With a *whump* the canister shot a cloud of glittering dust into the cell. The spirit screamed and battered the window, and then, with a flash, it dissolved. *Iron powder. They're killing people and spirits here, trying to make more food for Arkwright.* She felt like vomiting or, better, like rushing out and attacking every calm-faced worker overseeing this horror. But she knew that would help no one. She pressed her hands into the floor until the shaking passed.

The tall woman and her colleagues were moving toward another cell. Two workers struggled behind her.

"Would you hurry, please? Arkwright will be here soon, and if we haven't made progress—"

"We're trying, but his false leg is bloody heavy," the man just behind her said.

Molly's eyes snapped to the thin, drug-addled man between them. *Croyden!* The sanatorium drugs had sapped all expression from his face. *What is he doing here? Oh God, they're going to kill him!*

They pulled him forward, the tall woman opening a door for him. *What do I do? How do I stop this?* This wasn't just a factory where a few overseers kept an eye on laborers too weak to stand up for themselves. There were at least two dozen staff in this place, and their iron suits would keep Ariel from fighting them effectively. *How can we stop them all?*

Croyden slumped to the floor inside the cell, his artificial leg clanging against the wall.

Molly heard more footsteps above her in the truck. *The traps!* She slid to the rear of the vehicle and watched as two men stepped out, carrying more traps. As soon as they were gone, she slid out from under the truck and hopped up into the cargo area. Half of the traps were gone now, but some of the largest were still sitting in the back corner. She ran forward and found the dials to open the vents and feeding hatches on all the traps. She crouched down in front of them. "Can you hear me? Can any of you speak English?"

There was no answer, though she could hear air wheezing through the vents, and one of the terric traps had begun to rumble.

"No, of course you won't talk to me. Why would you?" she said softly. "Okay, I'm going to talk, and I hope some of you can understand me. I want to let you out—no, I'm *going* to let you out. It's up to you what you do after I open your traps. But I'm hoping some of you might stay and help us shut this place down so they can't hurt any more people or spirits here. I really, really hope you're not so angry that you attack me or the other humans who are victims of this place." She stopped and listened. The wheezing of air through the vents had softened. "Did you understand any of that?"

"Trick," said a low, rippling voice from the largest aqueous trap. "Lie."

"No," Molly said. "Not a lie."

She moved closer, examining the trap. There was a prominent valve on one side that seemed promising. She tried it first with her bare hands, then pulled the wrench from her belt and stuck its handle through the spokes of the valve, using it for leverage. It turned slowly until the top of the trap opened with a *pop*. She lifted the lid off and set it down quietly.

Nothing came out of the open trap. She peered over the side and saw something dark and glimmering pooled at the bottom. It flowed away from her, bunching against the far side of the trap. Molly could hear a hiss where it touched the iron sides.

"See? No lie. You can go or stay. You should know the workers here are wearing iron though. It'll be dangerous to fight."

She turned toward the other traps. She started at the top of the pile and worked her way down, releasing each spirit in turn. Several burst out immediately when she gave them a path. After the first few had fled, she heard a rushing behind her and turned to find the aqueous spirit sitting at the edge of the cargo area. It looked like a crested wave almost as tall as her. The water wasn't blue, but black, speckled with small points of light like reflected stars. Its liquid body rippled slightly, and the crest of the wave turned toward her.

"We go?"

"That's up to you." She continued through the rest of the traps.

When she released the rumbling terric spirit, it leapt from its trap, hitting her in the chest and knocking her backward. Its legs, crystalline and jagged, dug into her ribs, and she whimpered. It seemed to be made up almost completely of legs. It looked down at her with multifaceted eyes and raised jagged crystal claws over her head. It paused, looked toward the open back of the truck, then leapt away, colliding with the door.

She heard a cry of alarm from outside and scrambled to her feet. "Go, go!" she hissed at the spirits still nearby, and she quickly to opened the rest of the traps. Just as the last spirit flew free—a silver dragonfly with human eyes, wings flapping weakly—she heard a bang from outside. She jumped out of the truck.

The facility had been thrown into chaos. The two laborers who had been unloading the truck were fending off the crystalline terric spirit with empty traps. Even the iron didn't seem to dissuade it. The sanatorium patients followed placidly behind shouting workers, who were shoving them through the narrow doors. The tall woman was wrestling with a canister, and there was already a glimmer of iron powder in the air around her.

Most of the spirits who could fly had fled to the upper reaches of the room, where the iron powder wouldn't reach them. They hid inside tangles of pipes and walkways— leftovers from the building's previous life as a genuine factory, it seemed. Ariel dropped down beside her. "Are you sure this was the best course of action, Molly?"

"The best I could think of anyway. I think they're trying to make more spirit-touched people, but really they're just loosing confused spirits on helpless people. Can you do something about the woman firing off the iron powder while I get the doors?"

"I can certainly try," Ariel said. She flew back up to the ceiling directly above the woman and began battering one of the walkways with strong winds. It trembled and shook, its moorings coming loose from the ceiling.

Molly didn't wait to see if Ariel's plan worked. Instead, she turned and began running. Everyone was too distracted to take any notice of her as she hurried across the room to the front door. She threw the deadbolt and kicked the door open. Her father and brothers shielded their eyes against the light that suddenly flooded out at them.

"What's happening, Moll? We heard shouting," her father said.

"I released a lot of spirits."

"I thought we were going for quiet," Rory said.

"I had to do something. Croyden's here, and they're going to kill him."

"Croyden?" her father said, stepping forward. "Where?"

"In one of the little cells, but he's drugged. We have to get all these spirits and people out."

"I count at least a dozen people," Kiernan said. "And is that iron they're wearing?"

"Two more behind the truck," Molly added.

"So how the heck do we stop them?" Rory asked.

"The cells," Molly said. "They've been locking people in those cells. Maybe we can do the same to them."

There was a crash, and Molly turned to see the wreckage of a walkway splayed across the floor. The tall woman was nearby, unhurt, but she no longer had the iron powder canisters in her hands.

Her father nodded. "Let's get to it. Boys, you take the five on the left. Moll, we'll be on the right. Be careful, everyone!"

He started running, and Molly had to hurry to keep up. The nearest two workers were busily stuffing patients into cells while being harried by the silver dragonfly Molly had seen. Despite its small size, it was making quite a nuisance of itself, rushing in at the workers' unprotected faces, blinding them and pushing them back with puffs of silver-blue wind. One of the workers moved away from the patients and raised iron-plated gloves to try to catch the spirit.

He was so focused on the dragonfly that he didn't see Molly's father, who barreled into him and sent him flying backward through the open door of the cell. The patients inside fell, too addled to catch themselves, and the other worker stumbled back.

"Hey—" she said feebly before a burst of wind from Molly sent her into a cell after her colleague. Her father rushed into the cell and pulled two patients out by their shirtfronts, while Molly grabbed the door and slammed it closed.

"Molly Stout!" a booming voice shouted, and Molly turned to see the tall woman glaring at her across the wreckage of the walkway. "It's Molly Stout! To the weapons, everyone!"

Rory and Kiernan had managed to overpower another of the workers, but the rest turned from their struggles and ran for the back of the factory, where lines of lockers stood.

"Remember, do not kill the girl! Arkwright wants her!"

Ariel flew in from across the room and bowled several of the workers over with a gust that swept the ground, but she could not stop them all. They reached the lockers and threw them open, grabbing guns that glimmered red with igneous energy. The tall woman took the first gun and leveled it at Molly's father.

"Stop now, or he dies!" she shouted.

Molly and her father froze.

"Molly, the lockers!" her father hissed at her side.

"What? What about them?"

"They're metal!"

"So what does—"

"METAL CONDUCTS ELECTRICITY!" he shouted at her.

"Oh. Oh!" She planted her feet and looked inside for her anger. Given what she had just seen, it wasn't hard to find.

Lightning arced from her and hit the lockers, spreading across their metal surfaces. The workers who had been gathering weapons were blown back to lie steaming on the floor. The tall woman turned toward the sound, and as soon as her weapon moved, Kiernan began running. The tall woman saw him and brought her gun back around. She pulled the trigger when Kiernan was only a few feet away, and a flare of fire hit him in the chest. He screamed, and his legs buckled. He lay sprawled at the woman's feet.

Molly's father was shouting, and Molly thought she might be too, but she couldn't hear it over the sudden ringing in her ears. She and her father were sprinting, but they wouldn't reach Kiernan in time. Molly tried to gather lightning, wind, but the ringing cut through her brain, scattering her thoughts before she could form them. All she could do was run.

She saw the weapon rise again, pointed at her brother's face. He was on fire now. She saw the woman tighten her finger on the trigger.

Then there was a *crack*, and Molly gasped. But the sound hadn't come from the gun. There was something clear and shining climbing the wall behind the woman. *Is that ice?*

The ice climbed halfway up the wall, and then let out a *thump*. The ice and the wall both burst, sending shards of frozen concrete out across the ground. The tall woman flinched, her finger sliding from the trigger, and in that moment Molly's father reached her and punched her on the jaw. She fell, jelly-limbed, across the wreckage of the wall.

Molly ran to her brother, batting at the flames on his chest. She put them out quickly, but his blackened skin still smoked. "Is he okay?"

"Okay? No," her father said. "But still breathing."

Another sheet of ice climbed the wall behind them, cracking it apart. The roof groaned. Molly spotted the strange aqueous spirit near the back wall. It seemed to be directing the ice.

Rory was suddenly beside them, holding several fragments of ice in his arms. "Here. Will these help?"

Their father took the ice and spread it over Kiernan's chest. Kiernan gasped and shuddered, his eyes flickering open and closed.

With a thump another piece of the wall collapsed, and fragments of pipe rained down around them from the ceiling. Powdered concrete drifted through the air.

"This place is going to collapse," Molly said. "I asked the spirits to help shut this place down, and I think one of them took me literally. We have to get out of here. We have to get everyone out of here."

Her father nodded. "Molly, Rory, you get the others out. I've got Kier."

"Are you sure? He's—"

"Don't bloody talk! GO!" he roared, heaving a whimpering Kiernan into his arms.

Molly stood, turning toward the tall woman, who was still unconscious in the wreckage. She knelt down and found a set of keys on her belt. She took them and ran back to the cells.

She went to Croyden's first, trying three keys before she found the right one for the small cell. Croyden sat on the floor inside, his mechanical leg stuck out at an odd angle. Rory grabbed the keys from her hand.

"Croyden!" Molly shouted. "You have to leave!"

"Molly?" he muttered. "But you're not here."

"Of course I am, you idiot. Now get up." She bent down and slid her head under his arm, trying to lift him. *This leg really does weigh a ton.*

"No, no. They said they killed you."

"Still alive, Croyden." She heard another wall crash down. "But I won't be if you don't move."

She finally got him upright, and he shuffled halfheartedly forward. When they emerged from the cell, she saw a crowd of white-clad men and women being ushered out the front door by Rory. Ariel was helping, pushing the slow ones along with gusts of wind.

"Ariel!" Molly called, and the spirit flew to her side. "Can you carry him? He can't move himself with his leg."

"I believe I can, as long as his leg contains no iron." She swept in around Croyden, and his feet lifted slightly off the ground. His head lolled toward Molly, and he looked at her blearily. "I can take him," Ariel said. "You gather the rest."

"Molly?" Croyden muttered sleepily. "They said they killed you." And then he was carried forward to join the crowd.

Molly snatched the keys back from Rory and moved to the cells, freeing the patients and sending them shuffling slowly toward the door. As the last of them neared the exit, the final piece of the back wall caved in under the aqueous spirit's ice, and a corner of the roof came down with it, narrowly missing the tall woman.

Molly turned to the last cell, the one containing the workers. She unlocked the door and opened it cautiously. "Are we going to fight, or are you going to get out of here?" she asked them. Without a word they rushed past her and out through the collapsed back wall, slipping on the ice.

The spirits had gone, save for the aqueous one still dismantling the building. The patients were out, and Rory was at the door. The ceiling was bent and cracked, looking like it would collapse at any moment. Other than Molly and the spirit, there was only one person left in the building: the tall woman.

Molly scowled. The thought of helping her made Molly's stomach clench. Still, the building was going to come down on her, and that thought was even worse.

She ran across the room. "You've done enough!" she shouted to the spirit as she ran. "Get out before it comes down!"

The spirit flowed across the rubble of the walls toward the outside. Molly reached the woman and bent to try to pull her up, but she and her iron suit were far too heavy to lift. Molly grabbed her heels and started pulling.

"You probably won't...feel very good...when you wake up," Molly said, pulling the woman across the rubble with quick tugs, watching her head bang against the concrete and ice. "But at least...you'll wake up." They moved slowly, one tug at a time, the ceiling bowing and cracking above them.

Da is going to think I'm crazy, risking my neck for her, Molly thought. She pulled the woman up and over a huge chunk of concrete. *What am I doing?* The shoulder of the iron-laced suit caught on a corner, and Molly tugged until the straps broke and it came off. *She made her choices. She put herself here.* Another tug. They were almost clear now. *I'm going to get myself killed.* With a groan, part of a wall fell across the truck that had brought Molly inside, crushing it. She risked a glance up and saw the night sky through cracks opening in the ceiling. *Oh hell.* She braced her feet, tucked the woman's legs under her arms and heaved, skittering back as fast as she could. Concrete smashed down just beyond the woman as they slid out into the road behind the building, and Molly tripped and fell. Dust billowed out of the collapsing building, rolling over them and blocking out the world as Molly lay, face pressed to the cobblestones, breathing hard.

"Well," she whispered to herself, "no one died. I think."

"The night's young yet," a soft voice replied through the clouds of dust.

FIFTEEN

Molly scrambled away on all fours, moving until she hit the wall of the building opposite. As the dust began to settle, she saw a man walking toward her. He was in a dark coat that glistened oddly under the streetlights. He wore some kind of hood or helmet—something black and smooth that hugged the curves of his face, open only at the eyes and mouth. But she knew him instantly.

"Howarth," she whispered.

"Come quietly now. You've done enough damage for one night." He walked toward her with a calm assurance that reminded her of Arkwright. The black airship hovered above them. There were other figures descending from it, sliding down long lines to the ground around her.

Took too long. She pushed herself to her feet against the wall. She called on the lightning and sent it at Howarth. It struck his arm.

He didn't even flinch. "Rubberized clothes, grounded boots," he said, walking forward. "You can't catch us off guard anymore." He was within a few feet of her now, and not stopping. He had some sort of blade in his other hand.

"I don't want to fight you," she said.

"Well, that makes two of us," he said. "But in my experience, you're not one to come quietly, so I'm not—"

Molly brought the wind in under her as she jumped. It seemed harder than usual to direct, as if it didn't want to linger, but the gust took her up over his head and to the top of the building beside them. As she cleared the lip of the building, she pushed the wind away and let herself fall, rolling across the roof and stopping near the far end.

There was a thump behind her, and she turned to find two Disposal agents alighting on the roof. "How did—" she began, and then Howarth appeared over the edge of the building, rising lightly into the air and landing in front of her. *Do they have flitters? No, they're not using the wind.*

She braced herself and gathered the winds again, but Howarth made a cutting gesture. Something at the tips of his fingers sparked, and the winds fractured and vanished around her. "I told you," he said. "We know your tricks."

She looked over the edge of the building at the street far below. Midway down she could see a scaffold. *The spirit tricks won't work. Maybe I should try some of my human tricks.* The agents were rushing forward now. Molly ducked under one of their grasping arms and leapt backward.

The fall was far enough to hurt, but she landed well, legs folding and bringing her down into a forward roll to soften the impact. She'd made countless jumps like that aboard the *Legerdemain*. But the deck of the airship had been much sturdier than the scaffold. A moment after she landed, it creaked beneath her and began to tip sideways. Molly scrambled to the edge and held on as it fell, leaping clear at the last moment and coming to rest on the cold cobblestones.

She groaned and forced herself to her feet. The agents were still coming, gliding through the air toward her without using wind. Molly turned and ran, twisting and turning through alleys until the sound of their heavy boots faded behind her. To her right she saw a half-open loading-bay door, and she ducked inside, crouching down amid moldering crates. She was breathing so hard it was almost deafening. She forced her lungs to slow, sipping air through pursed lips.

She heard a thump outside. "Damn it." It was Howarth's voice. "Anyone see her?"

"No eyes on her, sir. She's gone," another voice shouted back.

"Bloody hell. Even with the new gear."

There was a series of thumps as more boots touched down. "We expected the lightning and the wind, sir. Didn't expect her to jump off a building."

"And her family?"

"Gone. Orders were to focus resources on the girl."

"All right then. Keep to it. Pair off, spiral search pattern. If you don't find her in ten, back aboard the Black Guard."

"Aye aye, sir."

Molly heard a hum and boots scuffing against the ground. She sank back farther, staying there even after all sound had faded. She counted slowly to herself until she reached one hundred before risking a look out the door. No one was there.

She peered farther out, then crawled into the alley. Between the hulking factories she could just make out the aft section of the airship, dark and ominous. The silhouette of an agent rose toward the ship, cutting through the winds and leaving them in tatters behind. *They've got something that stops the wind. They must be flying using gravitics, just like their airship.*

She turned and started moving away from the ship, watching the sky for the people still hunting her.

Hours later, her legs so tired they were beginning to tremble, she reached the Bantam's Rest and trudged down the stairs. When she was halfway down, the door burst open and her father leaned out. He stopped when he saw her and blew out a long, long breath. He reached his hand to her, and she took it, letting him lead her inside.

"Thank the Almighty you made it. You were gone so long, we thought maybe they got you."

"I walked," Molly said. "Stuck to the back streets. Sorry it took so long. How's Kier?"

"He's going to be okay," he said. "It's a bad burn. Probably be weeks before he's back on his feet again, and chances are it'll always give him grief. Ariel flew him off to Legerdemain, outside the city. He'll be safe."

Molly nodded and sought out Rory in the shadowy basement. He was sitting against the back wall on a half-broken chair, rubbing his fingers together. He didn't look at her, so she let go of her father and went to him.

"Heya, sis," he said without looking up from his hands. "Glad you made it back."

"You too," she said and put her hand over his. "Da says he'll be okay."

He finally looked up at her and faked a smile. "Yeah. Women like scars, right? Especially bloody big ones."

"I'm sure some woman somewhere likes bloody big scars," Molly said. "Or some man. Kier never told me which he fancied." She allowed herself to sink to the floor next to Rory's chair.

"I think he fancies airships," Rory said.

Molly nodded. "What did I miss? Did the patients all get away? Do the Unionists know what we found yet?"

"You just missed them," her father said. "They say they'll get the patients somewhere safe, and they've already started their press rolling on these." He held out a small book to her, and she leafed through it. It was a replica of Haviland Stout's handwritten journal, bound in thin leather. Printed on the front were three words: *HAVILAND'S TRUE JOURNAL*. The pages were stitched together with thick string. Someone had taken a great deal of care with it.

"Looks good," Molly said. "Theresa will be happy. And now I could really, really use a nap. Where are we spending the night?"

"Bascombe offered us a place, down near the wharf. Should be safe."

"More walking to get there though," Rory said, rising and extending a hand to Molly. "Got it in you?"

"Sure," she said. "Why not?"

They walked toward the door, but their father stepped in front of them. He looked at Rory, then at her, and his eyes were clouded with tears and yet clearer than she ever remembered seeing them. He gripped her shoulder, his hand so solid it was like granite, and then he was folding them both in a hug that almost knocked her over, it was so unexpected. He simply held them.

"This is because Kier got himself burned, isn't it?" Rory said.

"You're bloody right it is. Now shut up," their father said, and they did, standing uncomfortably while he held them for several more breaths.

"How much further until we can stop all this?" he asked softly, speaking into Rory's shoulder. When no one answered, he straightened and released them. "Do you think we've done enough, Moll? Can we leave it in other hands yet?"

Molly shook her head. "I don't want to, Da."

"Me either," Rory said. She looked into his eyes and was shocked to find they were wet too. She didn't remember ever seeing Rory cry. "And you, Da?"

"I'll be where you are. Likely telling you you're a bloody idiot."

"Are you sure?"

He nodded.

"Okay. So we keep going."

⚓

Molly woke the next morning to the scream of gulls outside her window. They were a few blocks from the water, but she could still hear the sounds of the busy docks—

voices raised, ships' horns, the bang of cargo loading and unloading. Air or water, docks always sounded the same.

She was in a small room with three cots so close together she could barely pass between them. She remembered coming into the room with her father and Rory but didn't remember falling asleep. Neither her father nor brother was here now. Molly rose from her bed and went to the window.

The sun was well up in the sky, meaning it was probably ten or eleven. She was on the second floor of a converted warehouse—a place the Unionists had been using for some time to funnel laborers and runaways to safer conditions, though they'd never invited Molly or her family in before. The window was small, and all she could see through it was the wall of the next building over. She closed her eyes and listened.

Besides the sounds of the docks, she could hear voices on the floor below her—dozens of conversations, all going on at once. *I hear Da, and is that Bascombe? But who else is here?* She listened for a moment more, enjoying the solitude, until she heard a fluting voice that sounded like Ariel's. Quickly she pulled on pants and shoes and left the room, heading toward the voices.

She navigated a network of rooms much like hers, found the stairs and descended into a wide room filled with crates and crowded with bodies. Half of them wore the white of the sanatoriums, while the rest wore the garb of laborers and factory workers. As she came in, conversations dried up and faces turned toward her. The eyes of the sanatorium patients were clear now, and they pinned her where she stood.

"Molly!" Theresa called from farther inside the room. Molly hurried forward into a clearer area with stools set up.

Her father was there, and Rory, as well as Bascombe and a few other Unionists she recognized. Ariel was hovering near Rory. And Croyden sat on a stool, his artificial leg stiffly extended.

"Am I interrupting?" Molly asked.

"Good you woke," Theresa said. "You should be here for this."

"We're talking through Theresa's plan," her father said. He stood and offered her his stool. She took it.

"Are all of these people from last night?" Molly asked. "I didn't think there were so many."

"Most are," Theresa said. "Some of the ones you freed along with me asked to come too."

"Oh. Okay." She looked around at all the faces, but dropped her eyes to the floor when she saw how many of them were watching her.

"Bascombe has told me that the journals have already begun distribution," Theresa said. Bascombe nodded. "Which is a start."

"You called it a seed," Molly said. "Something about seeds and rain."

Theresa nodded. "Yes, the rain. It will take a few days for the journals to find their way into the right hands, the right minds, but we'll need that time to prepare for what comes next."

"Which is?" Bascombe asked.

"Molly, why don't you tell them?" Theresa said.

Molly frowned. "But I don't—"

Theresa put her hand on Molly's knee. "Remember what we talked about in Twillingate? About me?"

"You mean…finding out about Charles Arkwright? About the wool?" Theresa nodded. "Okay." Molly turned to face everyone. "Theresa said that the best way to get people to change isn't to tell them what they're doing wrong. It's to show them who pulled the wool over their eyes."

"Exactly," Theresa said. "The journal puts the right ideas in their heads. Now, if we can show them who's been lying to them, the ideas might just stick."

"We have to reveal Arkwright," Molly said. Theresa smiled grimly at her.

"And how the hell do we do that?" Rory said. "I mean, he's kept his secret for decades now. Everyone thinks he's dead."

"He's careful. Always," Theresa said. "Only reveals himself to people who directly benefit from him running things. And when one of them turns, he shuts them up in the sanatoriums. We need to draw him out. And we have the one thing he might risk exposure for."

"What?" Molly's father asked.

Theresa's eyes turned to Molly. "You."

Molly breathed deep and nodded. "Yeah, I thought of that."

"What are you talking about?" Molly's father said. "Because she's a danger? Because he wants revenge?"

Theresa shook her head. "It's simpler than that."

"I'm food, Da. He needs someone spirit-touched to feed on."

She could see the thought working its way into her father's mind. The confusion creasing his brow, the disgust curling his lips, the anger glittering in his eyes.

"As far as we know, you are the only person so changed by spirits in Terra Nova," Theresa said. "Unless the mystery man from Twillingate is still here."

Molly shook her head. "Wîskacân. He's gone home now, and I doubt he'll ever come back here."

Theresa nodded. "So. We give the journals a few days and keep Molly out of sight. Let Arkwright get hungrier and more desperate. We choose a time and place, then bring her into the open."

"Wait," her father said. "Why use her as bait at all? If Molly's the only one he can feed on, why not just let him starve?"

"Believe it or not, if Arkwright dies before we reveal him, we've lost our best opportunity to change how things work in Terra Nova," Theresa said. "He is the living proof of his own lies. He is a tool we need if we want real, immediate change. If he's dead, we'll find ourselves arguing against a ghost and a history people have believed for generations. We can't win that argument."

Molly's father did not look happy, but he didn't argue further.

"You think he'll just stroll out where we can nab him if we offer up Molly?" Rory asked. "Why wouldn't he just send his lackeys to take her?"

"I have no doubt that he will come," Croyden said. His voice was quieter than Molly remembered, and he did not look up as he spoke. "I saw Arkwright in the sanatorium where they held me. He was weak and in pain. He could not walk without help, could hardly move. He is in need of sustenance, and even a few extra moments could be too many. He will come. But I very much doubt he will come gently."

"No," Theresa said. "Not gently. Disposal is in his pocket, and they will bring everything they can muster. Which is why we will need those few days to prepare our response."

"What kind of response can there be to that?" Bascombe asked. "To the full weight of Haviland Industries and the authorities of Terra Nova?"

"The people in this room, for one," Theresa said. "We've all enjoyed the tender care of Arkwright and his machinations. I suspect most of us will stick around for the finale." There were heads nodding around the room—not all of them, but most.

"I know a great many once-trapped spirits who would happily join us," Ariel said. "And Legerdemain, as always, will be where Molly goes."

"We'll have to be careful, bringing spirits into the fight with Disposal," Molly said. "They hunt rogue spirits, after all. And when they were chasing me yesterday, they had something that stopped me from calling the wind. If they can do the same to you or Legerdemain, you might be in trouble."

"They've got that damned airship that doesn't even fly on the wind too," Molly's father said. "How do we fight that?"

"I might have an idea about that," Molly said, trying to ignore all the eyes that fell on her. "I think they're using some kind of gravitic engines to fly around without wind. But do you remember Loam—the terric spirit we freed, I mean—and what it did to the tunnel rat?"

"It made it fall sideways," Rory said. "And then it crushed it."

Molly nodded. "It shifted the gravity. Enough to bend metal. So if we asked him to help with those gravitic engines..."

"It could overload the engines," her father finished. "That might work. Gravitic engines are finicky things. But that spirit crossed over to its own world. Could you even bring it back?"

"I think I can find it," Molly said. "After that, all I can do is ask. But I doubt we can fight Disposal and Haviland Industries and win. There's got to be more to the plan."

"Once we reveal Arkwright for what he is, things should shift," Theresa said. "Even most Disposal agents don't know about him. The plan is this: we and the spirits keep Disposal busy, while you, Molly, find a way to drag that bastard out into the light before we're all brought down."

Molly swallowed.

"Good then?" Theresa said. "We all have to prepare. And remember, whatever we do, we must keep Molly out of sight."

"But how do we know when the time is right? When do we do all this?"

"I will handle that, I think," Theresa said. "The other preparations are not exactly in my wheelhouse. But I know the right time to deliver a message. If no one has anything else?" Theresa rose to her feet at these last words, looked around the crowd and then walked away.

Molly watched the others file out, leaving in twos and threes. Most of the sanatorium patients stayed—they seemed to be collecting new clothes from some of the crates. A group of Unionists stood in heated discussion around Bascombe.

"I know how you feel," Molly heard Bascombe say, "but you've read the journal, you know what they found at that factory."

"What do you figure?" Rory whispered at Molly's side. He was watching Bascombe too. "Think they'll kick us out before we bring more trouble down on their heads?"

"I don't know," Molly whispered back. "I know they think we're crazy, but we're talking about shutting down Haviland Industries. That would close half of the factories in Terra Nova. They probably wouldn't mind that so much."

"Except they still think Charles Arkwright is dead, just like everyone else."

She watched Bascombe, who was mostly listening while others spoke now, not saying much. He hadn't said much during the meeting and the planning either. *He always looks so tired. Or disappointed maybe.* "I don't know what he thinks," Molly said. "I'm going to go upstairs."

Rory let her go, and she made her way back to the small room filled with cots. She went to the window and breathed the salt air in deep.

Almost immediately there was a knock on the door.

"It's just me in here," Molly said. "And I could use a few minutes."

"I know you could, but I want to talk to you anyway," Theresa responded from the other side of the door.

"Okay." Molly took another deep breath and turned around as Theresa entered. "Something else you need me to do?"

Theresa shook her head. "No. But I want you to be ready for something. I already know when we're going to bring you out, you see. But I wanted to talk to you about it first."

Molly frowned. "Oh?"

"It's the right time. It's the best time we have, and it will reach the right ears. There is no better—"

"You're just making me nervous now," Molly said. "When are we doing this, and why are you afraid of what I'll say?"

Theresa sniffed and nodded. "In five days' time, your sister will be making a public speech. Nothing prerecorded, but live on a stage below the docks—a sort of rally. That's when we need you to show up."

Molly was already shaking her head. "No, I don't want to involve Brighid. She's—"

"She's involved herself, and we need you to talk to her."

"You don't know my sister. She doesn't listen."

"It's not for her. It's for the people watching. So they can hear your voice, see your face. They know the stories about you, but they don't know you. And seeing Arkwright might change a lot of minds, but seeing you, a human being instead of the hobgoblin your sister describes, will change more. We need to give these people so much reason to doubt that they have no way to turn their back on the truth."

"But I haven't even spoken to her since the *Gloria Mundi*. Since I set free the spirit that broke her ship, and she started making her speeches, and…what would I say?" Molly breathed in and out, but there didn't seem to be any oxygen in the room.

"That's why I wanted to talk to you first," Theresa said. "I knew it would be hard. I'll tell the rest of them once you've had a few hours."

"There isn't—"

"There's no other time. If you want this to work, to change things, this is the best way." She let herself out, closing the door behind her.

Molly turned back to the window, but the bright sun stung her eyes. She sat down on the bed, then curled up on it. Gravity seemed heavier than usual today.

SIXTEEN

Five days passed, so slowly they might have been years. Molly kept to her room, save for the one time she was allowed out to seek help from the spirit world. The sun came and went from her small window, and she slept and spoke little, the others all busy with their preparations. She tried not to think of her sister—and thought of nothing else.

Her father came to see her when he could. "This is probably great for you," Molly said to him on his second visit. "Me stuck in here, safe. You'd probably keep me in here if you could."

He chuckled. "Tempting, but…No. In here you're not you." He sat with her and spoke of nothing until he was called away yet again. She was alone in the silent room. Hiding, and hating every moment of it.

And yet, when the day came, she almost couldn't bring herself to leave her room. When she stepped out of the Unionists' building, it was with the feeling she was plunging into fathomless water with no winds to accompany her. Theresa and her father ran through the plan again and again, their words washing over her.

In the early evening they headed to the foot of the docks and went their own ways. Rory clenched Molly's hand tightly, and she squeezed him back. She flew with Ariel up to the rooftops and looked out on the open circle surrounding the umbilical, taking her assigned place, and feeling she was sinking down into darkness.

Breathe, Molly. Breathe. She rubbed her eyes, slapping her cheeks lightly. *Focus. You have a job to do.*

The fug in the air here was thick. Molly could taste grease, soot, burned things. She felt grit between her tongue and the top of her mouth.

Up above, the floating docks blocked out the moonlight, leaving the area below to be lit only by a few soot-encrusted igneous lamps. But more lights were soon brought in and placed around the small wooden stage they had constructed at the foot of the umbilical. One of them was turned on, and a beam of light swung across the rooftops as they positioned it. Molly ducked below the lip of the building where she sat, hoping her dark clothes blended with the shingles.

The light finally settled on the center of the empty stage. Soon, Molly knew, Brighid would appear to begin her speech.

You'll know the right time to step in, Theresa had told her when they all left to take their places. *Trust your instincts.*

But my instincts are telling me to run, Molly thought now. *Not so helpful.*

"I always hate this part," Ariel said softly beside Molly. "This moment on the cusp of greater things. The waiting is almost worse than being in the midst of it all."

Molly nodded. "Me too. It's weird, because I know once it starts I'll be in constant danger, and so will everyone else. But I still wish it would just start. Even if..."

"Even if we fail, and Arkwright brings us all down?"

Molly nodded. "I'm sorry. I know that's selfish, just to want it done."

"There have been times, during the past century, when I have wished the same. That I could slip and let Arkwright finally do away with me, simply so the struggle might be over. I have been fighting a long, long time. And you are only fifteen, but you have spent a year and a half of your short life engaged in this revolution. It is selfish, true, but there is nothing wrong with selfish thoughts. Sometimes they provide good counsel. But those thoughts must be tempered with more generous ones, lest we follow the path of Arkwright and forget that the world is filled with beings of equal significance to ourselves."

Ariel fell silent, and Molly sat staring at the reflection of her light in the small black stones in the shingles.

"I never said thank you," Molly said.

"For what?"

"For believing in me. For showing me Haviland's journal and thinking I might understand. For bringing me in to all of this. Letting me do something better. You're the one who really started this, not me."

Ariel was quiet for a time, her face turned upward. Molly looked up too. The sky was mostly clear, but Molly knew that somewhere up there Legerdemain was waiting, up so high that he was indistinguishable from the stars, where the air was so thin it could barely sustain him. She could feel him, his nervousness increasing her own.

"Identifying who began something like this is like picking out the stone that began an avalanche. It began somewhere, true enough—maybe with me, maybe with the first spirits Arkwright captured for his own use—but once it well and truly begins, we are all just stones moving together. One stone rolling down the mountain changes nothing unless others move with it." Ariel moved in closer. "So I should thank you too, Molly. For being my second stone."

There was a noise from below: applause. A man Molly did not recognize, in a black suit and a bow tie, stepped onto the stage. A small crew had set up an amplifier in front of him to carry his voice across the square. The entire area at the base of the docks had filled with people. At the front of the crowd were dozens of reporters, some with notebooks in hand, others with the black boxes of cameras strapped to their chest. Most of the people looked like sailors and harvesters, the laborers who fed Terra Nova and all the other industries within it by trapping and selling spirits.

"Are you ready?" Ariel whispered.

"No," Molly said. "I never am though. But here we go."

"People of Terra Nova!" the man shouted, and the amplifier in front of him sent his voice rippling through the air all around them. Molly guessed it would be audible even dozens of blocks away. "You have come tonight to hear firsthand of the terrible downfall of the Stout family. Over one hundred years ago, when the great explorer Haviland Stout discovered the scourge of spirits and taught us how to protect ourselves from it, he set the world on a path that has changed life as we know it. What he could not foresee was his own kin falling under the pernicious influence of the spirits.

"But you are not here to listen to me tell you the tale, right?" There were murmurs of agreement from the crowd. "You are here because the one survivor of the disaster, the last unpoisoned descendant of the Stout line, is here to tell you, to warn you, of the way the spirits can find their way inside the minds of even the most noble families. Her story is heart wrenching, and I hope you listen well. Here she is, folks. Brighid Stout of Haviland Industries!"

As he swept his hand back, Brighid climbed the steps to the stage and emerged into the light. She waved to the crowd. The man who had announced her disappeared into the shadows as she took his place.

Molly's breath caught in her throat. Her sister looked like another person. Her skin was pale but smooth and clean, every scar and pockmark smoothed away under a layer of makeup. Her hair hung in ringlets around her face, not tied back the way Molly had always seen it. She looked like someone pulled from the stages in London, someone dreamy and glamorous. Not a real person at all.

"Hello," she said, the amplifier carrying her voice. The simple familiarity of her voice warred with the strangeness of her appearance.

"Thank you for coming here tonight," she went on. "My story is important, now more than ever. Six nights ago my sister Molly, and with her my father and brothers, struck another factory, freeing the spirits and killing dozens, some of them children." Molly's legs tensed, but she felt Ariel's cool arm around her shoulders.

"Not yet," the spirit whispered. "Bear it a little while longer."

Molly forced herself to relax.

"We do not know when they will strike again, but we know they will. We must always be alert. At this point they do not care about the human lives they ruin. The spirits have turned them too far for that, as I can attest. The last time I saw my sister was aboard the *Gloria Mundi*, where she released the spirits to slaughter the crew and left me to die."

It felt like something was crawling up Molly's throat— a bundle of words she couldn't say, knotted together, blocking her breath. It rose until she could feel it sitting heavy on her tongue.

Her sister went on, outlining Molly's flaws and mistakes as Molly had heard her do on the projections and the radio. She mixed truth and fiction expertly, spinning a story that made more sense than the truth.

Molly tried not to listen to the words as her sister went on, playing their family's pain like a fiddle for the audience. "Not yet," she whispered to herself. "Not yet."

"I did everything I could to keep Molly away from the spirits," Brighid said, and Molly nearly shouted in rage. "When she was young, I sang her to sleep. When she grew older, I taught her her knots and read books to her. But she was always drawn away to the engine, until my father made the biggest mistake of his life and promoted her to be our engineer, against my warnings."

Molly exhaled long and hard, until there wasn't a scrap of air left in her lungs. *You liar*, she thought. *How can you say all of that? You, who were hardly a part of the family, even years before you left. Taught me my knots? The ones no one would teach me, so I had to learn them myself by watching the deckhands? Read me books? How could you have through that damn door you always kept closed?*

"Anger alone will not persuade anyone," Ariel whispered. "Remember, they need to see you, see you are not who they say you are."

Molly breathed in and out through her nose and nodded.

"Despite everything, I loved her," Brighid continued. "How could I not, when I remembered holding her in my arms, changing her diapers, feeding her milk?" Here she paused again. "I loved her, and it blinded me to how bad things were. But now, she's..." She sobbed and turned away from the stage. Molly couldn't tell how genuine the show of grief was. She wasn't sure she cared.

"Now, Ariel," she whispered and began to hum.

Ariel bent the wind around her, sending it in twisting patterns across Molly's mouth to carry the sound of her voice across the area just as the amplifier did for Brighid's. Molly's hum grew louder, and people began looking around for the source. As Molly stepped forward to the lip of the roof, some in the crowd caught sight of her. Some screamed. "It's Molly! Molly Stout is here!" Others simply stared. Molly glanced down and saw the cameras turning toward her. She kept humming, the tune ragged and faltering in her throat. As it continued, Brighid finally looked up, eyes wide, staring directly at Molly.

"That's the song you used to sing me," Molly said. "Or the best I can do. I'm not much of a singer, I know, and I don't know the words. But I remember you singing it to me, on the deck, sitting against the mast."

Molly's heart was pounding in her chest, but her hands were still at her sides. She was vaguely aware of the huge crowd below her, but all she could see was her sister's face, the light of the lamps reflected in her eyes. Her face was different, and her hair, but the eyes were the same as ever—dark and deep, like a pool run through with moss.

"I missed that song, when you stopped singing it to me."

"I didn't know you remembered," Brighid said, her soft voice carried by the amplifier. There were people swarming between Brighid and Molly now, some kind of security guards, but they didn't have a way to the roof, and Brighid didn't move from the stage. "You were so little then."

"Sometimes I wish I didn't remember. But I do."

"I didn't know how much you could remember, once the spirits got into your head," Brighid said, speaking louder. "Once they turned you into—"

"That's not how it works, Bridge. I'm me. I'm Molly." She could hear her own name echoing off the walls of distant buildings, but she focused through the sound, the bright light of Ariel's winds, refusing to shift her attention. "The spirits got into my head right enough, but just in the same way you got into my head when you sang that song. I'm still me."

"The little girl I knew would never have released a powerful spirit on the—"

"You never knew me!" Molly roared, the anger in her chest blazing up. "When you knew me, I was a baby!

Barely a person at all! And once I grew up, you closed the door on me!"

"Because I—" Brighid began, but Molly wouldn't be stopped.

"And when the door wasn't enough, you left the bloody ship! Abandoned your family, your father, *me!*"

"Because it wasn't safe!" Brighid shouted back. "Because I needed to save myself from you! If I hadn't left the ship—"

"You left us a long time before you left the ship, Bridge."

Molly's eyes flickered to the side, and for a moment she felt dizzy. There were so many faces, so many eyes. Molly had expected people to flee when she appeared, afraid of the dreaded Molly Stout. But no, they were all just standing there, watching her, waiting for what would happen next. If she focused on the crowd, she would freeze up. She pulled her eyes away. She was here for Brighid. Brighid, who was still staring up at her, looking lost and afraid in a way Molly recognized all too well. Molly's anger suddenly drained out of her, leaving only sadness in its place.

"I mean, I know our family was hard. I was born, and Ma died, and Da spent fourteen years sinking deeper into his bottles. And we weren't…we weren't right. It hurt a lot of the time. But still…

"You know Da hasn't had a drink in over a year? It got uglier for a while. When you left, when we lost the ship. But then Da stopped, and you weren't there for that. And our brothers. Kier is hurt right now, but he got hurt saving people, working on something we all believe in. Rory, too, who used to skive off while the rest of us kept the ship running. He's so brave, Bridge, you wouldn't even believe it. He's kept me sane better than anyone. You missed all of that."

"Kier?" Brighid said. "Is he…" Then her eyes flicked to the crowd, and Molly saw her jaw set in a way that was so familiar it ached. "So you're getting our family killed now too. I knew you would eventually."

Molly took a deep, shuddering breath. "I never forced him. He wanted to, and now he's hurt. I don't want that. I want to bloody stop all this so no one else gets hurt. But the people you work for now, that's how they power their machines. On pain, on lives stolen from—"

The winds in front of her shivered and broke apart, and Molly's voice was suddenly normal again and too small to reach her sister. She turned to Ariel, who was grasping at the winds as they dissolved. Molly looked up and saw a dark patch in the wider streams of wind above, growing steadily, a silver sword just visible around the curve of a black hull.

She looked around and saw dark vans moving in at the edges of the crowd, Disposal agents spilling out and heading straight for Molly.

"Okay, it's happening," Molly said. "Ariel—"

But Ariel was already rising into the air, her light growing until Molly couldn't look anymore. Her cool blue glow illuminated the entire area around the umbilical, and the eyes of the crowd turned away. The light only lasted a moment, but everyone had seen Ariel's signal. Dozens of red glimmers danced out into the crowd, heading toward the stage. These were the spirits of the lamps in Molly's sanatorium, who had come flocking back at Ariel's call. And behind them came more spirits, and men and women pushing their way into the crowd. Molly tried to find her father, but she couldn't see him. She looked down in time to catch Rory, though, jumping out the open window of the building below Molly's feet and racing for the crowd of reporters at the front of the stage. The myriad threads of their plan were unspooling in front of her, and she couldn't track them all.

"Molly!" a voice shouted from above her, and Molly turned upward. There were people in the air, people in black with dark helmets, gliding silently toward her. "Molly!" the voice repeated, and she realized it was Ariel, who dodged back as one of the airborne Disposal agents swung something metallic at her. "Go! Run!"

Right. Molly looked back out at the crowd, at the agents already grappling with sanatorium patients, the free spirits creating ripples of panic as they surged through the crowd— igneous and aetheric spirits skipping above people's heads, terric and aqueous spirits wending between their feet. There were so many, but there were more Disposal agents than Molly had ever seen, more than she knew existed. And above it all, two more airships pierced through the bright winds. *They've got three of those ships?* Molly felt panic rising—it was all too big, and happening too fast.

Focus, Molly. This doesn't change your part of the plan. You need to distract the airborne agents and draw them to the south. And if Arkwright is in an airship, like we suspect, then… She shook her head. *No. One thing at a time. You just need to run and not get caught.*

One of the dark-clad agents alighted beside her and grabbed for her arm. She jumped away, running along the edge of the roof. She could see winds around her, but they were all cut to shreds, nothing she could use. She could hear more agents landing behind her. She sped up, planting her foot at the very edge of the roof and leaping across the alley.

The next roof came at her fast, and she rolled and landed back on her feet. To her left, the first Disposal airship had descended so low she might have been able to jump and touch its hull, and the other two were following close behind. Spotlights flared on their prows, fixing on her. She glanced over her shoulder and saw the agents with their antigravity packs lifting off from the roof, giving chase. This wasn't going to be easy without the wind to help her. *Just run, Molly,* she told herself. And she did.

The agents were at her heels, and the spotlights never lost her. But Molly ran from roof to roof, never stopping, the shingles rolling beneath her heels in a blur. The agents were faster than her, but they weren't as nimble—once they kicked off, they tended to keep going in the same direction. So Molly constantly changed direction, moving up and down levels, traversing roofs and gutters, away from and toward the base of the docks, never letting them keep moving in a straight line.

As she clambered up a gutter pipe and onto a wide, flat roof, a blaze of blue light broke through the clouds, and the thrill of flight surged inside her through her connection to Legerdemain. *He's coming down. That must mean the fighting is getting serious.* She looked out over the square and saw that the Disposal agents on the ground had brought out weapons, wide-mouthed things that spewed clouds of iron filings into the air. A few got shots off, but as Legerdemain descended he brought a wide swath of wind that poured across the crowd, sending the iron filings flying back.

Legerdemain stopped in the air, beating his wings to keep the wind flowing, to keep the weapons from cutting down the spirits who were even now converging on the journalists and, more important, their cameras. But she also saw people stretched out on the ground, people who were meant to be keeping Disposal away from Molly and the spirits. And yet, despite the fallen allies, there were more people fighting than Molly had known they had. *Are those the Unionists? I didn't think they wanted to be involved in this part.* She knew Ariel was in charge of coordinating the efforts on the ground, and it wasn't her job to worry about the others, but she couldn't stop herself from watching.

Molly felt fingers on her arm, and she ducked. An agent sailed past, landing a few feet away. She doubled back.

Just as she leapt off the roof, she felt a hand on her heel. It knocked her sideways, and she fell short of the next roof, barely catching herself on the gutter. Someone landed just above her, and a dark helmet bent down.

"Come now, you must be getting tired," said Howarth. He was breathing hard but still eerily calm. Molly glanced down and then let go.

She landed on the awning of a storefront and broke through to land on the cobblestones below. With a grunt she got to her feet. She looked up at the docks floating far above, trying to judge her position by the jagged shape of their outline. *I'm on the south side now. I'm almost in position. If I can—*

Something crossed her vision. The airships had all been chasing her, as she'd hoped they would, but one was veering away now. The prow turned and pointed straight at

Legerdemain. The immense steel umbilical was between the ship and the spirit, shielding him, but it wouldn't be for long. Molly began to curse.

"This is needless," Howarth said, and he descended through the hole she had made in the awning. "You should stop before—"

Molly didn't let him finish. She leapt up and grabbed the lip of the awning, pulling it down hard so it fell across Howarth. As he struggled to break free, she jumped on him and scrabbled at his shoulders, reaching through the hole in the awning to access his antigravity pack.

"Get off," he said, his voice finally showing some frustration. Molly found a buckle and snapped it open. He batted at her, but the heavy awning tangled his arms. Molly found another buckle and reached down and yanked at the pack, pulling it free and rolling away.

"Don't mind if I borrow this, do you?" she asked. There was a small dial on the bottom of the pack. She turned it and saw the pack's straps float up, unimpeded by gravity. Molly clasped the pack to her chest and jumped.

She and the pack went straight up, sailing beyond the top of the buildings. One of the spotlights swung past her, blinding her for a moment, and when she could see again, she was only a few feet from the hull of one of the airships. She hit it, tumbling upward along its curve as she scrabbled for something to hold on to. But the hull was smooth metal, with no gaps she might use. Her fingers finally closed around a cleat on the deck, and she came to a stop. The spotlight shone down on her from the small forecastle just a few yards away. She could hear the crew shouting, feet pounding toward her.

She turned and looked out. The airship that was heading for Legerdemain was above them, drifting around the umbilical. *It'll have a clear shot in a moment.* She aimed and jumped, soaring straight through the air.

She hit the second ship's hull hard. The pack in her arms spun loose. She snatched at its straps, but it sailed away from her, floating weightless through the air. As it moved away, gravity found Molly again. She wrapped an arm around the ship's railing before she could fall, then pulled herself up and over, onto the deck.

She'd only ever seen the black airships from below. She knew from their shallow hulls that they were built strangely, but from above she could see that they were constructed more like submersibles than airships. The top had a small deck, circled by a railing, but other than a few crew members manning the spotlight at the forecastle, there was nothing there save for a few access points to the lower decks. No sails, no visible engine.

The crew at the forecastle hadn't noticed her—and she wanted them to—so she ran for the prow as quickly as she could, shouting. As she drew closer, she realized that the forecastle was actually a cabin. There were windows all around its perimeter, and through them she could see a dozen people. She ran straight at the cabin and banged against the windows, setting every head inside turning toward her.

In the middle of the cabin there was a chair on a raised dais, and Arkwright was sitting on the chair.

Molly was at the side of the cabin now, and he was turning toward her, but he was moving so slowly that his eyes hadn't found her yet. He'd looked like a cadaver before, but now…She shuddered. *He looks like a strong wind would tear him apart.* His skin, stretched tightly over his bones, was gray and peeling, and his mouth hung open. The whites of his eyes had turned yellow, and the green glow of his veins glimmered sickly on the metal of his chair. Molly stared for a moment, until his eyes found her. She leapt back, heart hammering. The hunger in those eyes was so strong, so eager, that she had to look away.

The crew was running toward the hatch at the back of the cabin now, coming out to catch her. *Got their attention, I guess.* She pulled herself back and looked to the sky. Legerdemain was in clear view, beating his great wings and keeping the wind below flowing, but no one seemed to be focused on him anymore.

Okay. Now what?

She looked around. There were no lifeboats that she could see, and if the ship held more of the antigravity packs, they certainly weren't kept on deck. She looked down, but the nearest airship was so far from her that even if she managed to land on it, she would break every bone in her body—and she couldn't count on using the wind to save her, not with the agents able to pull it from her grasp. *Where do I go?*

Her eyes landed on the umbilical, and she was running even before a plan had fully formed in her mind.

There was a cable car just below them on the umbilical. It was one of the old ones, held on with straps that wrapped all the way around the giant cable's circumference. She sped up, aiming for the car.

She heard the crew behind her, feet beating against the metal deck plates. Molly reached the far railing and jumped, sailing out into the air, curving toward the cable car.

She landed on its roof with a bang and steadied herself before looking up. The airship was just above, a dozen crew members hanging over the railing. And it was moving toward her again and away from Legerdemain.

Good. She lay across the roof of the cable car and stretched her arm down to pull the door open. She swung herself inside and examined the machinery. There were five wheels, pressed against the umbilical but jutting through into the interior of the car, all attached to a central engine. From the way the engine gurgled and murmured, Molly guessed it was aqueous. She took hold of its lever.

"Sorry for this," she whispered to the engine as she pulled the lever down full. The cable car jumped to life, speeding downward so fast that even Molly, used to life aloft, felt a lump rise in her throat. As they descended, she pried at the engine with her fingers. The faceplate came off, and she found the trap holding the spirit inside. She leaned out the door and watched the ground rushing up at them. When they were only a few yards above the base of the umbilical, she turned and began yanking out cords. The engine quickly let go of the wheels, putting them into genuine free fall. Molly kept pulling at the engine's interior until the trap cracked open and something short and scaly, with huge wet eyes, tumbled out onto the floor of the cable car. Molly gathered it up, moved to the door and leapt free just as the car collided with the ground. She hit the pavement and rolled, coming up bruised and dizzy but still moving.

"Can you move?" Molly asked the spirit. "Can you get away?"

It gurgled at her but didn't seem to understand. She wondered how long it had run that old cable car. The airships were still descending, and all three spotlights had found her again. She checked her position against the docks above, then bolted through the crowd, carrying the spirit with her.

All around her, clusters of Disposal agents struggled with Unionists and patients from the sanatoriums, spirits flitting in to help from time to time. Disposal was clearly winning the fight—they were better trained and better equipped. Still, Legerdemain's winds were at least keeping the agents from employing the worst of their weapons. But as the airships drew closer to the ground, following Molly, Legerdemain's winds began to falter.

Molly finally cleared the outer edge of the crowd, pushing past a Disposal agent who saw her and recognized her for just a second before she hurtled past. She kept running, between the buildings at the outskirts, down a southern street. Up ahead she saw the intersection she was aiming for.

Just a little farther.

She looked up just in time to see boots coming down at her, and she stopped short. One of the flying agents landed in front of her, settling back into gravity. Molly kicked out at her before the antigravity pack lost its effect completely, and the agent went sailing several yards away. Molly ran on, trying to measure the distance to the intersection. *Twenty yards.* The airships were just above her, one so low it was scraping the brick walls of the buildings. *Ten. Five.*

Agents dropped down all around her, and she had to stop. She was still cradling the small spirit in her left arm, and she raised her right in a fist, but even she knew it was useless. Some of the agents chuckled.

"Come with us now," said a broad-shouldered woman with short hair and a scar across her lips. "We're under orders not to hurt—"

The ground beneath them shook. The agents stumbled but kept their feet.

"What was that?" another agent asked. He had his answer a moment later when Loam burst out of the street at the intersection, only a few yards away. The spirit towered over them all, glimmering with golden vines. It pounded the street with its feet, and the earth shifted sideways. This time everyone, even Molly, fell to the ground.

They all watched, frozen, as Loam's huge eyes turned upward to the airships just above them. Molly could feel the gravity change, her body becoming heavier, but she knew the worst of it was focused far above, on the airships. The metal hulls groaned, and a length of railing fell down so fast that it embedded itself in the cobblestone street. Molly scrambled away, the agents too distracted to stop her. At the side of the road, she gently put down the aqueous spirit and turned her eyes skyward.

The whine of the gravitic engines rose in a crescendo until they were screaming with effort, and then all three ships began falling at once. The lowest one tipped sideways and crashed into the street nose first. The second trembled and stayed even, but Loam pulled it inexorably, until the ship's engines finally broke from the strain.

It plummeted straight down, its hull cracking over the edge of the first ship.

The third airship—the one that Arkwright inhabited—was still in the air. It was caught in Loam's grip, but it was fighting, and it wasn't falling. *It must have stronger engines,* Molly thought. *I should have known. Arkwright wouldn't want to risk himself. What do we—*

A hammer of wind came down on top of the airship, and it dropped several yards lower, almost touching the roof of one of the buildings. Legerdemain swooped in, great wings flashing, calling out with a sound like thunder that set Molly's bones humming.

The winds around the airship broke up almost as soon as they appeared, but Legerdemain was relentless. He poured hurricane winds down on the ship faster than it could dissolve them. As the ship sank lower, Loam's golden lights flared brighter, the gravity around Molly increased and finally the airship was crashing down. Molly whooped, but at the same time she saw something dark pivot on the airship's port side. *Cannon!*

At the same moment she recognized the dark shape, it spat fire. A metal ball soared through the air and straight through one of Legerdemain's wings. The spirit's rumbling cry turned to a piercing shriek. His wing crumpled, and he fell, landing on the roof of the building across the street and then sliding off into the alley beyond.

"LEGERDEMAIN!" Molly cried, and she could feel his pain under her skin. She ran across the road blindly, tripping over one of the stunned agents, clambering clumsily over the rubble the crashing airships had thrown everywhere. She banged off the corner of a building and into a narrow alley. At the end of the alley she could see the curve of Legerdemain's belly, turned up to the sky. She put her hand on the bricks of the building next to her, and she could feel them vibrating with Legerdemain's cries, just as she herself was.

She stumbled forward and placed her hands against his cool skin. He was stretched out in the alley, his vast body filling the narrow space. His one unbroken wing strained upward, still reaching for the sky, while the other lay crumpled beneath him. He cried out again and again, and then Molly was crying out too, the pain too much for either of them to endure. She collapsed against him, shouting into the night until her throat was ragged.

Legerdemain's flank heaved against Molly, moving in and out with his breath. "Oh, Legerdemain, I'm so sorry," she wheezed. "I'm so, so sorry."

She opened her eyes, though all she wanted to do was curl up against him. Ahead of them, down the alley, there was still dust drifting through the air. She couldn't see Loam, but the Disposal agents were still lying on the street where they had fallen. *Why aren't they coming to finish us off?* They weren't unconscious—she could see them moving, shifting on the ground, sometimes rising a few inches before falling back, like they were struggling against an unbearable weight. *Loam. Loam must be holding them down.*

That means we have time.

She forced herself to her feet, though her connection to Legerdemain was so strong that she felt she was dragging a broken wing behind her. She moved along the spirit's body, leaning against him. His eyes roiled like storms, full of anger and panic, and as she looked into them, Molly fell to her knees again and pressed her cheek against his.

"I'm…I'm so…" she stuttered, but she couldn't even get the words out. She sank into his panic and pain, and for a moment she felt nothing else.

I need to help, she thought. *There must be something I can do.*

She dragged herself back up out of the feeling, pressing her back against the bricks of a building to steady herself. *What can I do?*

She heard Loam's booming footsteps from the next street over, and the answer came to her. *Loam was almost dead, but the spirit world healed it. I healed there too. I need to get Legerdemain to the other side.* She stood up straight and walked past the end of Legerdemain's nose, whimpering slightly as she stepped over the crumpled tip of his wing. She gave herself a few yards of space and then called the wind.

The storm that had been under Legerdemain's command had dissolved, but the winds that had made it were still nearby, spinning between the buildings. Molly brought them all in, every gust and stream that could hear her call. They came rushing through the alley, skittering along Legerdemain's skin and nearly knocking her over. She braced herself, raised her hands and set to work.

It was hard, in the closed space of the alley. She set the winds spinning in a tall oval with its peak above the roofs of the buildings. She kept adding wind after wind, blinded by their light, uncertain how long she had been working at it. Her arms were trembling, and it was hard to catch her breath.

She stumbled and fell to her knees, but she continued to work the winds.

And finally, with a thump that she felt in her bones, the winds became a font, a black tear forming in the center of the oval.

Molly turned and looked back at Legerdemain. His eyes were on the font, watching it. His one wing beat against the walls, trying to push him forward, but it couldn't move him. He couldn't get to the font.

Molly rose to her feet, took a long, shuddering breath and closed her eyes. She felt the font above her, its winds spinning endlessly. She raised her hands and pushed.

The font drifted forward, touching Legerdemain's nose, and she heard the spirit exhale, relaxing. The font passed over him, first his narrow head and then the greater bulk of his shoulders, his body, his wings. His tail pressed down into the ground, pushing him up and through, and then he was gone. Molly's connection to him suddenly vanished. She stopped pushing and fell flat to the ground, exhausted.

She breathed in and out. Without Legerdemain's anguish so close and so heavy, she felt life flowing back into her. She was tired, but she knew this wasn't done. She forced herself up and looked around.

I still need to get Arkwright before it's too late.

She thought about dismantling the font, but there was no time. She started running lightly down the alley toward the airships. Back on the street she saw Loam hunkered down just beside the Disposal agents. There were at least twenty of them, all pinned to the ground. Loam turned to her, and she nodded to it before turning to look back toward the base of the docks.

The struggle was still going on. But the storm had faded, and the Disposal agents were letting off shots of iron filings into the air. Spirits were screaming and retreating into the safety of the streets. And without their help, the people wouldn't hold out for long.

Where's Da? Where's Rory?

She looked over to the stage. Many of the journalists were still there, still filming with their cameras. Rory was there too, trying to put on a camera of his own. Her audience was waiting, but if she didn't hurry, she knew Disposal would shut the cameras down.

Not over yet. But it will be soon.

SEVENTEEN

Arkwright's airship was beyond Loam, lying on the street with its prow buried in the wall of a building. She ran and leapt up to its deck, pounding across it until she reached the small cabin at the front.

Through the windows she saw wreckage—navigation equipment and spiritual machinery all jumbled together. The chair where she had seen Arkwright was tipped over and empty.

She peered in through the glass, wiping dust away. There were people there, though none looked to be conscious. And there was Arkwright, his glowing veins creating a pocket of green light in the wreckage. His eyes turned and fixed on her.

There was no expression on his face. He simply sat, watching her. *I don't think he can even move*, she thought. She tried the door, but it seemed to be locked. She raised her foot and kicked at the window, but it didn't crack no matter how hard she hit it.

She went around the ship, trying each of the access hatches to the lower decks, but none would open. She went back to the window and stared in at Arkwright, then turned to look back toward the umbilical, where people were still fighting, still falling.

He's in there, helpless, and I can't even get to him. But if I don't, the fight won't end until Disposal has finished us all off. She kicked at the door, the metal plates ringing. *How do I get through a solid metal door?*

She turned and looked at the glimmering winds of the font she had created, just visible over the roof of the building next to her. *There is no metal door on the other side.* She took one more look at Arkwright and started running.

As she went, she carefully counted steps and direction. *Twenty paces, down off the hull, another ten, now turn here.* The font was still open but flexing uncomfortably in the confined alleyway. Molly ran for it and jumped through.

She came out onto rolling hills, so unlike Terra Nova that she felt dizzy. The stars glimmered in the sky, and clouds that pulsed with light sailed overhead, streams of blue and purple winds wending through them.

Legerdemain was there, lying on the ground just behind her, and her connection to the spirit flared up again as she came through. She could feel the pain of his wing in her own body, but his panic had gone. She heard his wheezing breath passing evenly in and out of his great lungs.

"I wish I could stay with you," she said. "But this isn't over yet." The spirit trilled slightly and fluttered his unbroken wing at her, sending winds spinning around her.

She pulled the font apart and wrapped some of its winds around her. She gauged her direction—difficult, with all the buildings gone—and retraced her steps, turning where the alley would end, running across the hills until she stood where she thought the airship would be. She aimed for the cabin where Arkwright sat and brought her winds forward to form a new, smaller font. With one last look back at Legerdemain, she stepped through.

Her head banged against something, and she fell a short distance to the ground, colliding with a metal ladder. Molly looked around. Her font glimmered in the middle of a metal passageway with no windows. She was at the foot of a ladder that led up to a hatch.

She had missed the cabin. *But at least I'm inside the ship.* She pulled the font apart and climbed the ladder, turning the wheel on the hatch at the top and pushing it open with a bang. She could see the wreckage of the cabin on the other side.

Good. Then Arkwright should be—

Hands suddenly reached down and grabbed hold of her, yanking her up into the room. She started to yell, but the breath was knocked out of her as she was slammed down onto the floor, just beside Arkwright's broken chair.

"Yes, hold her there," a soft, sputtering voice said somewhere near her head. "Now the machine."

Molly looked up into the faces of two black-clad Disposal agents. She struggled against them, but they were too strong. And a third one was moving in now, pressing something cold down on her chest—Arkwright's machine from the sanatorium. She fought harder, and lightning crackled across her skin. But the agents were protected, their hands gloved.

"Keep her steady," said Arkwright's wavering voice. She could see him now, pulling himself up with difficulty. His legs clearly couldn't hold him, but he was crawling toward her, and she couldn't move.

"Ariel! Loam!" she screamed. She knew the terric spirit must be just outside, still holding the other agents down. If she could get its attention, it could help.

The machine on her chest whirred to life. Molly tried to concentrate through the rising panic, focusing the lightning that flowed through her, willing it toward Arkwright. But one of the agents swiped a gloved hand through the electricity, and it dissipated. She tried to bring it back, but all she could manage was a small crackle across her arms.

Arkwright had reached her, his trembling hands on her arm, her stomach, climbing the machine to the grips. He was making adjustments on the machine now, preparing it with his palsied fingers.

Molly rocked herself back and forth, and the machine tipped, but it was quickly steadied. "Hold her still, damn you," Arkwright hissed to the agents. They pinned her arms and legs down with their knees. She could feel the machine beginning its work, pulling at every emotion inside her.

Molly searched the room desperately, looking for something she could use. The two agents held her arms in their gloved hands, while the third, who had brought the machine, pinned her legs, but...

The third agent wasn't wearing a helmet or the thick jacket the others were. Or gloves.

She closed her eyes and breathed. The machine was tugging away her panic, her fear, her worry for her family. She wanted to lie down, not move, let it be over. And then she didn't want at all. But she was still angry, beneath everything, and before that too could be stolen, she focused all her anger and sent it down to the clammy hands that held her ankles.

The agent yelped and convulsed as lightning coursed into him, and before the others could respond, Molly brought her knees up hard. The machine and Arkwright both tumbled away from her, and Molly gasped as she felt her emotions flowing back into the void the machine had created. She kicked at the other agents until they let go, then pulled herself to her feet, hobbling for the door on legs that prickled as if they were still half asleep.

She turned the wheel on the door and pushed it open. It banged against the outer wall.

"You know we won't let you run," she heard a soft voice say behind her. She turned to see Arkwright standing on his own two feet. He hadn't finished feeding, but it looked like he'd gotten enough. As she stared at him, the two agents with protective gear came to her side.

"Not...running," Molly panted and reached out for the wind.

It came thundering into the room. The agents raised their hands, swiping at the streams of wind to break them up, but Molly hadn't been trying to hit them in the first place. The winds came in across the wreckage in the room and sent it all flying through the cabin, fragments of machinery filling the air. The agents went down under the onslaught, and Arkwright tumbled backward.

The wind stilled, and Molly stepped forward, weak and panting. She could see Arkwright struggling to stand on the far side of the cabin. "You're going to come with me," she said, stepping over what must once have been the wheel of the airship. "We're going to show everyone—"

The third agent—the one she had jolted—climbed up out of the wreckage and leapt at her. She tried to move, but she was too slow, too weak from what they had done to her. The agent brought her down hard on the wheel and gripped her arms, pinning her.

Her forehead was pressed into one of the spokes of the wheel, and she looked through to the detritus beneath. Four wood-handled cylinders lay on the floor, and Molly stared down at them.

Flares! She wrestled harder, twisting and turning until she got a hand free to reach down and grab one of the wooden handles. She pulled its cap off with her teeth and then ground the head of the flare against the ship's deck with as much force as she could muster, closing her eyes at the same time.

The flare ignited, and she raised it above her shoulder. The agent on her back shouted and fell away, either blinded or burned. But Molly didn't wait to find out which. She stood quickly and looked to where Arkwright had been.

He wasn't there.

She searched the cabin. There were the three agents, one lying nearby with his hands over his eyes, the other two struggling out from under heaps of broken machinery. Arkwright was gone. She looked back to the doorway and saw a slim figure sliding away down the side of the hull.

"Oh no, no you don't." She ran after him, the flare in her hand turning the world red around her. She ran to the end of the deck and looked down. There he was, running away from the umbilical, from the crowds, from the spirits and from Loam and anyone who might stop him, faster than she thought he could move. He turned a corner and vanished.

"Arkwright!" Molly shouted and gave chase. As she ran, her heart beat faster, and it seemed like the harder she pushed, the less tired she felt. Her legs stopped prickling, her breath came easier and her muddled emotions came back one by one—fear, anger, hope, exhaustion. *He won't escape. He won't get away with this anymore.* She called the wind to her, and it urged her faster until her feet barely touched the ground.

She rounded the corner and saw him ahead of her. He was no longer alone. He stood in the middle of the street, not fleeing, someone held tight in front of him. Molly slowed, her wild heart lurching in her chest.

No. Oh no, please don't let that be who I think it is.

But as she drew closer and the red light of the flare illuminated the scene, she saw that it was indeed Brighid. A blade glinted in Arkwright's hand, pressed to her sister's throat.

"Arkwright, what are you doing?"

"Ensuring that I will not be stopped. Ensuring that I can continue my work, keep humanity moving forward."

"Molly?" Brighid said, her voice transformed by fear. "Molly, what's happening? Is this a spirit? What is he?"

Molly let the wind fall away around her. She stepped forward, and Arkwright raised the knife. The red glow of the flare glinted off its tip.

"Don't think I won't kill another Stout."

"Molly?" Brighid said. She seemed to be struggling against him, but Arkwright was holding her easily, despite the strength Molly knew Brighid had. *It's because he fed on me,* Molly thought. *That's mine. That's my strength you're using, my strength you stole.* With one hand, Arkwright held both of Brighid's wrists tight.

Molly stopped and considered. No one else was close enough to help. Brighid was right in front of Arkwright, so Molly couldn't hit him with lightning. Perhaps a wind around his back, to knock the knife away—but she had never been great at fine control.

"What do you want?" she finally said.

"You, of course. You to sustain me, and to stop all this ridiculous fighting so we can resume my work."

"And you'll let Brighid go?"

"She is of no use to me. Not once I have you. You know I am a practical man."

Molly sighed. Her skin crackled with lightning, but it had nowhere to go. Brighid's eyes were on Molly now, full of fear—fear of both Molly and the blade at her own throat. Molly roared in frustration and took another step.

Brighid cried out, and a rivulet of blood flowed down the pale skin of her throat. Molly froze.

"You wouldn't want to kill her now," Arkwright said. "Would you?"

"Don't you put that on me," Molly said. "You're holding the blade."

"All the same, I am waiting for your decision."

Molly bounced on her heels. "Why should I want her? She's been of no use to me either."

"That's true enough," Arkwright said, as calm as if they sat at a table with a cup of tea. "But you want her all the same, don't you? The Stouts always were more sentimental than was healthy."

She curled her hands into fists and considered rushing him, but he was right. He had her sister. The only choice Molly had was whether to trade herself for Brighid's life.

She didn't remember ever seeing Brighid afraid before. Angry, petulant, sad, but never so baldly afraid. She looked at her sister, and her sister looked back at her.

What happens if I give up here? What happens to Da and Rory and Ariel? What happens to the spirits?

But how can I let him kill my sister?

Molly groaned, and her head fell forward. "Yes," she said softly.

"Pardon?" Arkwright said. "I couldn't quite—"

"Yes, okay?" Molly shouted. "I'll go with you. Just let her go."

A tight smile split Arkwright's lips, and Molly wanted to retch, but she dropped the flare and spread her arms in the air beside her, plainly visible, and began walking slowly forward.

"I have a length of iron wire in my pocket," he said. "When you are close enough, you will bind yourself with it."

He released Brighid's arms and reached into his pocket. Molly waited for her sister to act. But she didn't. She stood there, like she was stuck on the point of the knife, no fight in her.

And then a dark shape burst out of a nearby alley and bowled both Brighid and Arkwright over.

"Get! Off! Her!" Molly's father roared, tumbling with Arkwright to the ground. Brighid rolled away across the cobblestones.

"Da!" Molly shouted. She started running as her father raised his fist. The fist didn't come down.

Arkwright's blade flashed in the red light of the flare, and Molly's father toppled sideways. Then Arkwright was standing, turning to Molly, his face illuminated by the sickly glow of his own veins. Molly leapt at him, but he braced his legs and plucked her from the air, holding her by her neck out in front of him. She pulled at his hands, but they wouldn't budge. She was too weak, her strength taken and turned against her.

"You know, when I was trapped in all those machines, I never realized I could be like this. Strong and capable in more than my mind. I thought time had taken this away from me. Perhaps you did me a favor."

Molly stopped fighting. She felt helpless and afraid, and she could feel tears running down her face. She didn't know how to fight anymore. It had all come to this, the struggle of so many people, so many spirits, to bring her to this man who had twisted the world around him to keep himself alive, and she couldn't even hurt him. And she was so very, very tired.

But there was her father on the cobblestones, and her sister sobbing behind her, and Legerdemain lying broken on the other side of a font, and Toves ground to dust, and the city, all around them, fed by the lives of countless spirits. And she was angry. From the bottom of her soul she felt anger, pounding away under her skin like the fierce winds of a storm. She could hear the rumble of thunder inside her ears.

She stared into Arkwright's contented eyes, and she let her anger out. Lightning arced between them, her chest to his, and for a moment he looked surprised. But then he calmed, and the lightning began to bend away, around him and down, to disperse against the ground. The lightning still didn't want to touch him.

But the lightning was not like the wind. The wind went where it wanted, and Molly could only ask it for help. The lightning came from inside her, from the storm that had been boiling beneath her skin for as long as she could remember. Since she had been born without a mother, with a father who could hardly see her through his own pain. Since her sister had stopped singing, and Molly knew there was no one taking care of her anymore. Since she'd found her only friend in Legerdemain and been told he was a demon who must be caged. Whatever change the spirits had wrought in her had given it a way out, but the storm was hers. The storm was *her*.

It found its way back to Arkwright, and it did not falter. The lightning flowed between them, and Arkwright's lips shivered and pulled back across his teeth in a rictus of pain. His arms trembled, and she pulled herself free.

She did not stop. She kept pouring her anger into him until he fell to his knees, then to his back, and he lay steaming on the cold cobblestones, curled into a tiny ball. She stood over him and finally let the lightning go. It flowed back into her with a snap.

She watched him for a moment. He was still moving slightly, whimpering, but she did not think he would rise again. She turned away and went to her father.

"Da?" she said. "Da, are you..."

She knew the answer before she finished the question. Because there was the knife's handle, just beneath his ribs, and the blade was hidden inside him. She stepped forward into the pool of blood that was flowing out of her father onto the cold street. She knelt in the blood, not caring, and put her hands on her father's cheeks, turning him toward her. There were his eyes, already empty. He was gone.

"Da," she said. "Da. Da. Da." Over and over, as if she might call him back. But her words could not travel to where he was. Still she said his name and pressed her cheek against the rough skin of his forehead, feeling him still warm, trying to soak it up as if she could carry that last warmth away with her.

"Oh, Da. I love you," she whispered into his beard. She wanted him to say it back, more than she had ever wanted anything. But his lips were still, all their words spent.

"Is he dead?"

Brighid was standing beside her. Molly didn't look at her, didn't answer.

"Why did he do that?" Brighid asked. She sounded like she was speaking from a million miles away.

Molly raised herself, wiping her face with her sleeve to clear some of the tears and snot and then wiping the tears she had left on her father's face.

"If you had ever paid attention to anyone but yourself, maybe you would already know the answer," Molly said.

She stood and turned, keeping her back to Brighid, and looked down at Arkwright.

The storm was roiling inside her, but she didn't let it out. She called the winds, and they came rushing down around them, more than she had ever called before. Great torrents of wind swirling around them all, buffeting them until Brighid almost lost her footing. Molly brought the winds in under Arkwright, lifting him off the ground, spinning him through the air, and she and the wind carried him forward, down the street, toward the base of the docks and the melee there. She hardly saw Loam as she passed, or the Disposal agents still held down by the spirit's gravity. She walked past them all, unseeing, until she reached the stage and let Arkwright drop onto the wooden platform with a *bang*. She jumped up next to him, regathered the winds and wove them in front of her the same way Ariel had to amplify her voice.

"Stop!" she shouted, her voice so loud it hurt her ears. "Look!"

They stopped, Disposal agents and rebels, human and spirit eyes turning to look at Molly, shocked into stillness by her voice. She bent down and grabbed Arkwright. He was heavy in her arms, but she gritted her teeth and forced him up, one arm around his waist, her other hand holding his hair so that his face could be seen.

"This is Charles Arkwright!" she shouted, the winds still carrying her voice. "This is what we've been fighting about all this time! This man, who didn't want to die and thought he could spend other lives to keep his own!" At her feet she could hear cameras whirring, and the eyes of the crowd all pressed in on her. "He did this, all of this, for himself!

He killed Haviland Stout and demonized the spirits, and now here we are, and here he is, still alive after all he's done! Look at him! See what he is!" She found the strength to hold him up higher, and Arkwright groaned. His eyes were open now, Molly saw. He was staring out at the crowd, though his body still seemed to be trying to curl itself back into a ball. He looked so weak, for one who had done so much damage.

She let Arkwright slide to the ground, and she sat down herself. "Enough. Enough of all of this. Just please, make it stop." As the last word left her mouth, she realized that the wind was no longer carrying her voice—the amplifying winds sat just above her head, where she had stood. The crowd couldn't hear her anymore. But she didn't think she could stand. She looked out at the people, who looked back at her as the tears started flowing down her face. She searched for Kiernan—but no, he wasn't there, he was still healing somewhere far away from here. But there was Rory, camera pointed at her. When her eyes met his he stepped forward, jumping up onto the stage.

"Are you hurt?" he said.

She nodded and reached her arms out to him. Rory crouched down next to her and wrapped his arms around her awkwardly. The camera dug into her ribs, but she didn't pull back, just squeezed it harder between them.

"What's going on, Moll? Where are you hurt?"

"Da..." she said, and that was the only word she could manage.

Suddenly there were others on the stage with them. Molly felt a hand on her back and looked up to see Theresa's face, eyes tired and knowing. Bascombe was there too, hefting

Arkwright up with the help of others, shouting out to the crowd. "Put down your weapons, all of you! We need to talk!"

The fighting had stopped. Even the Disposal agents were still. Spirits drifted in closer to Molly and Arkwright, and no one tried to stop them. Through her tears Molly saw glimmering red shapes move in around them, igneous spirits casting warmth on her face, but their warmth only made her realize how cold she felt inside.

"You can go," Theresa said softly at Molly's side. "We can handle the rest of this."

Molly nodded. "We should go, Rory. We need to…" She couldn't say the words. She stood up with her brother's help, and they walked down the steps.

"Go where, Molly? I still don't understand."

"Neither do I," Molly said.

She let him go and walked on her own, though she felt she might fall at any moment. A cool wind flowed in around her and buoyed her up—no, not the wind, but Ariel, come to carry her on. But Molly shook her head. "Thanks, Ariel, but let me walk on my own."

"Are you sure? I can carry you."

Molly shook her head, and the spirit released her, following behind as Molly made her slow way down the street to collect what was left of her tattered family.

EIGHTEEN

"Are you sure you want to do this?"

Kiernan stood beside the door, hand on the doorknob, leaning into Molly. She considered him for a moment. It had been a few weeks since the battle at the base of the docks, and he seemed more or less healed, except that he now walked with a stoop in his shoulders. She wasn't sure if that was about his injury or about what they had all lost, but it made him look more like her father than ever.

She looked into his eyes and nodded. "Yeah. I'm sure."

"I mean, you really don't have to talk to him. There's no reason, nothing we need to know. We could just let him stay in there until he turns to dust."

"I know." She took a deep breath. "But I want to. For me, not for him or for the cause or anything. I want to talk to him before he's gone."

Kiernan nodded. "You're braver than I am then," he said, stepping aside.

"Or crazier," she replied and turned the doorknob. The door clicked open. "They don't keep it locked?"

"He can't even get up anymore. No point."

Molly nodded and stepped through, closing the door behind her.

The room was dark, the single lamp on the wall burning low. With all the igneous lamps being broken apart, there was a shortage of oil, and she doubted anyone wanted to waste much on this room.

In the corner was a single cot—the same thin-mattressed type that she had slept on for years aboard the *Legerdemain*. Arkwright lay on the cot, his long legs protruding over the end. As Molly entered the room his head turned slowly toward her.

In the weeks since they'd captured him he'd begun to fade again. His skin was an ashy gray, and some of the blue had drained from his eyes. She could no longer see his veins through his skin, though the corners of his eyes still glimmered with green light.

"Have you come to see me dying?" he whispered through lips that barely moved.

"Sort of, I guess," Molly said. There was no other furniture in the room, so she moved to the wall opposite the cot and sat down on the floor, legs crossed. "I wanted to tell you what's been happening."

He let out a gurgle that might have been a laugh and might have been a cough. "What does it matter now? There is nothing more I can do."

Molly nodded and sat forward. "Everything is changing in Terra Nova. Faster than I would have thought. Theresa—

you remember Theresa, right? She tried to expose you, and you locked her in a sanatorium—she had the idea to expose you like we did. It worked. People believe us now. That you lied. That maybe the spirits aren't monsters."

"They are monsters, or they will be, given time and opportunity," Arkwright said. "You do not understand how these things work. They are more powerful than we are, and if we give up our advantage, they will destroy us."

Molly shook her head. "You're wrong. But I'm not done yet. I mean, it's not easy, changing the way a whole city runs. Figuring out how to do things without spirits. No one knows how we'll heat the buildings when winter comes. We still haven't figured out how the hell to get the docks down without destroying half of the industrial district."

"So much lost—"

"You're wrong, but I'm still not done," she said through clenched teeth. "Even I've been surprised by all of it. I thought it would be the workers who changed their minds first—the harvesters, like I used to be, and the factory workers, the people who spent their lives feeling what it is to be under your thumb. But it was the Unionists. They were the ones who spread the journal, as a trade for me, but most of them read it along the way, and most of them believed it too. I'm not sure why, but even Bascombe, who told me he lost his wife to a rogue spirit—he changed his mind."

"Why are you—"

"And the spirits. After everything we've done, the spirits are helping, though I still don't know why. They're helping us grow crops so we don't all starve. There's a team of aetheric spirits holding up the docks so we can break up its engines without killing anyone."

"Damn it to hell, girl, why are you telling me all this?"

Molly watched him. He was wheezing now, his breath rattling in his chest. She stood up so she could see his face better, see the anger there.

"Because I thought it would hurt you. To know how quickly it's all falling apart. I mean, there are people who don't change so fast. People fighting, people locking themselves away, saying the spirits have infected the whole damned city. It's not easy. It's chaos."

He turned his face toward her with a monumental effort. "And that is what you've unleashed on the world. Chaos. All I ever wanted was to move us forward, to make sure humanity would come out on top."

"You're wrong. And you never did this for humanity."

"Look what I've accomplished," Arkwright wheezed. "In a little over a hundred years we conquered the skies, plumbed the oceans, built machines that could work magic—"

"And we would have gone further without you there," Molly said. "If it was Haviland who had survived, and not you. If we had done it at the spirits' sides, not on their backs. We could have gone further."

They both fell silent, staring at each other. Molly shook her head.

"None of that is really why I came here. Though I did hope all the news would hurt after what you did to me, to everyone. But I came in here because, I guess, part of me wasn't sure what I would do to you. And I needed to know."

She laced her fingers and squeezed until her flesh turned white.

"I thought I might kill you. I think you deserve it. You killed my da, and Haviland, and so many spirits we'll never be able to count them all. I wondered if I would do it, if I saw you again." She stepped forward. Arkwright flinched away, but she kept her hands gripped together tightly. She breathed in deep, staring straight at him.

"I brought you something," she said. She pulled a small leather-bound book out of the back of her belt and dropped it on his chest. His fingers twitched, but his arms lay limp.

"What is this?" Arkwright wheezed. He struggled to turn his head. "Is this…"

"Haviland's journal. The original."

"Why?"

"You asked me about it, right? For some reason I kept thinking about that. About why you cared when no one believed the journal was real anyway. And I thought about how you kept all of Haviland's stuff set carefully away in that room in your mansion. The room I stole this journal from. That room wasn't just a vault. It was like…a shrine to Haviland. You actually cared about him once, didn't you?"

Arkwright's arms came up now. The journal looked heavy in his weak hands, but he didn't drop it. He cracked it open, ran his fingertips over the pages.

"You wanted it back, right? Because it was his."

"Why would you do this? Why would you give this to me?"

Molly shrugged. "I just wanted to see if I could, I guess. Wanted to see what I would do if I saw you again."

She turned and walked back to the door.

"I won't come back. You can't feed anymore, and I won't bother you again. So you'll die soon, I guess." She stood in the doorway a long time, trying to think of something else to say. But she kept thinking of her father, and his blood glistening in the light of the flare, and she couldn't find any words. She didn't look back as she let herself out of the room.

Things seemed jarringly normal back at their old house in Knight's Cove. They'd never been rich enough to have much spiritual machinery in their home to begin with, so nothing had changed for them as spirits were freed across the city. The woodstove still ran, the lamps still worked as long as their oil held out, and their beds still welcomed them in.

And yet, everything was different. Brighid sat at their kitchen table for the first time in years. She didn't talk much, but she didn't leave either. And Ariel came to stay with them when she wasn't too busy helping the freed spirits find their way home. Da's room sat closed. Molly went in sometimes. So did her brothers, and she had caught Brighid just sitting and staring at the door more than once. But they hadn't touched anything in the room yet.

It was good, having Ariel and her brothers there. Molly felt like there was a huge, deep pit sitting in the middle of her, and she might slip in at any moment. But having them close pulled her farther from the edge.

It was suppertime, and Kiernan was cooking enough stew to feed two families—and Rory had brought enough whiskey for three. They all sat at the table, drinking, while Kiernan served. They even let Molly have a cup. She didn't like the smoky taste, but it reminded her of her father in a way that was painful and warm all at the same time. She sipped it slowly.

"How's Legerdemain doing?" Kiernan asked Molly as he handed her a bowl.

"Good," Molly said. "Getting better. His wing's not ready to use yet, but it seems like it'll heal, given time."

"He will return to the sky again, I have no doubt," Ariel said.

"Think he'll want to come back here? To this world?" Rory asked.

"Yeah," Molly said. "I'm pretty sure he will. How are things at the docks?"

"They're thinking of dumping them in the ocean," Rory said. "Cut the umbilical and fly the whole thing out over the water." He mimed dropping something and then a splash. "It means sinking the lot, but it might be the best solution."

"That would be good—to finally get it down," Ariel said. "The spirits holding it aloft are growing tired."

Brighid watched them all with her glass raised to her lips.

"Seems a waste," Kiernan said. "I wonder if it could be retrofitted to float. Get some airbags on it. Or even find a shoal big enough to hold it up. I know it has to go, but... I remember spending a lot of days there with Da. I'd hate to see it just disappear."

Rory nodded.

Brighid put down her glass abruptly and stood. "I think I'll go to bed," she said.

"Not going to eat your supper?"

"No, thank you." She walked to her room and closed the door. Molly stared at the door. She would have to go in later—it was where her bed was too, after all—but if she waited long enough, maybe Brighid would already be asleep.

"Maybe we shouldn't bring up Da for a bit," Kiernan said. "Every time we say his name, she goes and hides."

"No," Rory said. "We can't not talk about him. That's not right. He's not here, but he's still..." He shrugged.

"Still our da," Molly said.

"There you go," Rory said. "Listen to Moll. She knows." He smiled across the table at her, and she attempted a smile back. It almost worked.

"I don't want to stop talking about him," Molly said.

Ariel sank down to hover next to Molly. "So what do you want to say about him?"

Molly looked around the table. They were all watching her. "I mean, I didn't have anything in mind. Just... in general."

"What would you say to him if he were here?" Ariel asked.

Molly grimaced. She braved a larger swallow of whiskey, then spent several minutes coughing. Kiernan brought her a glass of water, which she took gratefully.

"Should we drink to him or something?" Rory asked. "I don't know the proper form here."

"Seems weird to drink to him, given that he just kicked his habit at the end," Kiernan said. "I mean, it seems inappropriate somehow." He looked at Molly and saw the tears in her eyes. "Hey, Moll, are you—"

"Yeah, yeah. I'm okay." She turned her face away. "I just...I didn't ever understand, and I hoped I would. Why he did it all."

"All what?"

"Fighting with us for the spirits. I mean, I know he believed the spirits were innocent. But he never seemed the type to get up and do something, you know? I keep thinking he probably wouldn't have done any of this if it wasn't for me. If I hadn't...I don't know. I just don't understand."

"Are you asking if you are to blame for his death?" Ariel asked gently.

"No," Molly said. "Maybe. I don't know."

"You never coerced him into acting," Ariel said.

"But that's the thing. I know sometimes he wanted to stop, but he never did."

"He didn't want to stop," Kiernan said. "He wanted *us* to stop. All of us. And...I think he was there because of you, but that doesn't make it your fault."

"Oh. That clears it up then," Rory said.

"He just wanted to stick with you. Protect you if he could."

"He did. None of it would have worked without him."

"Let's not talk about him like he was a saint now that he's dead," Rory said. "He spent a lot of years screwing up. He threw Molly out of the bloody house once, remember, and he wasn't exactly kind and comforting to me either."

"I know," Molly said, raising her hand to her face where her father had given her a black eye that night long ago. "He didn't do such a good job most of the time. But I miss him."

"Me too," Kiernan said.

"Yeah, me too, I guess." Rory raised his glass. "To Da, sometimes drunk, sometimes not." He emptied his cup. After a moment Kiernan did the same. Molly drank more slowly.

"Think she's listening?" Kiernan said, gesturing to Brighid's door.

"Of bloody course," Rory said and raised his voice. "Maybe one of these days she'll even come out and join the conversation."

The talk went on, Kiernan and Rory falling into old rhythms with each other, the sound of their words almost as soothing to Molly as the creak of sails and the whisper of wind. She stared down at the table, watching the light of the lamp play through the whiskey in her glass.

"Molly? Do you feel well?" Ariel asked.

"I need some air, I think." She got up and walked out the front door. She looked up at the sky—the winds dancing, the stars blinking sleepily at her. Oil lamps flickered in the windows of the houses around her, and she stood in their dim glow, breathing in and out until her chest unclenched. She knew it was in her head, but the air seemed to smell fresher already, now that the factories had been stopped. The air above was still stained brown, and yet…She filled her lungs again.

"It wasn't what you think it was."

Molly jumped at the unexpected voice. It had come through the open window of her own bedroom.

"Brighid?" She walked to the window. It was dark in the room, but she could see Brighid sitting on her bed.

"When I left the ship. It wasn't like you said."

"Oh?" Molly's fingers gripped the windowsill.

"You never knew Ma. And the boys were so little when she died, they hardly remembered her. But I did. And I remembered how Da was before too. For a while I could stick it out, because you needed me. But then you didn't need me anymore, and I was stuck there thinking of Ma, watching Da waste away. I didn't…I wasn't trying to get status or money. It just didn't feel like my family anymore. Not the one I knew."

"That's not how families are supposed to work," Molly said.

"I know that," Brighid replied.

Molly opened her mouth and closed it again. She didn't trust herself to say anything more, not with so many emotions washing through her—anger and disappointment and, worst of all, the hope that the sister she remembered might come back to her. She stood at the window, waiting, but Brighid lay down in the bed and turned her back to Molly.

She suddenly longed to have the air all around her, to feel nothing but the wind on her skin. Molly went back inside the house.

"Ariel?" she called.

Ariel rose from the table and drifted closer. "Yes, Molly?"

"Do you have anywhere you need to be? Do you think maybe we could go see Legerdemain again tonight?"

"I would like that," Ariel said.

"But you already went today," Kiernan said. "It's getting late."

"I know. I just…I sleep better with Legerdemain. I'll be back in the morning."

"Fair enough. If I'm not here, you can find me at the Unionist building."

Molly nodded. "I'll find you."

She and Ariel stepped out into the night air. "Can we fly?"

"It would be faster to make your own font and cross over here," Ariel said.

"I thought maybe we could try to find one. Spend a little extra time in the air. If you don't mind."

"I do not," Ariel said. "If you are ready."

"Yes," Molly said. "Please."

Ariel lifted her off the ground, and Molly closed her eyes, feeling the air rush by, the pull of gravity lightening. She spread her hands and felt the wind passing between her fingers. She held it for a moment, pulling it along with them, and then released it again. Her muddled thoughts about Brighid scattered behind her with the winds, and she smiled.

She opened her eyes. Terra Nova was stretched out below her, the docks still glimmering above, held aloft by a nest of winds woven by powerful, and free, spirits. She looked down at the city. It was changing, and she didn't know what it would look like when it was done. Maybe it would never be done.

"What am I going to do now?" Molly asked.

"What do you want to do?" Ariel asked.

"I don't know. Just go see Legerdemain right now." She stared down at the buildings below. She had played a part in starting the changes, but she didn't know what part she might play in seeing them through. There were things that gave her hope—people working with spirits, people understanding when the spirits were too angry to work with humans. And there were still spiritual machines out there— they were such an ingrained part of the city that it would take ages to find them all and release the spirits. There were companies hoarding their supply of machines, who wouldn't listen to reason. *More work to do. Always more work to do.*

Maybe I could go traveling, she thought. *Spend more time in the spirit world. Or go see where Wîskacân is from, if he would let me.*

They flew past the city, out into the darkness beyond, following the course of the winds in the upper air. Molly closed her eyes again. She could feel Ariel all around her, tight against her skin. It was so quiet up here. They were flying, and no one would try to stop them.

"I do not see any fonts nearby," Ariel said. "Shall we land?"

"If you're tired."

"I am not."

"Then let's keep flying."

ACKNOWLEDGMENTS

Having Molly's story find its way into the world, into the hands and hearts of readers, has been a dream come true for me. I want to thank everyone who helped it happen.

First, the staff at Orca Book Publishers, who are unfailingly fabulous people. They've championed this story and also fielded all my new-author questions with patience and wisdom. Second, my editor, Robin Stevenson, without whom this would be a very different (and very much worse) book. Thank you for seeing the book it could be and helping me get there.

My children are a constant inspiration, reminding me how clever and how powerful the young can be. Soon enough they will take the lead, just like Molly, and I'll be struggling to keep up and give support where I can.

And lastly, the one who has helped me more than any other: my wife, Alexis. You've given me unceasing support as I pursued this unrealistic dream. Thank you for all the years we've had, my love, and for all the years yet to come.

SHANE ARBUTHNOTT grew up in Saskatoon, Saskatchewan, and now lives in southern Ontario with his family. *Dominion*, his debut novel, was released in 2017. His short fiction has previously appeared in *On Spec* and *Open Spaces*. When he is not writing, he can be seen chasing his three adventurous children, trying to convince them to eat green things. For more information, visit www.shanearbuthnott.com.